"In *If the Shoe Kills,* author Lynn Cahoon gave me exactly what I wanted. She crafted a well-told small town murder that kept me guessing who the murderer was until the end. I will definitely have to take a trip back to South Cove and maybe even visit tales of Jill Gardner's past in the previous two Tourist Trap Mystery books. I do love a holiday mystery! And with this book, so will you."
—*ArtBooksCoffee.com*

"I would recommend *If the Shoe Kills* if you are looking for a well written cozy mystery."
—*Mysteries, Etc.*

"This novella is short and easily read in an hour or two with interesting angst and dynamics between mothers and daughters and mothers and sons . . . I enjoyed the first-person narrative."
—*Kings River Life Magazine* on *Mother's Day Mayhem*

FIVE FURRY FAMILIARS

Lynn Cahoon

Kensington Publishing Corp.
www.kensingtonbooks.com

KENSINGTON BOOKS are published by

Kensington Publishing Corp.
119 West 40th Street
New York, NY 10018

All Kensington titles, imprints, and distributed lines are available at special quantity discounts for bulk purchases for sales promotion, premiums, fund-raising, educational, or institutional use.

Special book excerpts or customized printings can also be created to fit specific needs. For details, write or phone the office of the Kensington Sales Manager: Attn.: Sales Department. Kensington Publishing Corp., 119 West 40th Street, New York, NY 10018. Phone: 1-800-221-2647.

First Printing: March 2024
ISBN: 978-1-4967-4079-3

ISBN: 978-1-4967-4082-3 (ebook)

10 9 8 7 6 5 4 3 2 1

Printed in the United States of America

This is dedicated to all the furry creatures in my life, past and present. You all make life interesting and magical.

FIVE FURRY
FAMILIARS

CHAPTER 1

Mia Malone sat at the kitchen table, wishing she didn't have to go into work for the meeting today. Frank Hines, her new boss, insisted on the two-hour torture session every Monday morning. They would do a blow-by-blow of last week's catering events, then a plan for the upcoming week. If they didn't have an event, he insisted on doing an inventory of the Lodge's linens, table-ware, and place settings that week. Just in case one of their servers was making their rent money by stealing the silver. Frank had a no-trust policy in his work life as well as his personal life. Rumors circulated around the Lodge that Frank's first wife hadn't been as committed to their marriage as he'd been. Mia knew the feeling after her failed engagement, but that hadn't turned her into a modern-day Scrooge.

Mia wasn't sure that this job wouldn't though. Working with Frank was killing her. But as James, the kitchen manager, had leaked to her when he encouraged her to take the job, the Lodge wasn't outsourcing any events. Not even small ones. Her catering company had depended on these types of events before this new catering director job had been created. In order to save Mia's Morsels, she had to suck it up and figure out a way to work with her unyielding boss.

At least for a while.

Christina Adams, Mia's second-in-command and roommate, stumbled out of the hallway and into the kitchen, stepping on Mr. Darcy's tail as she moved toward the coffeepot. The cat hissed his displeasure and then jumped up on the window seat where he glared at her.

"Sorry, Mr. Darcy, or Dorian. I'm just a little tired." Christina mumbled as she settled in at the table, "I know we're cooking today but I could have used another couple of hours sleep."

"You should have come back to Magic Springs yesterday afternoon. Or stayed the night at your mom's after the party." Mia studied Christina. "You look beat. I worry about you driving the mountain road so late at night. You know deer are active then."

"I didn't want to get up early and drive. Besides, Mom's being weird. Clingy. I'm not sure what's going on with her, but ever since she bought me that car, she expects me to drop everything and be at her beck and call. Last week, she wanted me to drive home to Boise to go to the pharmacy for her. I told her Isaac could pick up her prescription. Or send Jessica, his new arm candy." Christina sipped her coffee and sighed. "And then she got mad at me."

"Your mom likes things to go her way." Mia had

her fill of Mother Adams when she'd been engaged to Isaac. The two had never gotten along. Christina had never been the woman's favorite child. At least not up to a few months ago. "Maybe she misses you."

"I think she misses having her assistant. Dad apparently decided that Mom didn't need an assistant since she's supposed to oversee the house stuff and there's no kids in the house anymore. He's cut her budget and she's scrambling." Christina closed her eyes, leaning her head into her open palm. "Maybe Abigail will be late today."

The parking lot alarm went off, notifying them to a car coming up the driveway. Mia pointed to the television monitor they had set up in the kitchen. "No such luck. She's ten minutes early."

Christina groaned. "I'm missing my old boss."

"Not as much as I'm missing my old job. Frank is impossible to work for. Maybe we should switch places and you can be the Lodge's catering director?" Mia asked, hope seeping into her words.

"Not on your life. He's mean. Everyone says so." Christina stood and picked up her coffee. "I'm getting in the shower. Tell Abigail I'll be right down as soon as I'm dressed."

"Sure, go hide so she can't yell at you." Mia smiled as Christina nodded and left the kitchen. Mia went into the living room. Abigail had taken on the responsibility of running Mia's Morsels while Mia was playing Lodge catering director. Mia had set up the system before she'd interviewed, just in case, but she still wasn't sure it was the best decision. Best or not, it was what they had to work with.

When she saw Abigail on the monitor, at the

front door, she buzzed her in and spoke over the speaker. "Hey, come on up, Christina's running late. I've got a few minutes before I have to leave. I'd like to hear how it's going."

"I'll be right there." Abigail was always chipper. She exuded happiness. Not a trait Mia had or aspired to have. At least not now. Or any time soon.

Mia pulled out her calendar from her tote. She liked to keep up with what the business was doing, just to keep her hands in the pie, so to speak. She opened the apartment door and returned to the kitchen and her coffee. When Abigail came into the kitchen, she filled a cup for her and sat down. "Good morning. Christina got in late last night."

"Her mom really needs to cut the cord a little. She can't be driving back and forth to Boise every weekend, working, and going to school. It's too much." Abigail rubbed Mr. Darcy's head. "Good morning, sir."

Mr. Darcy meowed and not for the first time, Mia wondered if Abigail could talk cat. Or if she somehow had a mind meld with Dorian, the spirit trapped in her cat's body.

Abigail nodded and turned to Mia. "Christina was clumsy this morning, I take it."

"Yeah, he got his tail stepped on. I'm not sure he's forgiven her yet."

Abigail sipped her coffee. "I'd say that was true. Anyway, I'm supposed to tell you that Dorian is afraid the wards are slipping again. He's been seeing wisps around the side of the building."

"I'll get someone over here from the coven to check. I had a feeling the patches would need to be updated sooner or later, but I was hoping for later." Mia wrote a note on her calendar. This time she'd see if she could get someone from leadership out to check the wards on the old schoolhouse. She'd done a lot of renovations inside to change the building from being an abandoned witchcraft academy to the new home of Mia's Morsels. She had two classrooms on the ground floor for lecture teaching. However, she wanted to remodel a couple with individual stations so students could cook along with the teacher, rather having a watch-and-learn class. So many plans, not enough money.

It was the story of her life.

"So, Abigail, how have you been?" Mia needed to leave soon, but she wanted to hear about the week ahead. Unfortunately, Abigail liked a little small talk before they got down to business.

"Oh, it's been a madhouse over at the Major's house. Thomas is off for a week of hunting and of course left everything until the last minute. I hate to say it, but I love having him gone. Before I worked for you, I would just sit in the living room with a fire on and read for hours. I ate when I wanted to eat. I slept when I wanted to sleep. Thomas likes more of a routine." She rolled her shoulders. "Although I admit that I also like not being on call twenty-four seven. He called from his way to Boise and wanted me to run to town, meet him at the airport, and take him a hoodie he left in the kitchen. I told him it wasn't happening. He can buy a hoodie at the airport to take with him. I do believe I spoiled that man way too much."

Mia had to agree with that. But she took the polite route and only smiled. "Sometimes men need to miss us to realize what they have."

"Isn't that the truth." Abigail narrowed her eyes

and stared at Mia. "Do not tell me that son of mine is acting like his father. I'll talk to him if you want."

Another reason Mia didn't like Abigail running the business. She was way too involved in Mia's relationship with Trent now. Although, for all Mia knew, Trent might have kept his mother in the know about them before as well. They were a close family. She sipped her coffee. "No, Trent is lovely. We're doing great. In fact, he's meeting me at the Lodge for dinner tonight. We used to go on Mondays so that I didn't have to cook after getting deliveries ready, but now, we just kept the tradition."

"Well, you two lovebirds have fun. And don't worry about Mia's Morsels. We signed three new delivery clients last week. I'm giving them a free welcome dessert tomorrow. I bet they stay on." Abigail started chatting about the business and caught Mia up. By the time she was done, it was almost eight thirty.

"I've got to run. Our staff meeting is at nine. Thanks again for stepping in at Mia's Morsels. I'm not sure what I would have done without you." Mia knew that losing most of her catering business had tanked the profit she needed to pay living costs. Mia needed the money she got from the job to pay the payments on the school. Having Abigail work the delivery portion of the business as well as any catering jobs they did get, gave Mia the time to work at the Lodge and still teach a class once or twice a month. "I'll be in the kitchen as soon as I get home Tuesday to get ready for the soup class Wednesday night."

"Well, you just let me know if you need my help. I'm all by myself this week, so I'd love to keep busy." Abigail finished her coffee and grabbed her tote.

"If you want to help with prep tomorrow night, that would be great. Christina has a date with Levi, so I could use an extra set of hands." She followed Abigail out of the kitchen.

"Sounds like a plan." Abigail called down the hall. "Christina, come on down when you're ready. We've got a lot of cooking to do today."

They walked together downstairs and paused at the foyer. Mia got her keys out, and hesitated. "Thanks again for doing this."

"Mia, it's a season, not a lifetime. You'll either get enough catering gigs on your own so you can quit or that idiot of a boss of yours will realize that having an in-house catering director is too much for such a small market. You'll be back in control of your life in no time." Abigail gave her a hug and then went to open the kitchen and start cooking.

Mia got into her small, old, okay, so it was ancient, car, but it ran. She'd been saving for a new van, but when she had to take the Lodge job, she needed transportation that wasn't her side-by-side. Especially in winter. She drove to the Lodge and parked near the kitchen back door. James left it propped open so that he and his kitchen staff could sneak out for a cigarette without going through the main lobby.

On the way through the kitchen, she waved at the cooks who were dealing with the morning breakfast rush and found James in the hallway outside her office. "Good morning, why are you here stalking me?"

"You forgot, didn't you? I know it's Monday, but you're the one who set the appointments." He pointed to three people who were sitting outside her door. "Do you have time to interview them before the meeting or do you want me to help?"

"Take one and I'll take one and hopefully, whoever is done first can get the last one interviewed before the meeting. I'm so sorry." She pulled off her coat and unlocked her office. "Who was here first?"

A tall girl stood up. "I'm Jenna McDonald and I'm in a class with Christina Adams. She said you were looking for serving staff for events?"

"Perfect come on in my office." She turned back to James. "This guy will interview the next to arrive."

The man popped up out of his seat. "That's me."

Mia smiled at the last woman. "Someone will get you in for an interview as soon as possible."

"That's fine, I brought a book to read." She held up a paperback novel. "I never leave home without one."

Mia hung up her coat and turned on her computer, shoving her tote in the bottom drawer of her desk. She got out a notebook and sat down, pen in hand. "So, Jenna, tell me about yourself. Christina is a great reference so you're already one step ahead of everyone else."

"I'm twenty-four, I'm in my first year of culinary studies, so I need some flexibility in a job. Just for classes. I can study around class and work time. I'm a hard worker. I waitressed for two years at the Ponderosa before it shut down last month." Jenna handed her a résumé and the completed job application form that James must have given everyone when they arrived. She rattled on more about her high school grades and extracurricular activities.

As Jenna talked, Mia watched her body language. Jenna was cute, personable, had a strong work ethic and as long as Christina said good things, Mia thought she was going to hire her. Mia explained the job and the irregular hours. She told her the salary. When the woman nodded rather than blanched at the low hourly pay, Mia continued. "I can probably keep you busy full-time, maybe more during holiday season. And yes, you'd get overtime. I promise I'll work around your school schedule. If your references check out, when can you start?"

"Anytime. I'm going crazy hanging around with nothing to do. I've been acting as a private chef to fill in the time and for some cash, but I'd rather have a W-2 job." Jenna stood and held out her hand. "I know you're busy, so thank you for spending some time with me today."

Mia stood and shook the woman's hand. She really hoped the references checked out because she liked Jenna. She said goodbye and interrupted the last woman's reading time.

When she got to the conference room, she was the last to arrive. Frank narrowed his eyes as she went over to the credenza to get coffee and a donut.

She slipped into her chair at one minute to nine. Everyone at the table heard Frank's sigh.

"Miss Malone, I wonder if you ever heard the saying if you're not ten minutes early, you're late?" Frank stared at her.

"I have but I was interviewing applicants for the

catering positions. James and I had three good prospects this morning so I'm sure that is worth the fact that technically, I was in my chair and ready before nine. Of course, with this discussion happening, we're now running a little late according to your agenda." Mia glanced down at the agenda. "Yes, see, it's a little after nine and you should be done with your weekly welcome and inspirational saying by now."

He turned a little red. "I'm sure we'll catch up soon."

The discussion started and James leaned over and whispered in her ear. "You're going to get fired."

"Please, dear God." She smiled sweetly at him and then focused on her donut. She wasn't sure she could listen to another one of Frank's motivational sayings which he repeated three times to make sure the team really took the saying to heart, then he'd explain the saying, just in case the people in the room were imbeciles.

When it was her time to give her update, she stood, listed off the catering jobs they completed last week, a summary of the comment card results, and any new jobs for this week. "As you know, we've been shorthanded with servers for the last month and James has been kind enough to let us borrow his kitchen staff. But since that would be overtime for his servers, that's been costing us more than what's been budgeted. With three new hires, we should be able to limit James's staff involvement to emergencies and illnesses. I hope to hire five total positions, but interest has been slow. People can make almost twice what we pay here if they work in Sun Valley. We've been training their staff for the last quarter. They get a couple of months with us, then transfer to the higher paying job in Sun Valley. We may need to look at increasing our starting wage."

"I'm not going to corporate to ask for more money. We just need to hire smarter." Frank announced, then he went on to the next topic.

"Hire smarter?" Mia asked James as they walked out of the meeting together.

He nodded. "Hire great people but keep them in the dark on what they could make somewhere else."

"Sounds like a plan. Maybe we could lock them in the basement when they aren't working." Mia paused at her office door and opened it.

"Don't suggest that to Frank, he might implement the plan." James headed to the kitchen. "Stop by for lunch. I'm working on a local trout dish for the menu. I need a taste tester."

Her phone beeped and she answered the call as she walked into her office. "Hey, Trent. Don't tell me you're canceling."

"Actually, no, but can we meet at your house? I'm running late and I want to take you to a new place in Twin Falls rather than the Lodge. It's getting great reviews."

"Sounds great. Besides, it gives me time to change out of work clothes. How fancy is this place?" She moved the stack of résumés to the middle of her desk. She needed to get these people hired and run through the HR gauntlet so she could get them on the floor.

"Not black tie, not a drive-in." He said something to someone in the background that Mia couldn't hear. "Sorry, the delivery truck is here. I'll see you tonight."

"Love you." Mia hung up and then reviewed the notes James had made on the guy he'd interviewed. She'd call his references first.

By the time she left the Lodge, she thought she had three people to call tomorrow and offer jobs. She still needed to find out what Christina thought about Jenna. She'd do that as soon as she got home. Tomorrow, she might have almost enough servers for the weekend events. Hallelujah.

She pulled her small car next to Christina's Land Rover which made her ten-year-old sun-faded Honda look even older. She got out of the car and noticed a black Escalade parked on the other side. She raised her eyes to the sky and prayed that Mother Adams wasn't popping in for a quick chat. When she got to the door, a man stood from his place on the bench outside the doorway where he'd been watching her.

"Can I help you?" She tucked her purse closer to her body. Clearly, this was the Escalade driver, but you couldn't be too safe.

"I'm Todd Thompson. I'm looking for Christina Adams?" He tossed back his too-perfect blond hair and smiled. "I'm her fiancé."

CHAPTER 2

Mia froze, staring at the man. "I'm sorry, you're what?"

He grinned and she wondered if he got away with a lot with that smile. It was perfect, but just a little too perfect for her taste. It didn't look real. "Sorry, I guess I should say I was Christina's fiancé. We had a little falling-out a few years ago when I went away to Harvard. I'm here to correct that mistake now."

"Okay, then, but you should know, she's involved." Mia wanted to say that Christina hadn't just pined away for the guy, but it wasn't her place. Besides, this was Mother Adams's handiwork. Mia could see the emotional trailings of the woman on the guy. He'd talked to her just before driving to Magic Springs.

"She'll see me. Things will work out. They always do." He leaned against his car and examined his nails. "Should I wait out here while you fetch her?"

Mia wanted to tell him where he could wait, but she bit her tongue. "No, come on in. You can wait in the lobby while I track down Christina."

She unlocked the door and motioned him inside. She stomped off the snow from her boots and then slipped them off, putting on a pair of slippers she kept inside the front door. She looked down at Todd's fancy boots and nodded. "Please take those off. We don't want you to slip and fall on melted ice inside the building."

He glanced around, taking in the waiting room. It must have met with his approval as he sat down on the bench and pulled off his boots. "Next time, I'll bring my own slippers."

Hopefully there won't be a next time. "Socks are fine." Mia pointed to the couches in the sitting area. "Make yourself comfortable. I'll go get Christina."

She didn't wait to see if he followed her to the kitchen. Mr. Darcy was sitting on the stairs, watching the newcomer. If he went snooping, the cat would let her know. Or at least Dorian, the witch spirit that shared Mr. Darcy's body, would let her know. Her life was strange, but adding the visiting Todd into the mix, just upped the strangeness by a few degrees. She went to the downstairs kitchen first.

Abigail and Christina were just finishing up the prep work for tomorrow's deliveries. They looked up as she came inside the room. Mia closed the door behind her. "We've got a problem."

"I thought Trent was taking you out to dinner tonight. Do you need us to add a new delivery? We have extras so we can add up to ten plates. Maybe

more if some of them are children's portions."
Abigail reached for the delivery schedule.

"No, it's not about the deliveries." Mia nodded
to Christina. "I think I know what your mom's
been working on. You have a visitor."

"Mom's here?" The blood ran out of Christina's
face as she looked down at the stained T-shirt and
jeans she'd been cooking in all day. "She knows I
work on Monday and Tuesday, why would she
come today?"

"It's not your mother." Mia glanced at the door
and lowered her voice. She didn't want to say this
in front of Abigail, since she was Levi's mom, but it
was what it was. "Todd Thompson is here. He's
come to win you back and ask you again to marry
him."

Christina burst out laughing. Not the reaction
Mia had expected. "Todd's here? In Magic Springs?
What, was the entire Eastern seaboard closed down
for the week?"

"Wait, Todd's an ex-husband?" Abigail's eyes
widened as she listened to the back-and-forth.

Christina shook her head. "No. He asked me to
marry him via email from his dorm room at
Harvard when I was still in high school. I said show
me a ring, we'll talk. I guess he took a while to find
the right ring."

"So he's an ex-boyfriend." Abigail blew out a
breath. "I was beginning to get a little concerned.
Especially since you'd never mentioned being
married before."

"Don't worry, Abigail. I'm free and clear to be
dating Levi. I'm not legally or morally tied to another man." Christina patted Abigail's hand. "You
should see your face."

"Well, I like the idea of you and Levi. What can I say." Abigail closed the notebook. "We're done here. I can finish up if you want to go break the news to Todd."

"I've got to go get ready. Trent's going to be here soon." Mia met Christina's gaze. "Unless you need backup."

"Come with me for a minute and let's play it by ear." Christina took off her apron and put it in the laundry. She flounced out her hair in an exaggerated motion. "I'll go talk with him and let him down easy. I'm sure it's going to break his little heart. But I'm a one-man woman. No matter how many men my mother tries to throw at me."

The last time Mother Adams had tried to set Christina up with an appropriate match, Mia had been at the party wearing Christina's image. The man had seen through the glamour, mostly because he was also a Magic Springs resident witch. But Mother Adams still gave Christina hints about looking the guy up if she broke up with Levi. Mother Adams definitely had bad taste in men. And this Todd looked like he was going to be another failed matchmaking attempt.

Mia followed Christina out into the living room.

He saw the door open and he stood, opening his arms for a hug. His face dropped when he saw her coming toward him. He quickly forced back on the plastic smile he'd given Mia. "Christina. Well, your mother said you were working, but she made it seem like an event planner position, not a kitchen maid."

"Cook. I'm not a maid, I'm a cook." She ignored his attempt for a hug and sat down at a table.

"What do you want, Todd? I'm busy. I have a life here."

"I've graduated and am starting at the law school in the fall. I thought this would be a perfect time to get the wedding out of the way." He pulled out a Tiffany blue box. Opening it, he sat it on the table with a bow. "And here's the ring you requested."

"Todd, I'm not marrying you. I didn't say yes in the email. We haven't talked in years." She glanced at the ring and reached for it. Then she shut the box and pushed it toward him and the end of the table. "You might as well go back to Boise."

He took a breath, watching her. Then he nodded. "I see I've made an error in the production. I'll ask you again when you're in a better mood. I'm staying at a cabin at 1440 Lovers Leap Lane. Come have dinner with me tomorrow. We can catch up. I told your mother I'd check in on you."

"You rented a cabin?" Christina stood and started walking toward the door. "You should have just rented a room. I'm not changing my mind."

"I'm skiing for a few days while I'm here. No use wasting a drive to one of the best ski resorts in the country without some slope time." He leaned down and kissed her on the cheek. "Especially if you decide not to accept my offer."

"I already told you I'm not marrying you." Christina walked him to the door and then leaned down, handing him his boots.

"Then I'll have to console myself with days of fresh powder." He smiled as he sat down to put on his boots. "And dinner with you tomorrow night. I really do want to catch up, tadpole."

She laughed. "No one's called me tadpole in years."

"See, I didn't know that. What else has been happening that I didn't know about?" He stood and slipped on his ski jacket. "Tomorrow night at seven. I've hired a chef to come in so she'll do all your favorite dishes. At least the ones I remember."

"Todd, I'm not marrying you."

He held up his hands in surrender. "I hear you. I just want one dinner to talk with an old friend."

"Okay, one dinner." She gave him a quick hug. "It's good to see you."

He kissed the top of her head. "And you, tadpole."

Christina slapped his arm. "Stop calling me that."

Todd nodded to Mia. "Thank you for your assistance."

He left through the door and Christina went and sat on the stairs next to Mr. Darcy. Mia locked the door behind him and then leaned on the banister. "Are you okay?"

"Todd's harmless. He just isn't told "no" a lot. I'm pretty sure he expected to step back into my life and whisk me away. He sees himself as a white knight." Christina stood. "Levi's on his way to pick me up. I better go shower. He's going to kill me for letting Todd talk me into dinner."

"Why do you say that?" Mia followed her up the stairs. She had to get ready as well.

Christina paused at the second-floor landing. "My mom told Levi the other day about Todd and how we were supposed to get married. He asked me about it then and I blew it off. Todd hasn't even contacted me in years. Now, less than two weeks later, I'm going to have dinner with him. It's almost like I lied to him."

"You didn't know he was in town." Mia thought there was one person who had known in that conversation that Todd would be showing up sooner than later and it had been Mother Adams. Was she trying to force Levi into a decision? Or just trying to break Christina and Levi apart? Mia didn't know, however she needed to get ready for her date with her own Majors brother. Trent would be here soon.

She'd just finished getting ready when he arrived, and as he helped her into the truck, she told him about Todd's surprise visit and weeklong trip to Magic Springs.

They were on their way to Twin Falls when Mia remembered she'd forgotten to ask Christina about Jenna McDonald. She pulled out her phone and shot her a quick text asking her what she thought of her.

Trent watched her key the message, amused. "You know we don't have service out here on the highway. The mountains block the signal."

"I know, but if I wait, I might forget. I want to hire this girl, but she gave Christina as a reference. I need to know what she thinks of Jenna." Mia finished the note and hit SEND. The phone immediately dinged. "And message not sent. Remind me to hit send again as soon as we cross the bridge going into town."

"Okay. So you got at least one person to hire?" Trent asked and then listened as she told him about her day.

She tried not to complain, but it never failed

that she'd have a "Frank story". Most of those sto-
ries ended with her wanting to put a resignation
letter on his desk the next day. Trent knew why she
was working at the Lodge and supported her. She
just didn't want to always be the complaining girlfriend. By the time she'd broken it off with Isaac,
most of their conversations had been about work.
She wanted this relationship to be based on more
than just one common interest. Finally, she ended
her monologue with, "I'd love to hire all three of
them."

"In my opinion, hire when you can because you
never know when someone's going to leave and
then you're behind the eight ball again with staffing issues. Of course, I don't have to run my hires
by a boss and the human resource department, so
I can hire for more than what some corporate
bean counter thinks I need to run my store." He
slowed down to the lower speed limit as they ap-
proached city limits. "You should be able to send
your message now."

"Oh, good call." She took out her phone and
tried to resend. This time the message went through,
and she quickly saw three dots in a bubble. Christina was already answering. "Funny, I thought she
and Levi were having dinner."

"They're probably fighting about Todd." Trent
grimaced. "My brother can be a pill when he thinks
he's being played."

"She's not playing Levi. Christina didn't know
Todd was going to show up. In fact, he was totally
out of her life. She's just having dinner tomorrow
night with a friend." Mia read the message.

Jenna would be a good hire. Levi is mad at me.

"Okay, how did you know they were fighting? I

just told you about Todd when we got into the truck on the way here."

"You're forgetting about my link with Levi. He tried to turn it off a few minutes ago, but I heard most of their argument. It's fine. Levi's just being protective and insecure. He'll get over it. He loves that girl." Trent nodded to the next light. "After we pass that light, no more talk about work or Christina and Levi or even my mom. It's just about us and tonight. Deal?"

Mia smiled. This was one of the reasons she loved Trent so much. He intentionally made time for them as a couple. She needed to be better at working that skill. She squeezed his hand. "Deal."

Pulling into the driveway at home, Mia was stuffed and sleepy from dinner. But not too tired to notice a shape near the side kitchen doorway. "I must have gotten a late delivery. Either that, or the ghosts are back. I guess Dorian told your mom that the wards are weakening again."

"Do you want me to call the coven or you do it? I'm supposed to stay out of witch business after my power transfer. I think they used to wipe the minds of those who passed on the power, but they found that problematic with their actual lives." Trent turned off the engine. "Do you have the kitchen keys? Or do you want to go in the front and let me in that way?"

"I don't carry around the kitchen keys anymore. Your mom has my extra set. I'll go through the front. I have a set in my office. I'll call the council. If this is even an issue. You have to realize we got our information from a cat. If it's not bad, let's let

it ride for a few months. I'm so tired of them recruiting me. If I call, they're going to send someone new to tell me all the wonderful things I'm
missing out on with not joining their group. If they
had health insurance, I'd sign me and Grans up in
a heartbeat. But no, they do parties and network-
ing. They need to up their game as an organiza-
tion." Mia slipped out of the warm cab of the truck
into the winter night. The cloud cover had disappeared so the temperature was cold and dropping.
She pulled her coat closer and hoped that whatever Abigail had ordered hadn't already frozen
solid by being left outside.

She hurried to the front and unlocked the door.
She slipped off her boots and left her coat and
purse by the door. She quickly relocked the door
and flipped on lights as she hurried through the
empty Mia's Morsels waiting room. It was a great
place for her to entertain guests as well. Especially
if she didn't want to have to invite them upstairs
into what she considered her home. It gave her at
least a little wall between work and life. Okay, so
not much, but she was working on a bigger work-
life balance.

She unlocked the kitchen door and paused, feeling a power greeting her. It wasn't negative, but it
was definitely there. She flipped on the switch and
the kitchen blazed with light. She could see Trent
standing outside, the box in his hands, but he was
staring into the box. She stopped and watched
him for a second. Had whatever power was in the
box already affected him? Was her boyfriend
going to turn evil and it would be her fault since
she sent him out to get the box? She picked up a

baseball bat that she kept by the kitchen closet, just in case. Then she moved to the door and unlocked the three different locks she'd installed on the door.

Trent turned around and grinned at her, stepping into the kitchen. "Man, it's colder than a witch's . . . I mean, it's cold tonight. It's a good thing we came home when we did and found them or they would have been popsicles by morning."

She set down the bat, Trent didn't appear to be possessed by an evil ghost or spirit. She'd been working on communication with the dead spells last week with Grans. Maybe that was what she was feeling. She relocked the door and followed Trent out to the living room. He set the box on the coffee table and pulled out one, two, and finally, a third kitten. They huddled by the box, still cold. Mia picked one up. "Who on earth would drop off kittens?"

"They do it to the store all the time. I feel bad for the mama cat. Sometimes they drop her off as well. Then she has to keep the babies warm until we can get them inside. We might want to put the box back out with a bowl of food just in case she was hiding when I came over." Trent had the other two in his lap.

"That's horrible." Mia lifted the solid black kitten to her face. "Look at you, little one. Is your mama around?"

The kitten meowed sadly and Mia pulled it closer to her chest. "I'll take the box out with a heavier blanket and some tuna and water. Then I guess we'll just have to watch for her."

"We need to find homes for these guys. Otherwise, my mom will take them all out to the farm and put them in the barn. It's warm there and they'd have a good life."

"Well, at least we have options." Mia didn't want the babies to have to be outside kittens. But she couldn't keep all three. Not with Mr. Darcy around. She'd be lucky if she could foster the babies until they found their furever homes.

CHAPTER 3

The next morning, Mia woke to Mr. Darcy sitting on her chest, staring at her. And he wasn't happy. She blinked and glanced at the clock. "It's six. I don't have to be at work until nine today. Can't I sleep in?"

Mr. Darcy swatted at her face, apparently the answer was no.

"Fine, what do you want?"

He meowed, then moved over to stare down at the floor. The three kittens were lying on one of Mia's pillows that must have fallen off the bed. Next to the pillows was a treasure trove of items they'd found and claimed as theirs. Including Mr. Darcy's favorite ball and what looked like a pile of the dry cat food that usually was in a bowl in the kitchen.

"Oh no, how did you guys get out of the box?" Mia leaned down and lifted the kittens onto the bed with her.

Mr. Darcy growled and jumped off the bed.

Walking out of the room, his tail twitched in disapproval of Mia's actions.

"They're not here for long. We're just fostering them," Mia called after the cat who didn't seem to care what Mia was calling it. The kittens were not welcome. She curled on her side and played with each kitten, using her finger to get their attention. Mr. Darcy wasn't happy that there were three kittens in his house. But Mia was delighted. "So how did you guys get out of the box. And you found me? Who's a smart kitten?"

The black one watched her talk then swatted at her hand. Apparently, he wanted to take credit for being the ringleader in last night's shenanigans.

"Okay then, you're the troublemaker." She gave the kitten a kiss on the nose. "We probably need to get up. Christina and Abigail are working today and we need to chat about the three of you. Maybe you'll all have new homes by the end of the day."

The black kitten stared at her while she was talking. He or she was very attentive. The other two, well, they were wrestling. He looked over at them and then walked up to rub his face against hers.

"So you think those two should go and you should stay?" She rubbed the kitten's nose. "I'm not sure Mr. Darcy would like that."

He sat and watched her talking. This kitten was tuned into her. Maybe he was the source of the magic she'd felt last night when they found the box on the back porch.

"Anyway, we need to get up." She moved all the kittens off the bed and went into her bathroom to get ready. The black kitten followed her. She looked down at him while she was brushing her teeth. This was not good. Bonding between a witch and a familiar happened fast. And she already had Mr. Darcy and Gloria. Having a third familiar didn't seem like a good idea. Especially one that Mr. Darcy didn't approve of. Mia heard Gloria's giggle from the kitchen.

She was in trouble.

When she got into the kitchen, her phone rang. She glanced at the number and quickly answered. "Hey Grans, what's going on?"

"That's what I need to know. Your energy is all over the place. I haven't seen it like this since you and Trent started dating. Don't tell me you've fallen in love with someone else. I like the boy. And it's going to cause problems with Abigail and the business. You have to know that." Grans rambled on.

Finally, Mia was able to get a word in edgewise. "Grans, slow down. Trent and I are fine. I think you must be picking up the energy from the kittens."

"What kittens?"

Mia told her the story about finding the kittens on the step and bringing them in so they wouldn't freeze to death. "I just hope mama cat is home with her family and the humans just dumped the unwanted offspring. I hate the thought that she's still out there and now missing the kittens."

"I'll be right over." Grans declared.

Mia started the pot of coffee she'd been working on since she came into the kitchen. The yellow-striped kitten was trying to climb the tablecloth. She pulled him or her off and set the kitten back on the floor. Then she took the tablecloth off the table, folded it, and put it in a drawer. She needed to kitten proof the house. Especially since no one could be home today to watch them. "Grans, I have to go to work this morning."

"No worries. Make coffee."

The phone went dead. Mia sat down to wait for the coffee to finish. "Grans is coming over to test you three. You need to be on your best behavior while she's here."

The yellow-striped kitten stalked the black one from behind and pounced as she was talking to them.

"Or maybe not." Mia stood and went to get her a cup.

"Oh, my goodness. Where did you come from?" Christina swept up the tabby into her arms. "You are adorable. But you know that, don't you?"

"Of course, I know that I'm adorable." Mia smiled at her friend. "Oh, you were talking to the kittens. Trent and I found them outside the side door of the kitchen last night when we got back from dinner. Someone dumped the three of them."

"How could they?" Christina sat down with the kitten in her arms. "Where's the mama cat?"

"Unknown." Mia poured a second cup of coffee and then set both on the table. "So do you know of anyone who's looking for a pet?"

"You're giving them away?" Christina held the kitten closer.

"Christina, I can't keep all of them. Mr. Darcy is already having a hissy fit about having them here temporarily. I don't think he likes kittens." Mia lowered her voice. "Although, if I hadn't gotten him fixed when I got him, these could have been his kittens. His mom was a tabby."

"I'll ask at school on Wednesday. But most of

the kids I know either live in the dorm or an apartment. I'm not sure anyone can have pets." She stroked the kitten who'd curled in her lap and was now sleeping. "So you liked Jenna?"

"I did. She was smart and funny. No issues I should know about?" Mia sipped her coffee as the other two climbed up on the window seat and found the patch of sunlight that Mr. Darcy liked to lay in each morning. She hadn't seen her cat since he'd woken her up this morning. She suspected that with Dorian's help, the witch soul that shared Mr. Darcy's body, the cat was outside, chasing mice out of the yard.

"I've only had one class with her. But my friend, Torrie, knows her better. They went to high school together in Boise." Christina set her cup down. "She seems nice."

"Okay, I'll check out her other reference and then I'll probably hire her." Mia glanced at the clock. She still had time before she needed to get ready to leave. "So, Todd. He seemed nice."

"Nice but clueless. I told him we were done but for some reason, he gets it in his head that I'm just sitting here, waiting for him to deliver a ring?" Christina shook her head. "It was a really nice ring. I'll give him that."

"Levi's not happy?"

Christina shrugged. "I told him about it while we were driving to dinner last night. When I told him I was having dinner with Todd tomorrow night, he turned around and dropped me back off at the school. So yeah, not happy is probably a good description."

"Sorry about that." Mia watched Christina as she gently stroked the kitten's fur.

"He'll either get over it or he won't. I had a life before Levi and if we break up, I'll have a life afterward. But I'm not marrying Todd in any case. He's what my mom wanted for me. In fact, I'm surprised she hasn't called this morning to see how the reunion went. I like him as a friend. We have history together. But he's not the one. I know that now." She sipped her coffee. "I just hope Levi realizes it before he says or does something stupid we can't come back from."

As they talked, Christina's phone rang. She sighed as she looked at the display. "I better answer. It's Mom."

Christina walked out of the kitchen after refilling her coffee cup. The tabby followed along.

Mia shook her head. A second bonding. This wasn't going well for Mr. Darcy.

The security system beeped and Mia looked up to see Trent's truck pulling into the driveway. She put on her slippers and went downstairs to greet him, careful to shut the door to the apartment. She didn't need kittens lost in the school. She'd never find them.

She met him at the front door. He had a bag in his arms. "Ooh, donuts?"

He shook his head. "Muffins, orange juice, kitten food, toys, and a second litter box. I assumed Mr. Darcy wasn't too happy with the new arrivals."

"You got that right. He woke me this morning and basically told me to take care of them. I haven't seen him since. Somehow, they got out of the box last night and found my bedroom along with some other items they claimed as theirs. Like his favorite ball." She shut the door as he came inside.

"Any sight of the mama cat?" He glanced toward the kitchen.

Mia shook her head. "I haven't been out there to see if she even ate any of the food."

Trent handed her the bag. "I'll go check, just in case. I'll be right up."

"Grans is on her way as well. I'm not sure why but she felt a need to be here." Mia moved toward the stairs. "I'll leave the door unlocked for her."

As Mia took the kitten supplies upstairs, she wondered just how busy her kitchen was going to be that morning. She had to leave the house no later than fifteen before nine which would allow her enough time to be in her office before Frank came looking for her. Or started calling. One other reason she'd loved running Mia's Morsels. She had more flexibility in her schedule. Now, she was on a short leash and Frank Hines was on the other end.

The black kitten was sitting on the couch, watching the door as she came into the apartment. He jumped down and followed her into the kitchen. The yellow-striped kitten still slept on the window seat.

Mia pulled everything out of the bag, then opened a can of the kitten food. Everyone was standing looking at her as soon as it was on the plate to be given to the kittens. "So you've had this before?"

Mia sat the food down and the kittens dug in.

Then she put away the rest of the supplies and set up the litter box near the supply closet in the kitchen. Mr. Darcy's box was in the spare bathroom. Hopefully, they'd use this one. When everything was done, she saw Grans's car pull into the parking lot. Trent must have waited for her because she saw him meet Grans at the door. She'd brought a suitcase and Muffy.

"Apparently she's staying awhile," Christina said from the edge of the kitchen. She came in and refilled her cup. "Should I make more coffee?"

"Please. And yes, it looks like she's staying." Mia glanced at the kittens who were just finishing their breakfast. Actually, the two yellow ones were already using the litter box and the black kitten was cleaning up the rest of the food. Mia cleaned up after them and set them all on the window seat where they promptly fell asleep.

When Grans came in the apartment, she went straight over and checked the kittens. "They look normal."

"What did you expect? Labels saying they have familiar powers?" Mia poured her grandmother coffee. "Why are you staying here?"

"You need someone to watch the kittens. If not, Mr. Darcy will take them out to the yard and lose them. Hopefully, if he does, he'll put them in a garage or something, but you can never tell." She sat down and snapped her fingers at Muffy. He came and lay under her chair, his eyes wide and watching the love seat. "I thought maybe they'd be a little more powerful. I've got a feeling that something unexpected is coming. But it's not them."

"My ex-boyfriend showed up with an engagement ring last night," Christina offered.

Grans shook her head. "Thank you, but the affairs of mere mortals isn't what I'm feeling. Are you getting married then?"

"No. I'm dating Levi." Christina pulled out cereal and poured it into a bowl. "Anyone else want Fruity Flakes?"

"No. But I would like some eggs and a meat. I need protein in the morning, not sugar on sugar." Grans nodded to Mia. "Do you have time to cook? Otherwise, I can."

"I'll cook but someone else is going to have to clean up. I've got work today." Mia paused at the fridge and pulled out eggs, sausage, butter, and the orange juice Trent had brought. The muffins were already on the table. "How do you want your eggs?"

"Nothing for me. Cereal will be fine. And a muffin and OJ." Christina got up and got out four glasses. The security camera beeped again. "Okay, five glasses."

Abigail Majors pulled her SUV into the parking lot. As Mia watched the feed, she got a casserole dish out of the back seat. "Looks like Abigail's bringing food too."

"I still want eggs," Grans said. "But you might hold off on the sausage. I think she's bringing her sausage and hashbrown casserole."

"You can tell that from watching the security feed?" Trent came into the room and poured himself a cup of coffee. "You're good. And your bags are in your room."

"I talked to Abigail this morning after I talked to Mia. She's feeling the same anticipation in the air." Grans swatted at Trent. "Thank you for carrying my luggage. But are you sure there's nothing you and Mia need to tell us?"

His eyes widened as he met Mia's gaze. "Not that I know of. Mia?"

Mia scrambled the eggs. "Can you let your mom in? And no, there's nothing. I'm not sure what you're feeling. Are you sure it's not Todd's arrival? That was a bit of a shock to all of us."

When Mia left the Lodge at the end of the day, she had several missed calls as well as a few messages. She called Abigail first. "Hey, everything okay?"

"Yes, the cooking went well today. I just wanted to let you know that we had a new customer call in an order. Christina's friend Todd called in a delivery for tomorrow. I guess he's planning on being here for a full week because he ordered enough food for several days."

"He said something about skiing. At least that's what I heard. Or maybe he just wanted Christina to have to go to his rental after their dinner tonight. I think she's trying to limit her contact. Levi's not happy." Mia started her little car. It would take a while to get windows cleared from the ice that had settled on the car since she'd arrived that morning. "I may not need you tomorrow night if Christina and Levi are still fighting. But if you wouldn't mind showing up anyway. Christina might not be in the best mood to help me run a class."

"I'm your girl." Abigail laughed. "She was a bit distracted and kept looking at her phone. She went upstairs earlier to get ready and I just saw her leave. I guess she's meeting Todd at his rental. She told me she wouldn't even go except that she promised her mother she'd have dinner with him. One of these days, Christina's mother and I are going to have a long talk about how to treat adult children with respect and love."

Mia laughed. "Better you than me."

"I'm running upstairs before I leave to check in with Mary Alice. Are you on your way home?"

Mia turned on her window wipers. A chunk of ice cleared off, but she still had some icing blocking her view. "I'll be on my way in just a few more minutes. If you're not still there, I'll see you in the morning."

"Girl, my evening is free so I'm going home and eating ice cream in the tub. Then I'm watching old movies from my bed as I do the crosswords. It's going to be heaven." Abigail said her goodbyes and Mia checked the other messages.

One was from her grandmother telling her that the black kitten was still watching the door for her return. "He has bonding issues."

Mia nodded as she hung up the phone. "I'm worried about that."

The windows were finally clear so she texted Trent that she was heading home and she'd talk to him then. She'd finish checking her messages when she got home.

Abigail's car was gone so Mia went directly upstairs when she got home. She was trying to let Abigail have more control over Mia's Morsels, at least the delivery part. She'd go down and check that she had what she needed for tomorrow's soup class after she checked in with Grans. At least the house felt a little calmer than it had been when she left this morning.

When she opened the apartment door, the black kitten ran to meet her. He put his paws on her legs and asked to be picked up. Mia set down her bag after closing the door. Then she picked up the kitten. "We really need to talk about this."

Her phone rang. "Hey, Christina. Is your dinner already over?"

"Mia, something's wrong. His car's here but he's not answering the door or his phone. Should I call Baldwin?"

Mia sat down and put the kitten on her lap. "Could he be skiing?"

"His skis are out by the garage. He's in the house. Lights are on and there's music playing." Christina paused. "I've got a really bad feeling about this."

"What time was he expecting you?" Mia glanced at the clock. It was already six.

"Five thirty. I told him it had to be early since we have deliveries tomorrow."

Mia tried to reach out toward Todd with her power. She couldn't, but when she saw Grans come in the living room, Mia knew. "Christina, call Mark. I'm on my way."

CHAPTER 4

Christina had parked in the rental house's driveway so now her car was blocked in by several vehicles including the ambulance, two Magic Springs police cars, and Mark Baldwin's truck that he used as his official vehicle. Mia parked down the street and walked up the hill to find Christina.

She was sitting on the house's steps, shivering. When she saw Mia, she hurried over. "Mia, Todd's dead. Baldwin called the rental agency and got the lock code and he went inside. He was on the phone when he came out. He told me to stay outside but I heard him say Todd was unresponsive. And the EMTs are in there with him now. Levi's not working tonight so it's a couple of his friends."

"You sure he's dead?" Mia glanced around at the people milling about. No one was in a hurry to get Todd to the hospital, which probably was a bad sign.

Christina shrugged. "I don't know for sure. But I've got a bad feeling."

"Where's Mark? I want to get you out of here before you freeze." She pulled out her phone and punched in Mark's number. She watched as the police chief walked outside, looking around for her as he answered her call.

"I take it you want permission to take Christina home?" He hung up the phone and walked over to where the two women stood. One inside the crime tape, one outside.

"Yes. There's nothing you can say to her now that you can't ask her later." Mia lifted the crime scene tape.

Mark pushed it down with his hand. "Hold on a second. I haven't even talked to Christina yet. Please come over here into the light. I need a couple of pictures of you and then I'll ask some general questions. Then Mia can take you home. But please, don't leave the area."

"Including going to Boise? My mom expects me on Saturday." Christina asked.

He shook his head. "Mrs. Adams is just going to have to come here to visit if she needs to see you. Come over here. Mia, we'll be about ten minutes. You can wait in your car. It's already freezing. and it's just going to get colder as it gets later."

"Twenty-eight degrees if the temperature gauge in my car is accurate." Mia met Christina's gaze. "Go get this over with. I'll be in the car waiting."

"Should I have a lawyer?" Christina asked as they were walking toward the driveway.

Mark looked up at her. "Do you want a lawyer? If you do, I can't talk to you now and you'll have to go to the station to wait for him to show up. I assume he'll be coming from Boise."

"I didn't kill Todd." Christina said. She looked

back at Mia who was still watching them. "I just came for dinner."

"Then I don't think you need a lawyer." Mark sighed and looked back at Mia. "Would you tell her I'm serious and I'm not trying to trick her?"

"I don't think he's trying to trick you." Mia called back.

Christina nodded. "My mom's going to tell me I'm an idiot, but I didn't kill Todd. So I'm going to trust you."

Mark nodded. "I'm sure she'll have some choice words for me as well, but let's get this done and get you out of the cold. You look like you were dressed for dinner, not standing outside."

Mia smiled as she watched them walk toward the house. She knew Mark. He wasn't going to trap Christina into confessing to anything she didn't do. Mark wanted to find a killer, not put in jail the first person on his radar. She started walking back to the car, then she stopped and took out her phone. It wouldn't hurt to document the scene. Just in case. She couldn't see what they did inside the house, but it occurred to her that there were too many people standing around. People that weren't in uniform. What did the cop shows always say, the killer always revisits the crime? Well, if he did, she'd try to get his picture.

When she got back to the car, her phone rang. "Hey Trent. I take it you heard?"

"Levi and I are heading to the school now. Where is Christina?"

"Talking to Mark Baldwin. He said he needed pictures of her before she could leave. Any idea why?"

Trent paused a minute. "Levi's been talking to

his EMT friends and apparently the house is covered in blood. The guy had to be stabbed twenty or thirty times. They were still counting. They're waiting for the coroner. So unless Christina came over, stabbed him, then went back to shower and change, then came back for dinner like nothing happened, she's not the killer. I think Baldwin's making sure she doesn't have blood on her."

"Well, she was with your mom most of the day, cooking. I guess that's her alibi." Mia started the car and turned on the heater. Her legs started bouncing, trying to get warm.

"You were at the Lodge all day?" Trent asked.

"Yep. And with people most of the time. We have a catering Saturday that I was working out the menu and taste testing the food with James." She yawned as she watched the lights flash against the snow. "Wait, why do I need an alibi? I just met Todd."

"You say. You were in the Adams circle for a long time. I just want to make sure you were covered."

Mia thought about Trent's concern. "I was with Isaac during the time she would have been dating this guy, but she dated a lot of guys during those years. I didn't think there was anyone special."

Trent laughed at something Levi said. "I don't think that's what Mia was saying. Levi's feeling a little slighted."

"He shouldn't. Most of those 'dates' were set up by Mother Adams. She's always putting Christina in a bad spot. Like this mess." Mia saw Christina hurrying down the road. "I'll talk to you at the apartment. Christina's coming."

Mia unlocked the doors and Christina jumped into the passenger seat, moving Mia's bag to the back. "This has been a horrible day. No, week, already. Todd shows up out of nowhere, then Levi freaks out. Now, Todd's dead. At least Baldwin didn't think I did it. I guess I should feel lucky."

Mia pulled the car out and slowly drove past the house and multiple official vehicles. Her mind was on what Trent had said. The murder had been violent and personal. Someone with a lot of rage had killed Todd. Someone who must have known him.

"Oh, my. I'm sounding like a spoiled child. Todd's dead and I'm worried about Baldwin thinking bad about me." Christina held her hands out to the heater vents to warm them. "I'm a bad person."

"No, you're not." Mia turned off the street and drove a circle to go back to the school. "You have had a bad week though."

Christina's phone rang and she checked caller ID on her watch. "It's Mom. I'm not answering. I'll call her tomorrow so she can yell at me about not calling the family lawyer. I'm beat. And, worse, I'm hungry. How can I be hungry when Todd's dead?"

"I'm sure there will be food at the house. Trent and Levi are heading there now. Levi was worried about you."

Christina snorted. "I'm sure."

When they got back to the house, the parking lot was filled with cars. Abigail must have returned. Trent's truck was there. Grans's car. And the delivery van. The only car missing was Christina's Land Rover. Mia pulled up and parked next to the van. "We'll get your car tomorrow morning before I go to work."

"Baldwin said we could go back tonight after they left. He'd call me." Christina got out of the car. "It was a nice ring Todd bought for me. I feel bad that Mom gave him the wrong idea about me. His folks are rich. Richer than Mom and Dad. This thing's going to blow up around Magic Springs."

Mia thought about what Christina had said as they walked up to the apartment. Maybe that was why the other kittens showed up. Maybe the Goddess knew they needed a distraction.

As they came into the crowded apartment, the black kitten zeroed in on Mia and stood on his back feet, asking to be picked up. She set down her purse and obliged.

"I think you've been chosen with this one." Grans said from her spot on the couch.

Mia rubbed his head. "I don't need a new familiar. I have Mr. Darcy."

At those words, Mr. Darcy sat up and meowed from his place next to Grans.

"See, he agrees." Mia handed over the kitten to Trent who was standing by the kitchen. "You deal with this one. What's going on here?"

"We decided we needed to talk about Todd." Levi said. He came out from behind Trent. "We need to figure out who killed the guy so we can get his people out of town."

"He has people in town?" Mia glanced back at Christina.

"I told you his death wouldn't go unnoticed. His family's big in Boise. I'm surprised the press isn't here." Christina picked up the tabby after she found a place to sit in the living room.

"They are. At least the advance team is. Several news vans stopped at Majors for supplies just now. I got a call from my night manager. The woman who was checking them out heard them say that it's going to be a big news day. They're hoping to stay around so they can get at least a few runs in on the mountain before they go home." Trent handed Mia a cup of coffee.

"Seriously?" Mia took the coffee and took a big sip. "I guess we need to talk about who wanted Todd dead."

"Besides me?" Levi held up his hand.

"Levi, I told you that there was nothing going on with Todd and me." Christina closed her eyes. "I was having dinner with him, then he would have skied for a few days and left town to the next appropriate eligible woman on his list. Besides, he didn't even know you existed."

"That's not quite true." Levi said.

Trent turned to give Levi more room in the living room. "Do you want to explain that comment? Don't tell me you did something stupid."

"Okay, I won't tell you." Levi shrugged. "But you're going to hear it from Baldwin. I went to the rental this morning and talked to Mr. Perfect. He told me to get used to losing. He said Christina would get tired of a townie and see the errors of her ways."

"You know that's not true," Christina said, her cheeks burning. "I'm not looking for a rich husband to save me."

"So what did you do?" Trent asked. Mia saw him close his eyes, expecting the worst. When Levi spoke, it didn't seem like Trent was surprised.

"I hit him, knocking him into a chair. Then I left." Levi went over to sit by Christina. "I'm sorry. He was such a pompous jerk. I should have left it alone."

"Yes, you should have." Christina leaned back in

the sofa. "I don't know why everyone can't just realize I'm a grown woman and I can make my own
choices, good or bad."

"Levi," Trent focused in on his brother. "Tell me
he was standing after you punched him."

"He stood and told me to leave. That he had
better things to do with his time than fight with
me." Levi put his face in his hands, then ran them
over his head, pushing back his long hair. "I told
him I was sorry and left. He was alive and talking at
nine this morning. He was going skiing when I got
there or at least he was dressed in his skiwear."

"So we need to see if he actually hit the slopes.
Maybe that's where he met up with his killer. What
did you do after the fight?" Mia was trying to figure out how to prove Levi wouldn't have done this.
He'd already admitted to punching the guy. Would
he have come back and stabbed him later? She
didn't think so but she needed him to have an
alibi, because he definitely had motive.

"Derek and I drove down to Boise to pick up a
new ambulance. I just got back about six when
Trent picked me up at the station. Of course, I
heard about the killing on the radio from the guys
who were on the call. It shook up the new guy. I'm
not sure he'll stay on."

Mia blew out a breath. Levi was out of town for a
good reason and had a verifiable witness that he
couldn't have been there. She hadn't thought
he'd kill someone, but now she knew he didn't.
Now she just needed to make sure Baldwin knew
that.

She looked at Levi. "You need to talk to Mark
and tell him you were at the house."

"Doesn't that make me look guilty?" Levi asked.

"You were in Boise or on the freeway home when he was killed." Mia pointed out. "He's going to find out you were there."

"What if he thinks I hired someone or asked someone to kill the guy?"

"Have you taken out a lot of money from your account recently or been hanging out with serial killers lately?" Trent asked.

"Trent, stop being mean to your brother." Abigail reprimanded her son.

"Mom, it's a good question. Levi doesn't have the money or the clout to hire someone to do something like that. I think Mia's right. Levi needs to tell Baldwin about being there. Otherwise, it's going to look like he's hiding something." Trent crossed over to his mom and put a hand on her shoulder. "He didn't do it. Baldwin's not going to arrest him."

Abigail took a deep breath. "You boys always make my life interesting."

The alarm went off and Mia went to the kitchen to see who was in the parking lot. Levi wasn't going to have to wait, Baldwin was here.

She went back to the living room. "Grans, Abigail, Trent, why don't you stay up here and get dinner ready. Levi, Christina, come downstairs with me and we'll talk to Mark in the living room."

Abigail grabbed Levi's arm as he stood to follow Mia downstairs. "Are you sure? Maybe you need to talk to a lawyer first?"

"Mom, I didn't kill anyone. I wasn't even in town when he was killed. I can talk to Mark. He's good people." Levi leaned down and gave his mother a kiss on the cheek. "Besides, I feel good about this. I think Mark's going to need our help to find whoever did this."

Abigail squeezed his arm and nodded. Then she released him and stood. "I think it's a spaghetti night. Trent, you make an amazing sauce. Let's get this started."

Trent put his arm around his mom and they and Grans left the living room to go into the kitchen. All three kittens followed them. Mr. Darcy stretched out on the couch. Mia held the door open and Christina and Levi went downstairs with her to meet with Mark.

She had them sit in the living room as she went and let Mark inside. He was stomping the snow off his boots when she opened the door. "Hey, Mark, come in."

"I'd ask how you knew I was here, but I know your security system." He came in and wiped his feet on the mat in front of the door. "I need to talk to Christina if you don't mind."

Christina waved her hand. "I'm over here. And Levi needs to tell you something too."

"Levi Majors. I guess I should have expected to find you here. You're my next stop." Mark glanced down at his boots. "Should I slip these off?"

"No, you're fine. Come on in. Do you want coffee?" She glanced at the stairs. "I've got a full house upstairs. I thought maybe you'd be more comfortable here."

"That's thoughtful of you. I'll need Christina alone for a few minutes, then Levi. But coffee would be great. And a cookie if you happen to have any. Sarah's banned all sweets in the house until after the baby's here. I think I'm going through sugar withdrawal."

Mia smiled. "Levi, come help me make some coffee. Christina? Do you want coffee or hot cocoa?"

"Hot cocoa would be amazing. I'm still frozen from earlier." Christina bit her lip and Mia could see she was thinking about being at Todd's rental.

"We'll get it done, then I'll bring them out. Levi can help me set up my supplies for tomorrow's soup class while he waits." She nodded and put a hand on Levi's back, moving him toward the kitchen.

When they were inside, he stared at the door. "I don't get why he has to be alone with someone to talk to them. She should have someone with her."

"The only person she could have with her would be a lawyer. And she doesn't want one." She nodded to the coffeepot. "You get coffee going and I'll make Christina's cocoa."

As they were working, the parking lot security alarm went off again. Mia went over and turned on the kitchen monitor. A dark colored BMW had driven into the parking lot. "Who could that be?"

"No one I know. Christina's got the most expensive car of any of my friends and that one's pricier than hers." He squinted toward the monitor. "It's a guy. In a suit, I think."

Mia poured a cup of coffee and grabbed a bag of cookies and dumped them on a plate. "Finish Christina's cocoa, then bring it out. I need to answer the door."

Levi nodded but kept his gaze on the monitor.

Mia opened the door and smiled at Mark. "Sorry,

we have another visitor. Here's your coffee and cookies. I'll be out of here as soon as I handle this."

"No problem. We were just finishing up." He took the coffee and took a sip. "You always have the best coffee."

Mia nodded as she hurried to the door. "I'll send you a bag. I get it from a place in Boise that roasts their own beans."

She opened the door just as the man was reaching for the bell. "Hello, how can I help you?"

"Are you Mia Malone?" He asked. He was in a suit with a long wool coat over the top of it and he had a red scarf around his neck. He wore a black fedora to top off the outfit, but his shoes were leather and more made for a conference room than the eight to ten inches of snow that Magic Springs had already collected. Thank goodness she kept her sidewalks and parking lot clear or he would have slid down the hill rather than been able to walk.

"Yes, I'm Mia Malone," she answered.

He nodded and looked at his phone. "I'm Bernard Brown, here to represent Christina Adams. Her mother said there's been an unfortunate event surrounding a former boyfriend?"

"You're a lawyer?" Mia frowned.

He nodded. "Yes, may I see Miss Adams please?"

"Of course, she's right inside chatting with our local police chief." Mia held the door open. She guessed there would be one more for dinner.

CHAPTER 5

Bernard Brown hurried past Mia and, looking around, found Christina sitting at the table with Mark. He held up a hand as he rushed forward, slipping on the tile floor. "Stop talking to Miss Adams. I am her attorney."

Mark stood and hurried over to pick Mr. Brown off the floor where he'd landed. "Mr. Brown, are you okay?"

Mia and Christina stood by as he struggled to his feet. He nodded and slipped off his shoes. "Sorry, I don't have the appropriate footwear for the location. You don't mind if I stand here in my socks, do you?"

"No, not at all. I hope you're all right." Mia held out her hands. "Let me take your coat."

He shrugged out of it and looked at Christina. "You are Miss Adams?"

"Yes, I take it my mom sent you?" She reached out and shook his hand. "I don't need legal representation in this matter."

"Please let me determine that." He turned toward Mark. "Thank you for your assistance earlier. You are the local police officer?"

"Police chief." Mark took out a card and handed it to Mr. Brown.

He took it and nodded, taking a slim case out of his suit pocket and putting it inside. He took out his own card and handed it to Mark. "If you don't mind, is there somewhere Miss Adams and I can talk, alone?"

Levi came out of the kitchen with a cup in hand. "Sorry to interrupt, but here's your cocoa."

"Thanks, Levi," Christina walked back to the table and took the drink.

"Can we offer you some coffee or cocoa or tea?" Mia asked Mr. Brown.

He looked around at the four people in the room. "Coffee would be nice. Black is fine. Miss Adams, I must insist we talk alone. At least for a few minutes, if you would."

"You can use my office." Mia squeezed Christina's arm. "Go talk to him. You know your mom is going to have a cow if you don't. I'll get him some coffee."

"Sounds good."

"Fine, let's go in here." Christina pointed to Mia's office. She turned toward Mark. "We'll be in there. Unless you still need me."

"Go talk to your attorney," Mark went back to the table. "Levi and I can talk while we wait."

Levi held up a finger. "Let me grab my coffee and I'll be right out."

He and Mia went to the kitchen. When the door closed, he said, "Mother Adams sent an attorney? How did she even know?"

"The same way the press knew. Someone leaked Todd's death as soon as Christina called the police." Mia poured a cup of coffee. "Or Christina's phone is being monitored."

He shook his head as he picked up his coffee and headed back to the lobby area. "I wouldn't put it past that woman."

Mia followed him out. "Neither would I."

Trent came down right after Bernard Brown and Mark Baldwin left the parking lot. "I've been sent to tell you the garlic bread just went in the oven, so you need to come upstairs."

Mia had just locked up the kitchen after making sure the coffeepot was off and drained. She'd left the cups in the sink as Christina told her she'd clean them up in the morning. Levi and Christina were talking on the couch.

"We're on our way," Levi stood up. "That was intense."

"Who was the guy in the BMW?" Trent went to put his arm around Mia.

Christina answered. "That was my mother's answer to every problem. She sent me an attorney to make sure I didn't say anything stupid to the police."

"How did she . . ." Trent saw Mia's nod and shook his head. "Never mind. I'm not sure I want to know."

Christina turned off the lobby lights. "I'm getting my own phone and phone plan tomorrow."

"You think she's bugging your phone?" Mia asked.

Christina turned to look at her. "You think she's not?"

Mia shrugged and headed upstairs. "I'm too tired to make a solid judgment."

They plated the food and after everyone had eaten, Grans stood. "Can someone take Muffy out for a walk? I'm going to my room and preparing a spell for poor Mr. Thompson."

"A spell?" Christina asked. "What does it do?"

Grans patted her shoulder. "It helps send his soul away to the next destination so he doesn't get stuck here. I think we have enough souls hanging around right now, don't you?"

Mr. Darcy made a yowling sound, then walked over to the apartment door. Dorian magically unlocked it and the cat ran outside, shutting the door quickly after him so the kittens couldn't follow.

"Grans, you upset Dorian." Mia shook her head.

"He'll get over it. Besides, it's the right thing to do when someone passes violently. Dorian knows that. Who's taking Muffy?" Grans asked as she paused in the hallway.

Levi stood. "I'll take him."

Christina stood as well and took his plate, putting it with hers in the sink. "I'll go out with you."

He started to say something, then he smiled and kissed her. "Thanks. That would be nice."

After they'd left with Muffy, Abigail let out a loud sigh. "Those two are going to kill me. That's all I can say."

"They'll figure it out." Trent stood. "Is there more garlic bread?"

After everyone had gone home, Mia was in the

kitchen doing dishes when Grans came in from her room. "Are you okay? How did the spelling go?"

"You never know with these things." Grans took a glass from the cabinet and poured water from the pitcher Mia kept in the fridge. "But it's done. Hopefully Todd's wherever his belief system told him he'd go."

"Like Heaven?" Mia rinsed the last plate before putting it into the dishwasher. She started the machine.

"Like Heaven." Grans sat down. "I'm still having that feeling. Something big is coming. I thought it was Todd's death, then that lawyer fellow. But no. It's something else. Something with a lot of power."

Mia turned off the water and picked up a towel to dry her hands. "What can we expect or look for?"

Grans pressed her lips together. "That's the problem. I don't know."

After she said goodnight, Mia went into her room and took a long bath. She thought about Grans's concern and tried to open her own thoughts to the universe. At first, she didn't notice anything, just the hot water and the smell of the bath bubbles. Then she heard a voice.

"Power isn't always a bad thing."

She opened her eyes when no more messages came. She shivered, realizing the water had gone cold. How long had she been out? All she could remember was a field of flowers, lightning in the sky and that phrase. Power isn't always a bad thing. She stood and wrapped a towel around her, letting the water out of the tub. As she did, she saw a flash of lightning and heard thunder. Snow lightning? That was unusual. Maybe the lightning had seeped into her vision from the real world. That happened at times. She went to bed, watching the flashing light show over the Magic Mountains outside her window. Finally, when the show stopped, she fell asleep. The message from the Goddess echoing in her head.

Power isn't always a bad thing.

The next morning, she was in the kitchen making a French toast casserole when she saw Trent's truck pull into the parking lot on the security monitor. She put on her robe and slippers and went to the door. Mr. Darcy was asleep on the couch and the three kittens surrounded him. He opened one eye and glared at her.

Trying not to giggle, she unlocked the apartment door and went downstairs to let Trent in. Muffy must have followed her because he hurried out to the snow-covered yard, did three circles, then did his business. He turned around and ran back into the house. Mia watched as he made his way up the stairs.

Her home was a zoo. She smiled at Trent as he put a bag over his shoulder and made his way to the door. She reached up on her toes and kissed him. "I didn't expect you today. Don't you have to open the store soon?"

"I do, but I need your help. You're not working at the Lodge, are you?" He moved inside and closed and locked the door. He handed her the bag then took off his coat and slipped off his snow boots. Trent had his own set of slippers at the school.

"Not today, why?" Mia started walking toward the stairs.

Trent caught up with her and handed her a blanket. "I need you to babysit."

"What are you talking about?" She unwrapped the blanket and a small white head with black eyes looked at her. The tiny dog barked. "Where did he come from?"

"Did you see the snow lightning last night?"

When Mia nodded, Trent continued. "Well, after the lightning show, I was compelled to check my porch. He was there in a basket with a note."

"What did the note say?" Mia reached out and the puppy licked her finger.

"Here's your familiar. His name is Cerberus." Trent handed her a blue envelope. "And it was signed by the Goddess."

"Wait, like the Greek dog with three heads? And the Goddess dropped off a puppy for you?" Mia stared at the little puff of fur in the basket. "Does that even happen?"

"She probably used a human, but yes, it happens. Mom got her first familiar that way. It's kind of a family tradition." He petted the puppy and he lay down under the blanket. "I think it's a Maltese. Why would the Goddess give me a Maltese as a familiar. Why not a German shepherd? Or a Bernese mountain dog? Something that could see out the truck window when we go driving."

Mia heard Gloria's laughter from the apartment. This time, Trent must have heard it too.

"It's not funny," he called back.

"So what are you calling him." Mia leaned in as she carried the little package up the stairs.

"I'm going to regret this, but his name's Cerby." They'd reached the third floor and Trent held open the apartment door. "Maybe you need another pet?"

The three kittens ran toward them as they came into the apartment. Then they all stopped, spat out their displeasure at the new arrival and ran back into the kitchen.

Mia glanced over at Trent. "I think we have the answer to that question, don't you?"

The puppy, Cerby, started whining. Trent reached out his hand. "He does that any time I set him down. I thought maybe he just wanted to be held, but it looks like he wants me to hold him."

Mia handed over the puppy and read the note from the Goddess. Or more likely, the Goddess's human helper. Sometimes people just got the urge to do something. Buy a coffee for a stranger. Speak a kind word. Usually, it wasn't as extreme as giving a puppy to a neighbor or putting a basket of kittens on a doorstep, but these things happened. Especially if the push was from a higher power that had a plan they needed help with. "And you want me to babysit?"

"At least today. I'll set up my office and get something that I can carry him in with me, but I'm not comfortable leaving him alone in my office at the store. Not for a while until he's bigger. Mom said she'd watch him, but she has deliveries today." Trent went over and poured himself a coffee. "We stopped at the store and I brought everything he should need. And some ingredients for breakfast. If you feel like cooking. Or I can cook, but . . ."

"Cerby won't let you set him down." Mia finished Trent's statement. "Well, the Goddess must be aware that the transfer of power from you to Levi was more of a sharing thing. How are you going to continue to hide this?"

"I don't know. Of course, I'm going to blame you for the puppy. The official story is you gave him to me." He held the puppy up to look him over. "Who's a good boy?"

Muffy barked from his place on the floor where he was watching Trent and Cerby.

Grans came into the room. "I guess you got your answer. Trent, I think that dog is more than just a familiar."

Trent stood and pulled out a chair for Mary Alice. "Can I get you some coffee?"

"Please. I've been up all night since the lightning storm. Something crossed over last night. Don't worry, it didn't feel maleficent or evil, but it's obviously from the other side." Grans reached out to the blanket on the table where Trent had left Cerby to get her coffee. She touched the puppy on the head. She jerked back as he barked at her. She took the cup of coffee from Trent.

"What's wrong?" He sat down and put the blanket and Cerby back on his lap.

"This is what I've been expecting." Grans pressed her lips together. She spoke again. "Trent, I think you have a hellhound there."

With Abigail and Christina out of the school on the food delivery run, Mia took Cerby and the kittens downstairs to her office. She needed to finish her presentation for the soup class tonight. Right now, she was working on her slides that she'd turn into handouts. The other two kittens were sleeping, side by side in the basket she'd brought them downstairs in.

The other two kittens hadn't liked Cerby at all, but the black one, he seemed to love him. Black and white fur, curled together, they looked like that yin and yang symbol Mia had seen in books.

Kittens and puppies weren't what she needed to deal with while she was trying to save enough money and build contacts to go back to running Mia's Morsels, or at least the catering part. If she could figure out a way to make the other two parts of the business, delivery and classes, more profitable, maybe she didn't need catering.

Mia refocused on the project at hand and by the end of the hour, she had the slides done as well as handouts for the attendees. She put the documents in a computer file under classes so she wouldn't have to reinvent the wheel when she taught this again and made a separate paper file for her file cabinet. Someday, she was going to write a cookbook. But she'd yet to have come up with a good theme for the book, unless she just called it Mia's Morsels. Maybe something on entertaining? She finished the cold coffee in her cup and glanced over at the basket. Both the puppy and the kitten were awake. They were staring at her.

"Okay, so what do you need?" She turned toward the basket.

The puppy barked and the kitten did a circle.

"You have to go potty?" She felt a little stupid, talking to the babies.

The puppy barked and she could swear the kitten nodded. Or she was just going crazy.

"Okay then, I'll take you outside and you can do your duty." She petted Cerby. Then she turned toward the kitten. "I'll take you upstairs as soon as he's done."

She picked them both up and put one in each pocket of her hoodie. "Then we'll have lunch. I'm starving and you guys are probably too."

As she opened the front door, she saw a black Land Rover pull into the parking lot. Christina and Trent had gone to get hers a few hours ago and it sat by Mia's ancient compact. No, there was only one other person that Mia knew who also drove a Land Rover. Mia's life had gone from busy to complicated.

Mother Adams had come to visit Christina.

CHAPTER 6

Cerby hurried and did his business while Mia waited in the doorway, watching Mother Adams park her SUV and then walk up to the door. Mia scooped the puppy up into her pocket, then smiled at the older woman. "Mrs. Adams, so nice to see you."

"I'm here to talk to my daughter if she hasn't been arrested for being stupid yet." Mother Adams leaned to the side and looked into the doorway. "I can't believe you left your job at the Owyhee Plaza to work out here in the sticks. Then you bought this run-down monstrosity? Mia, I always thought you had a brain."

Mia pressed her lips together so she wouldn't say the first thing that popped into her head. Instead, she put a hand on the heavy door of the school. "Actually, you knew I had a talent for turning old, forgotten buildings into something beautiful. Like I did for the house that Isaac and I bought. We doubled our money out of that place when we sold it because I'd restored it and made it a beautiful home. Just not a home for the two of us."

Mother Adams's left eye twitched. A tell that Mia had learned years ago that meant Mia had scored points in a verbal game she didn't even want to be playing with the woman who could have been her mother-in-law. "The Boise house was beautiful."

It was Mia's turn to blink. She'd never heard Mother Adams give in so fast. She decided to let the moment pass, gracefully. "Christina's out doing deliveries today for Mia's Morsels. She should be back about five. I could call her and let her know you're here if you need to get back to Boise."

"No need. Just tell her I'll see her tonight at seven for dinner at the Lodge. I have a room there for however long it takes for this problem to be cleared up." Mother Adams turned back toward her car.

"I think she has a date tonight." Mia called after her. "She was going to help me with a cooking class, but she already had plans."

Mother Adams turned back and stared at her. After a few seconds, that felt like hours, she spoke. "Tell Christina that this Levi person is more than welcome to join us. It's about time I met the man she's throwing her life away for. And Mia?"

She froze, wondering what horrible thing the women had been waiting to say to her. "Yes?"

"You look good. Less stressed. Maybe country life agrees with you." With that, Mother Adams went to her car and left.

Mia shut the door and leaned against it as she locked it. Whatever she'd expected when she finally ran into Mother Adams again after breaking up with Isaac, it hadn't been this. The kitten patted at Mia's jacket, reminding her of her promise. She went upstairs to make lunch and think about the visit. And call Christina.

With the soup class over, Mia found herself in the downstairs kitchen with Abigail cleaning up. She glanced at the clock on the wall. "Well, Christina and Levi were supposed to meet with Mother Adams at seven for dinner. Either it's going well, or they're at a bar somewhere drinking."

"It's almost nine, so I'd put money on the bar." Abigail dried the last soup pan. "I really enjoyed your class tonight. I always cook my go-to soups. I think I'm going to be more adventurous next week and throw in one from the class."

"I like making soup. Especially this time of year. The process makes me feel warm and the soup makes the kitchen smell amazing. And if I make some sort of bread or quick bread to go with it, well, that's heaven." Mia dried her hands on the towel and glanced around the kitchen. "I think we're done here."

"Thanks for letting me hang out tonight. The house can be a little quiet without Thomas." Abigail pulled on her jacket. "I've been thinking about taking one of your triplets off your hands. The yellow-striped boy?"

"Really? That would be great. I'm so worried about finding homes for them. I think the black one is staying since if I gave him away, he'd just find his way back. He's a little attached already."

"She's attached," Abigail corrected. When Mia just stared at her, she continued. "The two orange kittens are males. The black one is a female. Don't be embarrassed. It's hard to tell sex on a kitten. It's not like a dog."

"Well, then I'll have to start thinking of girl names. I was considering Ralph, but now, maybe Princess or Bella." Mia laughed as she went to lock the doors. "Or maybe I'll find a Greek goddess name, like Athena. Or maybe not, since we've got Cerby hanging around."

"Yes, the hellhound. I'm not sure what the Goddess was thinking, but this proves she has a sense of humor. We've been trying to keep Trent's powers a secret and she sends him a hellhound? Do you know how rare of a gift that is?" Abigail shrugged on her coat.

"Actually, no. I've never heard of a hellhound. I mean, I know what it is, but I've never seen one. Cerby seems so calm." Mia had been thinking about this all day. The puppy was cute as a button. Not what she'd expect from a hellhound.

"Well, I've never heard of the Goddess sending one before. I'm doing some research when I get home. It feels like something's building and she wants Trent to have a protector." Abigail remote-started her car. "I'm sure the fact that she sent the hellhound in the form of a white Maltese reflects the fact she wants to protect Trent's secret as well. She's always got a plan."

"Well, he's well hidden." Mia turned out the lights and followed Abigail out of the room. She locked the inside door as well, then walked Abigail to the front door. "The one thing I've learned in the last three years is things, people, aren't always what they seem. Maybe it's just a coincidence that Cerby is a hellhound."

"I've learned there's no such thing as coincidence. Everything has a reason. Everything's a piece of a puzzle. We just haven't seen the entire pattern, yet." She gave Mia a hug. "I'll see you on Friday. We don't have anything going on this weekend, but I put out a notice that we'd have open shopping hours Friday from ten to three in the lobby."

"Sounds good." Mia watched as Abigail made her way out to her car, then waved as she sat inside, waiting for the defrosters to clear her windshield. And she wondered, maybe the Goddess sent the hellhound to protect Christina from her mother.

As she went upstairs, she thought about Todd. Who had killed the young man, and why had he even thought that asking Christina to marry him was a good idea? Mia could answer the last question, Mother Adams had sent him. But for the first one, all she knew was it wasn't Christina or Levi who'd done the deed. Yet, they would both be the first people Baldwin considered. Was that a coincidence? Or would Abigail's motto hold up here too, which would mean someone wanted it to look like one of the two lovebirds would react emotionally and kill the interloper? If that was the case, who would benefit from having the wrong person framed. Or who would have the anger to stab someone so many times?

She didn't like to consider why one human would kill another. It felt like she was abandoning her values as a fledgling kitchen witch. But one of her own had been affected by Todd's death. And she needed to make sure that neither Christina nor Levi would be charged with the murder.

Grans was on the phone when Mia opened the apartment door. The black kitten came running as soon as Mia walked inside.

"I'll call you tomorrow, Robert," Grans said as she hung up the phone. She patted the couch next to her. "Come sit and tell me how the class went."

Mia did and the kitten jumped on the couch and into her lap. Trent had come by after work and picked up Cerby. "I thought it went well. I had ten signups for next week's class on roasting."

"That's good." Grans studied the kitten. "She's very attached to you."

"Yes, I've noticed. Abigail said she'd like to have the striped one. They're probably old enough to go to homes, right? It's not like the mama cat is here, feeding them." Mia stroked the kitten's fur and was rewarded with a strong purr.

"Robert said the road crew found a female cat out on the road near town last night. He said she'd recently had kittens. She's cold, but he thinks she'll survive." Grans reached out and rubbed the kitten's head. "Poor babies. I wonder who brought them here."

"Good question." Mia had figured the mama cat was elsewhere since she hadn't been in the basket with the kittens. But she'd hoped she was at least inside. Mia would pick up the untouched food and water bowl tomorrow. "So, anything on Todd's case?"

"Robert hadn't heard much. You know he's on the city council, so they don't get involved in the goings-on at the police station. But he did hear that Todd had rented the same house last month when he came to town to ski. Robert knows the landlord. She told Robert that Todd came up at least a few times last year too."

Mia frowned. "Wait, I thought he came here to ask Christina to marry him. Didn't he know last month or last year that she lived here?"

Grans shrugged. "The way he talked, it seemed like he left school, got into law school, and came to claim his bride. I think he hadn't been pining for Christina as much as he claimed. Anyway, I thought that was interesting."

"I do too." Mia rubbed Muffy's head who was sitting between her and Grans. "Do you want me to take him out?"

"That would be nice. I was waiting for Christina to get home, but . . ."

Mia stood, dropping the kitten off on the couch. "I can do it. I'm a little amped-up after teaching. I won't be sleeping for a while now."

"Well, I'm crashing so I'll leave my door open. I'm thinking we'll have a training session on Saturday before I go back home. Now that Cerby has made his entrance, I'm feeling less anxious about what's ahead for us."

Mia paused at the apartment door. "You think a Maltese puppy can save us?"

"Oh, my dear. You need to look with more than your eyes. He's so much more than a puppy." Grans stood and picked up her phone. "I need to put this on the charger. Tomorrow's going to be busy."

Muffy followed Mia out the door and hurried down the stairs. Apparently, the little dog had been waiting awhile. She opened the front door and let him out, then reached back and grabbed a coat off the rack. She pulled it on, then stuffed her hands in the pockets. It was Christina's pink puffer jacket. It looked like it wouldn't be warm at all, but with the down filling, the coat was amazingly soft and warm. She watched Muffy wander around the same small patch of grass where the snow had been cleared to give the pup somewhere to go besides the snowbank. Trent took care of a lot without her even asking him to help. Like Muffy's potty area.

She felt something in the pocket of the coat and as Muffy hurried back inside, she followed him and shut the door. She pulled out the item, thinking Christina must have forgotten it. She'd take it upstairs. Hanging the coat back up, she looked down at the item.

It was a Tiffany blue ring box. The one Todd had handed Christina with the ring.

Mia waited up for Christina to come home that night. When she did, Mia was sitting at the kitchen table. She moved the box she'd found into view. Christina came inside and grabbed a bottle of water.

"Hey, what are you doing up?" She froze when she saw the box. "Oh, well, I can explain."

"Why do you still have the ring?" Mia asked.

Christina sank into a chair at the table. "Todd left it on the table. I called him but he asked me to hang on to it until we had dinner. He said I owed him that. To honestly take some time and think about his marriage offer. I planned on giving it back to him at dinner. But then, you know, and now I don't know what to do with it."

"Maybe your mother can give it to his parents." Mia opened the box and looked at the ring. "It's beautiful and expensive. Do you want to keep it in my safe until you go see your mom again? Is she leaving soon?"

Christina shook her head. "Even with Levi there, I got the lecture on talking to the police without a lawyer. She didn't even seem to care that I didn't kill Todd. Her main concern was me refusing his marriage proposal and the police interview. Like I could take either one of those decisions back now. Anyway, she calmed down, we ate dinner, and then Levi took me out for ice cream. And I vented. I feel bad for him. He got the whole story of my poor little princess life."

"You had advantages, sure. But you also had your mother. You know, I never hear you, or heard Isaac for that matter, talk much about your father. I met him a few times over the holidays, but he was always busy with some deal or client. I'm not sure I spoke more than ten or twenty words to him total." Mia sipped her tea.

"Dad is always working. Even at those dinners and parties Mom asks me to attend now, I rarely see him in person. And if I do, it's for a family picture. I'm not sure he even knows you and Isaac broke up. Even with the new engagement." Christina sipped her water. "No, my mom was the one who raised us, well, her and the nanny. I think Todd's family is the same way except both of his parents worked. We were alone a lot growing up. There were people there, sure, but not family."

"This conversation explains so much." Mia reached for a cookie. "No wonder you were always over at our house. I figured you just liked the food."

"I did like the food. And, bonus, you let me cook with you. I'm pretty sure it's your fault I went to culinary school. I wanted to make memories with people, like you did with me." Christina yawned. "I've got to crash. Deliveries were crazy today. Everyone wanted to talk about Todd."

"Small town gossip trail." Mia glanced at her watch. "I've got to crash too. Hey, Abigail wants the yellow-striped kitten. Do you want the tabby?"

Christina paused. "I do, but I live under your roof. So it's up to you. I know you're thinking about keeping the black kitten. And we have Mr. Darcy. I'm not sure a third is a good idea."

Mia nodded. "Let's think about it and see how things go." Mia also worried about Muffy. Grans was staying more and more often. She also had to think about Trent and Cerby. Somehow, they had turned into a family with a passel full of familiars. The apartment was feeling smaller by the minute.

Gloria giggled. Mia stood and grabbed the ring box. "Since the apartment is feeling like Grand Central Station, I'll put this in the safe. Let me know when you want it back."

"Never sounds perfect." Christina held up a hand. "I know, I have to deal with it. I'll talk to Mom when I see her tomorrow. She's taking me shopping in Sun Valley for some winter clothes since I look like I'm homeless."

"I like that sweater. And I know you just bought those jeans." Mia checked the lock on the apartment door. Mr. Darcy was sleeping on the couch with the three kittens surrounding him. He opened one eye and glared at her as she turned off the light. "Sleep well."

He closed his eye and huffed out a sigh.

Mia tried not to giggle as she moved toward the bedroom. Adding two more personalities to the mix would probably be too many, but she wasn't sure how she was going to break the idea to the black kitten. That was a problem for tomorrow. As was finding Todd's killer.

CHAPTER 7

Thursday morning, Mia filled a travel mug with coffee before she went to work. The Lodge was quiet as she walked through the lobby. Christmas decorations had been replaced with a more generic winter feel although they'd start putting up touches of spring soon. Even though the landscape outside would still be more arctic north theme than springtime meadows. This was when the Lodge wanted the snow to stay around, hoping for an extended ski season. Putting up spring in the lobby was seen as tempting fate.

She made it to her office without any serious conversations. She waved and greeted staff as she went by, but no one needed to urgently talk to her. She was surprised to find James sitting in her visitor chair, a cinnamon roll on a plate on her desk. "Uh-oh, what's wrong?"

"Why does something have to be wrong?" James smiled from the chair. "Maybe I'm just happy to see you."

"Of course, that could be it." Mia broke off a piece of the roll and popped it in her mouth. "I take it that we have a new event this weekend?"

"How did you know?" James sat up, hands on his knees. "Did someone call you?"

She took out her planner and a pen. "You did. Tell me about it."

The Friday night event that Frank had booked yesterday afternoon was for a group of attorneys from Boise. They wanted dinner and drinks for fifteen couples. High-end dishes with at least two options for each course. And the guests would need to be able to let the kitchen know of their choices Friday afternoon. Mia finished writing and looked up at James. "It feels like Frank gave them their own restaurant for the night."

"Basically. I just hope that fifteen couples estimate doesn't turn into more. I can do three soups, three salads, three protein choices, that's fine. I can use the prepped courses for specials in the restaurant or room service. But if the event goes from thirty to fifty, it's going to strain my supplies."

Mia tapped her pen on the desk as she thought. "Maybe I can do some recon and see if that thirty is a hard and fast number. Do we know the law firm?"

After James told her the information, she dialed her mother. Theresa Carpenter Malone worked at a Boise law firm and she should have contacts with this one. Or at least Mia hoped so. When she got her voicemail, Mia left a message. Then she called Christina and asked the same question. Someone should be able to find out more about this emergency catering event.

When James left her office, they had a semisolid plan for tomorrow's event. And, if she was going to get more information, she should have it by the end of the day. It would make procuring the necessary proteins a little sketchy, especially if the number of participants increased, but it was doable. James told her he would start making the plans for thirty covers today.

Mia went through her phone calls and found one from Jenna. She dialed the number and got voice mail again. What, was everyone too busy to answer their phone?

She focused on writing up a plan for the event and reached out to the decorating staff as well as housekeeping to make sure they had the room set up early Friday. By the time she'd finished her planning it was lunchtime, and her stomach was growling. She called the kitchen and got James.

"Did you hear anything?" He sounded like he'd been running for the last three hours.

"Not yet. I need food." Mia ordered a salad and a pitcher of iced tea. She might be a little wired by the time she finished work today, but she needed to scramble to get the Friday night event planned and check on the plans for Saturday. At least she'd hired more catering staff.

With that thought, she realized she hadn't scheduled the catering staff for Friday. She went down the list, calling and marking them off when she got a yes. Calling Jenna again, she still got voice mail so she drew a box next to her name. When she finished the list, she still had five boxes to check.

A knock on the door announced the arrival of her lunch, and she spent the next hour eating and listening to podcasts. She found one that talked about the origins of soups. She made several notes and sent them to her Mia's Morsels account. She'd add them to the talking points for the next soup class. Why was it that these fun knowledge bits never showed up before she taught a class?

She was taking her tray back to the kitchen when she ran into Jenna. The girl looked tired. Mia remembered how hard it had been her first year of college to put everything together as an adult including going to school and having a life. Then she'd added a job into the mix. Christina had the same look most of her freshman year. "Hey, I've tried to call you back. Everything okay?"

"Sure. I was just checking in to see if you needed me this weekend. I came up to ski this afternoon since my lab was canceled." Jenna smiled.

"I'm glad you stopped in. I left a voice message. Yes, we need you for a few hours Friday night and then again the next day. Can you be here at five Friday and three Saturday? We don't have anything yet on Sunday, but you never know. Friday's a rush event so you'll get a higher rate that night. We appreciate people being available at the last minute." Mia rattled off all the information for Jenna's first event. "Oh, and wear black shoes. Comfortable ones. You'll thank me later."

"Sounds good." Jenna pulled at her blond hair. She wore it long and she looked a lot like Christina, only younger. "I'll see you tomorrow."

"Have fun on the slopes. I need to learn downhill. I try to get out and cross country at least once a month, but that's usually on a weekday. The slopes are less crowded and I'm never available to play on the weekends." Mia lifted the tray. "I better get going. Thanks for checking in with me."

Jenna waved and Mia headed to the kitchen to drop off her dirty dishes. At least she had done smart hiring. She had almost a full staff and until they left for better-paying jobs, she didn't need to interview anyone else. That idea made her day.

When she got back into her office, her cell rang. "Hey, Mom, any luck with the law firm?"

"Actually, I would have thought you would know this answer. It's the Adams firm. Their trust division is having a partners meeting. I'd heard rumors that they'd changed the location at the last minute, but I thought maybe they'd use a Boise hotel, not Magic Springs." Her mom's voice sounded a little hesitant. "It's odd. I'm sure this quarterly meeting was originally set up months ago. And they typically hold it at the Owyhee, probably to give that jerk of an ex-boyfriend of yours a booking."

Her mother did verify that the trust partners should be a group of fifteen at the most. So that was a solid planning number. That eased Mia's mind a bit.

She thanked her mom for the information and promised to stop by soon. She needed to go see her parents more often, especially after hearing about the train wreck of a family that Christina grew up with. As she hung up, she wondered if Todd's death had brought the meeting this way. Did his family have trusts with the law firm? But why the fast switch up? She was glad her staff was getting more work, but the logistics were concerning.

When she got home, Grans was in the kitchen cooking stew. The black kitten didn't run to greet her like she had the day before. Mia came in after shutting the door and sat at the table. "You didn't have to cook. I would have made dinner."

"You worked today. I didn't. I can cook." Grans stirred the pot. "Besides, it helps me think."

"Did you solve Todd's murder?" Mia joked as she flipped through the mail, sorting it into junk and bills. She threw away the junk and put the bills on a shelf to pay later.

Grans shook her head. "When I meditate on it, I keep getting money signs floating around my head. Did Todd have an inheritance? And if so, where did it go?"

"So you don't think magic was a factor?" Mia wanted her to say it wasn't. Because if Grans did rule out the use of magic, Mia could leave the investigation up to Baldwin. He would find the killer as long as the victim wasn't killed by a wave of a wand or a potion. Humans solved murders all the time. She'd be happy to give this over to Baldwin.

Grans made a huffing sound.

"What? You think there is magic involved?" *Please say no, please say no,* Mia repeated over and over in her head.

"You would think that, right? But no. He was bound by magic before he was stabbed. Whomever did this had magical skills, but they aren't strong." Grans watched Mia's reaction. "I know, not what you wanted to hear."

"As long as Christina and Levi stay off Baldwin's lists, I'm fine with staying out of this investigation. Mark only turns to me when he needs the skinny from the magic community. Even though he says he doesn't believe." Mia focused on the kittens who were sleeping on the window seat. Muffy and Mr. Darcy were lying near the doorway toward the hallway, watching them. "I've got three kittens to re-home. Well, two. And we better get those two gone before Christina falls for the tabby. I don't mind her having a pet, but with Mr. Darcy, I'm not sure it would work."

"Christina's going to be moving out soon. I'm sure she can wait until she has a place of her own." Grans laughed at the look Mia gave her. "What? Did you think she'd live with you forever?"

"I know her being here is temporary. But I've grown to like having her around," Mia admitted as she grabbed a soda out of the fridge. "I've been thinking that maybe Mia's Morsels was a pipe dream or just a stepping stone to this catering job."

"I didn't say you had to give up your business if Christina moves out of your apartment. She might not even move out of town. You are always looking ten years into the future without any idea about what might happen tomorrow. You need to slow down and just live for today. Otherwise, you're going to be planning your life away. Besides, there's always the issue of you and Trent to think about. He's got a nice house over by the river. You may be living there and Christina and Levi might live here." Grans stood and checked the soup. Then she pulled corn bread out of the oven where it had been keeping warm. "Time for dinner and to stop worrying. It's bad for your digestion."

"Trent and I aren't even close to talking about that." Mia focused on eating. She was hungry again. The salad she'd had for lunch hadn't been enough and she'd been thinking about food since three that afternoon.

"Argue your limits and you own them," Grans said as she dished out two bowls of soup.

After dinner, Mia excused herself and went to her room to write down all the things she knew about Todd and his death. With the Adams law firm's trust division coming into town tomorrow, she needed to find out what she didn't know about Todd. Maybe in the holes, she could find a reason for his murder. And she wanted to talk to Mother Adams about why after a few visits to Magic Springs, Todd finally realized that Christina lived here. She knew the woman had steered him here, but why? Was it just to make sure her daughter married into the right family?

She looked at her list. So far, all the questions and leads pointed to Christina or Levi. What she needed to know was who was Todd friends with when he came to Magic Springs? Or did he stay to himself. Where was he prior to this week? Boise? What did he do there?

Now that she'd changed the focus to Todd and his life, it opened up a lot more questions. But, as she rubbed Mr. Darcy's tummy as he lay next to her on the bed, she didn't have any more answers. Hopefully Mark Baldwin was having more luck with his search for a killer than she was having.

Mr. Darcy hissed, and Mia saw the kittens standing in the doorway. The three of them sat in a row, staring at her. What had happened to their mother? And why had someone dumped them on Mia's doorstep? Another mystery to be solved.

The kittens came inside the room and Mia put a pillow on the floor for them. Mr. Darcy glared at her but lay down to sleep on the corner of her bed. He wasn't giving up on his spot. Mia set the notebook aside and got ready for bed. She turned on the television and found an old movie to help her ease into dreamland.

The next morning, Mia was up early and made a French toast and sausage bake. The casserole was in the oven and baking before Christina shuffled into the kitchen. Her hair was in her eyes and she spilled the cream as she got herself a cup of coffee. Mia wiped up the mess with a wet cloth. "Rough night?"

"I stayed late at the Lodge helping Mom." Christina yawned. "She's having an event tomorrow night at the Lodge. The one you called me about. It's her. She brought all the trust lawyers up for their quarterly meeting. She thinks they needed a break from the routine."

"But you don't think that was the reason?" Mia refilled her cup and sat at the table with Christina.

"I believe that it's an excuse for her to be here watching me for the next few days. She says it's just coincidence. She thinks Baldwin is going to sweep in and put me in an electric chair any minute. She even had the lawyer who stopped here, Bernard, sit with me and explain the legal process to me last night. For over an hour. I swear, I would have fallen asleep at law school if I'd gone that route like she wanted me to do. And it's so adversarial. Why can't it be just about telling the truth?"

"Good question." Mia sipped her coffee. She was used to being up early on catering event days, she just regretted the fact she was losing sleep over an event her business wasn't catering. It didn't seem fair. "So is your mom going to be at the event tonight?"

Christina nodded. "She's hosting so she wants me to come as well. I'm her plus-one since Dad's busy in Boise."

"Okay then." Mia stirred her coffee. "I'm going to try to talk to her after the event about why Todd was here. If you don't mind."

"I've already tried but go ahead. She swears she hasn't seen him in years. But he even mentioned he knew where I was because Mom told him." Christina pulled her hair up into a clip. "She gets caught in her lies, then she just clams up and changes the subject. She's always been that way."

"So you're telling me I might not get any information." The bell on the oven went off and Mia went to pull out the casserole dish. "Are you hungry?"

"Starving. I barely ate last night. I was so nervous about what she might say to Levi. I swear, that guy needs a gold medal for going to dinner with me and my mom two nights in a row. She tried to get him to come to the event tonight, but I told her he had to work. I think she's trying to show him what life with me could be like." Christina got plates out of the cupboard. "Except if Levi and I got married, I wouldn't be attending all these events for the family. I could tell her I had a life."

"So what's stopping you from telling her the same thing now?" Mia poured a glass of orange juice. "It's not my business but since she bought you that car, you've been running yourself ragged going back and forth to Boise for your mother. Maybe you should tell her you have a life."

Christina stared at her. For a second, Mia thought she'd crossed the line. But then Christina nodded.

"You're right. I've been feeling guilty about the car so every time she asks me to do something, I say yes. Isaac didn't act this way. I remember when he got his car. He disappeared for days. Mom was always griping to Dad about how they never saw him for dinner." Christina took a bit of the casserole. "I'd forgotten about that. Dad would always laugh and say, 'You bought him that car.'"

"Is that the difference between men and women? We feel like we need to show we're grateful or that we deserve the gift?" Mia wondered aloud.

"Probably. Anyway, it stops now. Or after tonight." Christina groaned. "I have to go to this dinner. Hey, maybe you need me to help serve tonight."

"You want to work an event that your mother is hosting?" Mia laughed. "Even I know that's a horrible idea. She'd kidnap you and send you to some rich kid's camp to get you deprogrammed since I must have you in a cult or something."

Christina laughed and picked up the tabby kitten. He curled up in her lap and went straight to sleep. "I think you're right about that. I'll go to the dinner. Then that's it."

Good luck with that. Mia smiled rather than say anything at all. Christina needed to determine her own boundaries with her mother. That wasn't any of Mia's business. But she was going to figure out how Todd had found Christina. Something in her gut told her it was important.

CHAPTER 8

Mia didn't have to go into work until noon. James was handling the food prep so all she needed to do was manage the different departments to make sure the event went off without a hitch. So she spent the morning planning and scheduling different classes to offer for the next three months. Once that was done, she opened her laptop to find out any information on Todd Thompson.

There was more than she expected. Besides the current articles on his death, there was a lot of information about his high school and college accomplishments. If you took the local newspaper's word for it, the man was Boise's favorite son. She thought with all this, the family must have hired a publicist for every major event in the young man's life. As she scrolled through the articles, she saw a younger Christina on Todd's arm at charity events. Christina looked like Mia had remembered her at that time. Scared of doing or saying the wrong thing. The articles from the last four years were about holiday visits home and his charity events at school. She hadn't realized the local paper even had a "society" page, but maybe that was more her lack of interest. She had scoured the business notices and the home pages looking for new catering opportunities, recipes, and home remodeling articles. Especially around the older homes like the one they were redoing. She left the society bookings to Isaac. He and his family knew everyone. She focused on new businesses that might need catering.

She and Isaac had made a good partnership. Except for the fact that Mia never lived up to Mother Adams's dream girl for her son. Isaac had said she'd grow to love Mia, but as the years went by, the relationship got even more distant. Probably because both Isaac and Christina liked Mia.

Water under the bridge. However, Todd's death had brought up those old insecurities. Mia loved her new life. Her only regret now was how much time she'd wasted staying with Isaac. If he was going to leave, she wished he'd left earlier. For both their sakes.

She studied the notes she made. Local boy does good. No one hated Todd. He was popular both in high school and college according to the newspaper. Yet something Christina had said didn't match with this picture. She went to Christina's room and there on the shelf were her high school yearbooks. Christina was lying on the bed.

"Do you need me?" She took off her headphones and sat up.

Mia pointed to the yearbooks. "Can I look at those?"

Christina stood and pulled them off the shelf. "Sure. What are you looking for?"

"I need to know Todd." Mia took the books. Then she realized Christina might know. "This is a stupid question, but did Todd have a publicist in high school?"

"You mean you don't believe all the amazing news clips that were published?" Christina laughed and plopped down on the bed. "Mom said Todd's parents owned the society page editor. She was always griping that her events or even her kids didn't get the coverage Todd did. I guess when Jacob, his older brother, left town and told his parents not to look for him, Todd got moved up to the favorite son spot."

"Todd had an older brother?"

"Jacob. He was amazing. Personable, charming, quarterback, smart. Everything the Thompsons wanted in a son. Todd was always complaining that his folks didn't see him. Not until Jacob left." Christina reached for her laptop. "Jacob was Isaac's age. Isaac was always griping about him. Jacob was valedictorian. Isaac came in second. Then just before he graduated from college, Jacob came home for Christmas, and had a fight with his folks. For a few years, they never talked about him. Todd became their focus. But I hear Jacob is back in Boise and working at his dad's company."

She turned the laptop around and showed Mia a high school senior photo of a young man who looked like Todd but was more handsome. The man's smile made you want to smile back. "Why did he leave?"

Christina shrugged. "Mom never could find out. Or she never told me. I heard her say to Dad once that she'd asked Mrs. Thompson how Jacob was doing and she got froze out."

"Froze out?"

"Mom and Dad weren't invited to the Thompson's parties for a year. Mom saw her at a store one day and they started talking again, but she never mentioned Jacob's name again." Christina shivered. "I'm sure Mom was the same way when I went to Nevada for that disaster year."

"Gap year," Mia corrected. "You tried something new. You didn't do anything wrong. Your mom just didn't see it as a learning experience for you."

"I think she called it ruining my life." Christina grinned and pointed to the books. "Do you want me to look through those with you?"

"No, I'll do it. I don't know what I'm looking for." She glanced at her watch. "And I need to get ready for work. Can I hold on to these for a while?"

"You know you can." Christina grinned as she plopped back on the bed, grabbing her earphones. "I know where you live."

Mia set the yearbooks on her nightstand and got ready for work. By the time she got there, James was standing outside her door with a cup of coffee and a sandwich. "Okay, what's the fire today?"

"Why do you think there's a fire? I'm just being a thoughtful coworker. Bringing you food." He came inside her office as soon as she opened the door. "Okay, I wanted you to be prepared. Mother Adams, as you call her, is sitting in Frank's office. She has a few changes for tonight's dinner. You're supposed to go in as soon as you arrive, but I thought you might want to fortify yourself with some food."

"Thanks, but I ate breakfast at home. I always bake before a big event. It gives me an excuse to be up as early as I was this morning. Man, I'm going to crash Sunday morning hard." She took the coffee and grabbed the folder, a notebook, and a pen from her desk. "I'll let you know if there are any food changes."

"You know her. Do you think she'd actually change the food this close to the event?" James followed Mia out of the office and closed her door.

"I know she will. Or she'll try. I'll try to limit it though. The good news is tomorrow's catering event's all set and we know they aren't going to change up anything." She headed toward the front where Frank had his office right off the lobby.

"You had to say something like that. You know you just jinxed us, right?" James called after her.

Mia just held up a hand. She'd been doing the catering for the Blaine County Association for Estate Attorneys for the last two years. They always ordered the same thing. And they liked consistency. She wasn't worried.

Jenna came around a corner and Mia almost ran into her. "Good afternoon. What are you doing here so early?"

"I had a meeting with HR. Signed all my papers and watched two videos on sexual harassment and diversity training. I hope I don't do anything stupid like the people in those films." Jenna adjusted her shoulder strap. "I'm having lunch in the dining room, then I'll be ready to clock in at two to help set up. There's still an event this evening, right?"

"I'm hoping so. I'm on my way to a meeting right now. Go have lunch. Are you sure you want to just wait around until work starts?" Mia glanced at her watch. Even a leisurely lunch would have Jenna sitting around for at least thirty minutes to an hour.

"I love this old Lodge. It's historic. I feel like I've walked back into time when I visit here." Jenna patted her tote. "Besides, I always carry a book. You never know when you're going to have time and it's a long drive back to Twin, just to turn around and come back."

"I like planners." Mia smiled at her newest employee. She really needed to get to the meeting and she was stalling. "I've got to go. See you in the grand ballroom at two. Don't forget to clock in. The time clock is in the employee locker room."

Mia hurried through the lobby and when she reached Frank's office, she took a long breath to calm herself. Then she knocked as she opened the door. "Good afternoon, I was told you needed to see me?"

Frank and Mrs. Adams were sitting at his desk. Mother Adams had a notebook in front of her and Frank was furiously scribbling down notes. He finished what he was writing, then looked up. "Finally. I would have expected you to be here earlier on a catering day."

"I always come in two hours before my staff on catering days. We talked about my hours last week." Mia smiled and held out her hand to Mother Adams. "Mrs. Adams, so nice to see you. I hear you're busy planning Isaac and Jessica's upcoming wedding. It should be the social event of the season."

Mother Adams looked at the offered hand and shook her head, standing. "Now, you're not getting away with that. Give me a hug. We were almost family for goodness' sake."

Mia found herself swallowed in Mother Adams's arms. She lifted her own arms and surrounded the small woman. Mia's mind raced. This was new. In the ten plus years she'd known Mother Adams, she'd never hugged her before. Maybe there was something wrong with the woman. A health issue? She needed to call Isaac. He'd know. All of a sudden, she was standing alone. Mother Adams had ended the hug and sat down while Mia was trying to figure out the meaning of the physical contact. She croaked out a quick, "It's good to see you," and sat in the other visitor chair.

"Oh, I didn't realize you two knew each other." Frank blinked, clearly off his game. Now, he had to treat Mia like he treated Mother Adams. And he wasn't used to staff having the upper hand in the conversation.

"Oh, yes. Mia was engaged to my son. He was an idiot for letting this one go." Mother Adams reached out and squeezed her hand.

It all seemed so warm, so surreal. Mia squirmed in her chair, then opened the file and the notebook. "I'm sure Frank doesn't want to hear about our history. Are there issues with the event tonight? I'm so looking forward to showing you what a lovely dinner we can provide. I'm sure it will be up to your standards. The Lodge is known for its upscale food and service."

"Well, I was off on the numbers. We'll be hosting twenty couples tonight. I guess everyone wanted a weekend to get away from Boise for a while. I'm not sure how many of the men will want to be out on the slopes, but their wives do seem to get younger each year." Mother Adams laughed, but it had an odd tone.

Mia glanced up from her notebook to look at the matriarch, but Mother Adams turned away and focused on Frank.

"Anyway, that's what I needed to tell you. We'll be adding ten plates to our dinner tonight. You'll still be able to provide the three protein choices, correct?" Mother Adams pulled out her phone and checked her calendar. "And we'll start right at five with drinks and passed appetizers?"

"Of course we'll be able to accommodate your guests, correct, Mia?" Frank was seeing the profit for the event increase as the guest numbers went up.

Mia was seeing James's face when she told him. She had warned him. Mia smiled and wrote down forty at five with two bartenders and passed trays. She was so glad she'd already overstaffed for the event. Mother Adams was predictable in her last-minute changes. But that hug was new. Mia nodded as she set her pen down. "Not a problem. I'm sure the event tonight will be lovely."

Mother Adams stood and Mia and Frank followed. "I just hope we can get through this weekend without any more problems. Has your sheriff found Todd's killer yet?"

Mia shook her head. "At least I don't know that he did. I haven't talked with Mark since Christina found Todd. And there's the small fact he doesn't keep me in the loop with his investigations."

"Oh, I just assumed, small town and all, you would know more."

"I can call the police station and ask for you," Frank offered. "I'll send a note up to your room as soon as I hear anything."

"Thank you." Mother Adams moved toward the door. "And, Mia?"

Mia felt her stomach drop. This couldn't be good.

"Please dress for dinner and not an employee for this evening's event. I have some people I'd like you to meet. I'll send over an outfit to the house and you can get ready with Christina. That way, you don't have to drive that death trap of a car on these roads."

With that she disappeared into the hallway. Mia and Frank were left alone in his office. Mia turned toward him. "I guess I'll be going home to change about four. I should have everything ready by then."

"Why didn't you tell me you knew Mrs. Adams? I looked like a fool treating you like you were just an employee." Frank sat down and ripped out pages from his notebook and shoved them at her. "Here's what we talked about before you decided to show up."

"Again, I was here at my agreed upon time and I'm sorry you didn't know about my connection with the Adamses. I didn't think it would really be an asset. Especially since Isaac and I broke up a few years ago." Mia tried to explain as she took the crumpled paper.

Frank waved her off. "Just go talk to James. I'm sure he's going to freak. And tell him I'll approve any extra costs he might have because of this change. And staff. If you need more staff, it's approved as well. If we show them what we can do here, maybe we'll get more bookings from the legal community in Boise. That could increase our profit margin for the entire year."

Mia excused herself and let Frank dream about his newfound customer base. She didn't want to tell him that the only reason Mother Adams had moved the meeting was because of Todd's death. She wanted to be here just in case something happened to Christina.

Mia knew that Mother Adams still didn't believe that Christina had nothing to do with Todd's death. And that one fact had brought the mother bear out in Mother Adams. She wasn't letting her daughter go to jail. Not again.

CHAPTER 9

Mia had just finished training the servers for tonight's events when she saw Trent leaning on the doorway. She handed the checklist over to Julie who was her unofficial lead server since Frank wouldn't approve a new position or pay raise. "Finish up showing the new kids the tray pass, then we need to get these rooms set up."

Julie smiled and waved at Trent. "Your man is looking fine today. Kind of a rugged business woodsman vibe."

"Right out of a Hallmark Christmas movie, right?" Mia smiled and pointed to the group of servers in the room. "Keep your mitts off him and go do your work."

"Just enjoying the eye candy." Julie turned and called the three new servers to the front. "Okay, who wants to show these rookies how we do a tray pass?"

"What are you doing here?" Mia hurried over to

the ballroom doorway and gave Trent a quick kiss. "And where's the baby?"

"He's back at the store, sleeping in the office. I had to drop off more steaks for James. Then Levi called and told me that Christina said her mom sent you a dress for tonight. I didn't realize you were a guest tonight." He moved them over to a bench on the other side of the hallway.

"Expect the unexpected. It was always my motto when I had to deal with the Adams family. Anyway, it's no big deal, she wants me to meet some people. Maybe Christina said something about the business. All I know is it's better just to say, yes, thank you, than fight her on anything."

"I would have thought, now that Isaac is with someone else, you'd be off the hook for events like this." Trent took her hand in his.

Mia leaned forward and stared at him. "You knew I was working tonight. What's really going on?"

"I didn't think you'd be working in a ball gown." Trent shot back. Then he leaned against the wall. "Sorry, I'm letting my intimidation of big money cloud my words. I just want you to know that I'm here for you and I love you. So you don't go shopping tonight for someone better."

"Better than you? Is that even possible? Julie clearly doesn't think so." Mia teased, then realized Trent was at least a little bit serious. "Are you jealous?"

He shook his head. "No. Okay, maybe a little. That house in Boise is a mansion. And then there's Christina's new car. You were about to marry into a lot of money."

"No, I was about to marry a jerk who grew up

with money. Isaac didn't have money, except for his way too-high salary at the Owyhee and a small trust fund from his grandmother. We pooled our money for the renovations on the house. And when we split, he paid me back for it. Mr. and Mrs. Adams have money. And when they die, if they don't spend it all, Isaac and Christina should inherit money. But it doesn't mean that I would have married into money. Or that I wanted it." Now Mia was getting steamed. "It's the same with you and your folks. Your parents are comfortable. And they have that huge house on the river. But you're not rich. Because you don't count their money as yours. Why is Isaac any different in your mind?"

"Because it is." He stood and looked at her. "Rich people are different."

"Yes, they are." Mia stood. "And right now, I've got work to do. I'll talk to you tomorrow."

He started to say something, then his phone rang. He just nodded at her and turned around to answer as he walked off. "What?"

As she watched him leave, she took a breath. This is what being around Mother Adams caused. Angry words and hurt feelings. Although before, it was her hurt feelings and angry words to Isaac. She'd call Trent this evening when she got home and smooth things over. Right now, she needed to finish pulling off this dinner and then go home to dress up like a Barbie doll going to her prom. Hopefully the dress that Mother Adams had sent her wasn't hideous.

Looking into the mirror later that afternoon, with Christina lending Mia one of her large necklaces to show off the sweetheart neckline, the one thing Mia knew was that the dress wasn't ugly. It was beautiful and cut specifically to enhance Mia's body. Where Christina's dress was more of a long cool drink of water, Mia's was curvy in all the right places. "I have to admit, your mother did great on this dress. I'm just not sure why."

"Why she bought you a dress? Or why she got you one where you look like a million bucks?" Christina studied Mia in the mirror. "I've been wondering that myself. You know I've been concerned with her actions for a few months now. Like when she bought me a car."

"I can top that. She hugged me. In front of a witness." Mia saw the shock on Christina's face.

Her eyes widened. "Oh, my goodness. You don't think she's dying, do you?"

Mia didn't have time to answer before Grans came into the room. "I just wanted to check in with you two before you left."

"What's going on?" Mia sat down to slip on her heels. She checked the look in the mirror, then took them off and put on flats. She'd change into boots before they left the house, but she'd spend most of her night in the flats. Except when Mother Adams was showing her off to her friends. The things she did to gain business for Mia's Morsels.

"Well, don't you both look like you're going to the winter formal." Grans held up a finger. "Hold on, I'll be right back."

Christina wiped at her eyes. "I'm not even going to put that idea in my head."

"Good. Because you know your mom's too mean to die." Mia laughed as Christina grinned. "I wonder what Grans wants."

She didn't have to wait long before her grandmother came back into the room with her phone. Grans snapped several pictures, then ordered the two women to stand next to each other. "Go on, you never want to miss an opportunity to get a picture of you looking young and beautiful. Sometime in the future, you're going to miss that."

Mia smiled as she stood next to Christina. After Grans took several pictures, she tucked her shoes into a tote along with a makeup bag, just in case. Things happened in the kitchen. She had a second set of clothes in her office, if something horrible happened. But she hoped the dress would stand up to a catering event. She really loved it. "Grans, you're beautiful too."

"Yeah, but I really enjoyed being younger. At least for a while." Grans started to leave the room. The results of the aging spell reversal debacle a few years ago was obviously still on her mind. "Oh, Abigail wanted me to tell you she had a very good afternoon selling stock. She thinks we should have open hours at least once a week. Probably on Fridays."

"I'll call her Sunday after these events are done to chat." Mia glanced at Christina. "Since you're my ride, are we ready to go?"

"Okay, but I might leave you sometime during the night and come back for you when you're done. It depends on how excruciating the event is." Christina warned.

"If I could leave with you, I would. But since I'm in charge of the thing, I'll need to stay until the end." She followed Christina out to the living room. The kittens were playing on the floor and Mr. Darcy was up on the back of the couch, examining them like they were a puzzle to be solved. Muffy was asleep but not for long. The kittens were getting ready to pounce. She opened the apartment door. "We really need to start finding homes for the kittens."

"One of Levi's EMT buddies thinks his sister might want one. She's coming over tomorrow to look at them. Is Abigail still taking the yellow-striped one?" Christina followed her outside and closed the door before any of the animals could escape.

"You need to call her and make sure. I'm going to be working tomorrow again." Mia had noticed that the black kitten had ignored her as she walked through the living room. She hadn't been happy to hear that she wasn't staying but Mia didn't have time to raise a kitten. "I just want to make sure they all go to good homes. If they don't work out, they have to promise to bring them back and not dump them somewhere."

"You're a good foster mom." Christina said as they reached the bottom of the stairs. "It's hard to give them up, isn't it?"

"Yes." Mia pulled on her coat and slipped on her winter boots. "But they deserve a good home where they can get a lot of love and attention."

Still, as Christina drove them to the Lodge, Mia kept seeing the black kitten ignoring her. She wanted to keep all the kittens, but it just wasn't practical. So she'd have to do what was right for them, not just what she wanted. Which was what her life was all about right now. She'd taken this job to keep Mia's Morsels alive, not because she wanted it. Mia was going to have to find one thing she did for herself and celebrate it sooner than later. Or she was going to drown in her must-do list.

"Hey, are you okay?" Christina asked, as she turned the car into the parking lot. She pulled up to the valet line.

"I'm fine. Just feeling sorry for myself. I love the beginning of winter, but sometimes, it just goes on too long." Mia smiled and climbed out of the car. "I'll see you inside."

Christina got out and took a ticket from Hank, the head valet. "The keys are in the car. Charge it and a tip to my mother's room, same as last night. Mia, wait up."

Mia paused as she reached the door. "Christina, I'm fine."

"I know, but I wanted to thank you for everything. You let me stay with you when I was hiding from my mom. You gave me a home and a life here in Magic Springs. I just want you to know how much I appreciate it. And that I'm proud that you've built a life and friends here." She took Mia's arm and they walked into the lobby and toward the coat room. "Give yourself some slack."

Mia shrugged out of her heavy winter coat and the dress bounced back into shape. She slipped off her boots and gave those and the coat to the attendant. She straightened her shoulders and gave Christina a hug. "Thank you. I needed that."

As they made their way to the dinner, James hurried over and walked beside her. "You look nice."

"By order of the hostess for this event." Mia glanced over to see James's face. "So what's wrong?"

"The bars are already set up and people are drinking, hard. I'm going to send the tray pass into the room fifteen minutes early." James said in an undertone.

"Sounds like a good plan. And add another tray pass before dinner. We need to keep the mix of food and alcohol even." Mia paused at the doorway. She handed her bag to James. "Can you put this in my office?"

"Of course. As long as you don't go hide out there in the middle of this." He took the bag and disappeared back toward the kitchen.

"Oh, if only I could." Mia turned back toward Christina. "Let's go into the lion's den."

"You really are too good of a sport about this." Christina adjusted her dress and they walked through the door, together.

Mother Adams headed toward them as soon as they entered. A server was passing flutes of champagne, and Mia took one and gave one to Christina. "Carry this around. It will make people think that you're drinking."

"And they won't push a drink on you." Christina nodded. "Party etiquette 101. I take it Isaac taught you that?"

Mia nodded. "I should have realized you were already well schooled. Here's your mom."

Mother Adams reached them and gave Christina a fake kiss. Then she turned to Mia. "The dress is lovely on you. I'm so glad I remembered your size."

"Thank you for the generous gift." Mia smiled and leaned in for a fake kiss as well.

"I wanted you to look lovely tonight. Isaac's here and he'll be sitting by you tonight for dinner." Mother Adams's eyes twinkled in the dim light. "He's missed you."

"He's engaged." Mia reminded her.

Mother Adams shrugged. "He was before as well. Christina, I need you to come talk to Bernard. He's concerned that this unfortunate issue with Todd isn't over for you."

Mia watched as the two women moved over to the other side of the room. Behind her, a low whistle made her turn. Isaac stood there in a tuxedo watching her. "Isaac. Your mother just told me you were here. Where's Jessica?"

A brief show of emotion came over his face. Then it was gone. "She's otherwise engaged tonight. I'm here to talk to you."

"About?" Mia didn't like where this was going.

"You always were bad at small talk. Okay, let's get right to the point." He smiled and took her arm, leading her toward the other side of the room from his mother and sister. "I wanted to see if you still loved me. If there was a chance of us reuniting. We were good together. You're better than just working here in this small town. You could have your choice of catering director jobs in Boise. Or we could move to someplace bigger. We always talked about Seattle."

Mia stared at him. She couldn't believe this was all part of Mother Adams's plan. Probably even the hug. She wanted to confuse Mia so her son would have a chance to repair the relationship. "Isaac. You're engaged. To another woman." She added that last part because he seemed to have forgotten it. "I'm not going to be the other woman, not like Jessica was to me."

"I made a mistake letting you go." He leaned toward her, running a finger down the side of her face. "I miss you. We are soulmates."

A laugh escaped before Mia could stop it. Trent must have been subconsciously picking up on this game. "Whatever we were to each other, I'm pretty sure it wasn't soulmates. I'm sorry to cut this short, but I've got an event to run. I guess I'll see you at dinner since your mother sat me next to you. But Isaac, I'm not interested in reliving old times. I have a life here."

He bowed, kissing the back of her hand. "We'll talk more at dinner. I've got some ideas I think you'll love, especially for a long vacation on an island in a private villa. We could swim and drink and relax and talk about us. No pressure. You'd even have your own room."

"Isaac—" Mia started but he cut her off.

"Your own room, I promise." He squeezed her hand. "Just think about it."

As he walked away, Mia shook her head, watching him. What was it about this week and old boyfriends just showing up expecting to rekindle the relationship? First Todd, now Isaac? Her thoughts were interrupted by a server with a tray of caviar. Mia adjusted the tray on his hand. "If you don't hold it straight, you're going to dump five hundred dollars of caviar onto someone's dress."

"Yes, ma'am. Sorry." He blushed as she corrected him.

She straightened his tie and patted his chest. "Tray passing is a skill. Smile as you offer up the treat. We're enjoying ourselves, right?"

He glanced around the room and nodded. "I'm doing my best."

"You are now." Mia laughed and sent him on his way. Julie had tried, but obviously, she needed to do a remedial demonstration with the servers on the correct tray pass process. But it could wait until before tomorrow's event. Tonight, she'd just fix what she noticed.

As she wandered through the room, she heard Todd's name mentioned. Two men in the corner, whiskeys in hand, were in a heated conversation. She moved toward the bar and asked for a sparkling water to replace her untouched flute. The bartender winked, letting her know he understood, and then made a show of making a mixed drink. He gave the alcohol-free drink to her with a flourish. If anyone had been watching, they would've said she had a fully leaded vodka and tonic. She thanked him and moved closer to the two men, taking a seat at an empty table where she could hear more of the conversation.

"Todd was reckless. He came up here in a huff, thinking that marrying that Adams girl would solve the trust issues. Now we have a dead kid and a still empty trust." The taller man took a sip of his whisky. "I'm not going to jail for this. I didn't spend the money."

"Look, no one's going to jail. I just need some more time to figure out how to move around some funds. Do we know who was named in Todd's will? Maybe we can convince that person to just leave the money alone. As long as they don't ask for an accounting, we'll have time." The younger man sipped his drink, his gaze landing on Mia. He smiled at her and lifted his glass in a gesture of hello. Then he turned back to the man he'd been talking to. "Who knows, maybe I'm the heir."

Mia blushed and took a sip of her water and scanned the room. The guy clearly had thought she was interested in him rather than what he was talking about. Or maybe he didn't think anyone could hear their conversation. The room was filled with chatter and without Mia using a bit of magic, she wouldn't have been able to hear him.

Now she had more questions. Who were those men? And why did Todd have an empty trust? One he apparently knew was dry? Mother Adams had clearly thought Todd was wealthy as she'd been pushing Christina that way. So why would marrying Christina solve his money issues? Now she really needed to talk to Isaac at dinner. Which would totally give him the wrong idea. Trent was already freaking out about Mother Adams being here. What would he say if he knew Isaac was in town as well? And she was having dinner with him.

Mia glanced up as the doors to the ballroom opened. She sighed when she saw Trent standing there, looking around the room. She could tell when he saw Isaac standing by his mother and Christina. When Trent's gaze found Mia, he raised his eyebrows at the dress, then waved at her to join him in the hallway.

Whatever was going on, this wasn't good. She hurried to meet him.

CHAPTER 10

"In that dress, you look like you're a guest, not an employee," Trent said as she walked out of the ballroom to meet him.

"Mother Adams felt like I needed to be better dressed for this event." She smoothed the skirt. "It's pretty, but I prefer working in a suit. What's going on? Why are you here?"

"No, hi, Trent, nice to see you?" He glanced at the closed ballroom doors. "Looks like most of the Adams family showed up for the event."

"Yes, Isaac is here." Mia answered Trent's unasked question as she leaned against a wall. "He's feeling bad about cheating on me."

"Poor guy. Are you in a forgiving mood?"

She studied the look Trent was giving her. She wasn't sure what was behind it, but she couldn't have a fight now. Not in the middle of this event. Which would be what Mother Adams would want, even if she wouldn't say it. "No. Isaac had his chance. We've been over since I moved here.

And, he's engaged. I won't do to Jessica what she did to me."

Trent relaxed his jaw. "That's good to hear. Anyway, I came to tell you something. The rumor has it that Todd's brother is here. Jacob Thompson. You may find him in that room since he's a trust attorney with the Adams firm."

"I think I already ran into him." Mia told Trent about the conversation she'd just overheard. Then she glanced at her watch. "I've got to go back in. Dinner will be served in a few minutes. And before you ask, I've been seated by Isaac."

"That should be fun, catching up on old times," Trent said.

She patted his chest. "Actually, I'm more interested in finding out what was going on with the Thompson family. I think if we knew more about them, we might find a reason for someone murdering Todd."

"So you're investigating, not flirting with your ex-fiancé." Trent pulled her closer to him, leaning his head toward her neck. "You smell amazing. He should be putty in your hands."

"You're a dork." She kissed him. "Now let me go play Nancy Drew."

She turned and walked back to the ballroom door.

"Nancy Drew never wore a dress like that," Trent called after her.

As she entered the ballroom, she noticed the staff had already opened the connecting doors to where the dinner had been set up. James was standing by the opening, directing people. She moved toward him. "How's everything going?"

He nodded. "Actually, we have four empty seats

so two of the 'couples' Mrs. Adams invited either didn't show or are running late. I'm still charging her for all forty seatings."

"Make sure you email me when you send in your final changes to the bill. I'll back you up on that." She watched the group move into the room. "And make sure you add in the additional tray pass. Maybe we can make a standard measure of the amount of alcohol being consumed with mandatory food availability. For a safety measure for our guests."

"I like how you think." He smiled at her. "So you're also a guest?"

"And she's buying my dinner. I made that clear when she dressed me up like a Barbie doll." Mia twisted in the dress. "Although I do like the way it moves. Maybe I'm a ballerina instead."

"Girl, I've seen you dance. I'd stick with the Barbie analogy. You better get going. The first serving is about to come out. I suspect you want sparkling water rather than wine served in your glass?"

"Please. Although I'm going to have a few glasses when I get home tonight. Being a double agent has me all tensed up."

"Wait, a double agent?" James looked confused.

"Guest and employee. I'm not sure what to even say anymore." She paused before going in. "But I do know we need to do a refresher training on tray passing. We almost lost a ton of caviar."

She let that settle with James as she made her way to her spot at the table. Mother Adams raised her eyebrows and Mia mouthed, "Sorry, work."

Mother Adams glanced at James who was now directing the wine pouring and nodded.

"My mother thinks you've changed." Isaac said from Mia's left. "I think she's finally seeing the amazing woman you always were."

"Thanks. But again, you're engaged." Mia smoothed her napkin on her lap, then smiled up at the woman who was serving her wine. The server let the napkin drop a bit and Mia saw the label for an upscale sparkling water. She thanked the woman as she went back to the table behind them.

"You're always too nice to the help." Isaac watched as the woman returned with his white wine for the first course.

"And you don't see the people around you or show any gratitude at all." Mia bit her lip. Fighting with Isaac wouldn't get the information she needed. "Sorry, I'm just a little shook up. Was Christina dating Todd when she was in high school? I don't remember her talking about him when she stayed at our house."

"Christina dated a lot of people in high school. And unfortunately, Todd was one of them. Mom kept pushing Todd on her so he was usually her date for the formal dances, but mostly, she saw him as a friend, not a love interest. Mom always saw him as a potential spouse though, so when he came over to the house to propose to Christina last week, she was over the moon." He leaned back and let the server put down a plate with a seared scallop over a mushroom puree with fresh arugula over the top and a blood orange reduction. "This looks remarkable for such a small kitchen."

"Our chef is pretty amazing." Mia cut into her scallop. "Todd came to the house to propose. Didn't

he leave school in June? He waited nine months to
come by?"

"I guess he was sowing his wild oats. His dad
must have put the hammer down. I had heard
Todd was burning through his trust fund pretty
fast." He took a bite of the food in front of him.
"This is really good. Who is your chef?"

"Not telling you. I don't want you to tempt him
away with a big salary offer." She finished the plate
and set the fork across the plate, a signal to the
server that she was done. "So Todd had a trust
fund? One like the one you had from your grandparents?"

Isaac shrugged. "Todd's was a little bigger than
mine. I'd forgotten that I told you about it. Mom
didn't want me to mention it. And you can't tell
Christina. Mom doesn't want her knowing she has
access yet."

Mia closed her eyes. She should have realized
the fact. "Christina has a trust fund?"

Isaac took a sip of his wine. "Of course she does.
Our grandparents set them up for us to have full
access when we turned twenty-one. Mom's been
keeping Christina's a secret from her so she doesn't
waste it."

"On things like food and a decent car and college. Yeah, I can see how your mom would be
concerned." Mia lightly rubbed her eye. It was beginning to twitch. Now she remembered why
being around Mother Adams had always bothered her. Everything was a secret.

"Christina has a car that Mom paid for. So you
can't say that anymore. Mom's paying for her
school now. Of course, she would have from day
one if Christina had chosen to go to Brown or Yale

where she was accepted." Isaac held up his hand. "Sorry, I'm getting testy. This is why we don't talk about money. You put value judgments on things that are really just financial."

"Making sure your child has access to what belongs to her, that's not just a financial decision." Mia leaned back to let the server set a bowl of roasted butternut squash soup in front of her. The truffle oil on the top glittered in the soft light. "Okay, let's not talk about your finances. You said Todd was running out of money. Did he know Christina had a trust fund?"

Isaac didn't answer. He set his spoon on the table and finished his wine.

Mia set down her spoon and looked at him. His face was dark. "Isaac, what's wrong?"

"I'm an idiot. I'm the one who told Todd about her trust fund. We were having drinks one night before a charity event that Jessica and I were attending. We were catching up and I was grumbling about how all Jessica wanted to talk about was the wedding. I said how happy I was she didn't know about my trust fund or she'd go crazy with the spending. He asked if Christina had a trust too, and I told him. I was angry at Jessica and I didn't realize what I was saying. You think he was going to marry her for her money?"

"I think your mom wanted Christina to marry Todd for his money. Maybe she hadn't heard the rumors of his overspending." Mia took a sip of her soup.

"Man, that's cold. Christina's worth more than just money. She should be able to marry someone she loves." Isaac's voice had gone soft.

Mia turned to look at him and he leaned in and

kissed her. Her mind blanked but she pulled away, covering her mouth with her hand. "Isaac, what are you doing?"

"Trying to have my own happily ever after."

"Sorry, that ship has sailed." She decided to change the subject. "Have you tasted this soup? It's to die for."

During the rest of the meal, they made small talk. She could do it, she just hated playing that game. Isaac told her that Todd was one of three children. He had his brother, Jacob, who Mia had seen earlier, and a sister who was also a lawyer but hadn't made the trip to Magic Springs. Their father's business was having issues, so he was heavily borrowing money to stay afloat until things turned around. Their mother was a stay-at-home wife and mother who'd begun talking about working again for her personal satisfaction. Rumor was they needed the cash influx. Mia saw Mother Adams watching them. "Did your mom know about the financial issues?"

"Mom? No. She's been a little off the last few months. One, she's not happy with the engagement with Jessica. Which is why I'm here and you're in that amazing dress." Isaac held up a hand. "All I'm going to say is I'm really sorry I messed up us. I know. I've said it several times tonight. But I want you to know, I am truly sorry."

"I appreciate that. But honestly, I love my life now." Mia laughed as she spoke the words. "Funny, I didn't realize how much until just right now. I can't go back to Boise. Back to us. I have a great life here."

He watched her for a minute. "I can see you're happy. I really messed up, didn't I?"

"Isaac, with Christina in my life, we'll always be around each other. We need to just put the past away. We're over. I need to be clear on that. You need to be clear on that." Mia sipped her sparkling water as she watched him process her words. "All we can be is friends."

"You've been kind but direct. I'll inform my mom and hopefully, she won't keep trying to rekindle the flame." He smiled at her. "Thank you for being in my life. You've made me a better man."

Mia blinked at that, but before she could say anything, one of the servers gave her a note. She read it and nodded. "Sorry, Isaac, duty calls. Thank you for a lovely evening. And thank your mother as well."

He stood when she did and gave her a kiss on the cheek. "It's been a lovely evening."

Mia nodded and then left the table. Christina saw her from across the room and she stood as well. She met her at the ballroom door.

"Are you escaping my brother? I saw him kiss you." Christina glared in the direction of Isaac. "What is he thinking? I mean, I don't love Jessica, not like I do you, but seriously? He's so bad at commitment."

Mia laughed at that last bit. "You are so right there. No, we're fine now. I told him I wasn't mad anymore. I just was over him and me together. That we weren't going to happen. But I did find out some interesting information about Todd and his family. We'll do a huddle tomorrow morning with everyone and see what everyone has found."

"The Magic Springs Sleuthing Club to the rescue." Christina studied the room. "So are you leaving? Mom's giving me a dirty look because I got up before I finished dessert. She's got a new man in her sights for me. That guy is one of Dad's newest partners. And he's only thirty-two. I know all about him now since he wouldn't shut up during dinner."

"I've got to talk to James in the kitchen but I'm not coming back into the dining room. Meet me in my office when you're done and we'll get out of here. Let your mom know I'll have the dress drycleaned and sent back to her." Mia stroked the soft fabric. It was really beautiful.

"No need. She already told me to tell you to keep it. It's a late Christmas present." Christina groaned. "He's looking like he's going to come after me. I'll go finish dessert and break his heart."

"I think he's just worried that your mom will be disappointed in him." Mia put a hand on the ballroom doors. "See you in a few minutes."

When she got to the kitchen, James met her at the door. "Hey, how was dinner?"

"Amazing as always. My ex was trying to get your name so he could steal you for his Boise restaurant." She glanced around the almost-empty kitchen. "What's going on? What did you need?"

"One of your servers had to go. She was sick or something. And I wanted to tell you I put tomorrow's menu and schedule on your desk. You don't need to come in until two, unless you were serious about the tray passing training." James leaned against a table and watched her. "Rumor from the servers was your dinner companion was getting a little intense."

Mia laughed. She should have known that James would come to her rescue. "So this was my get out of jail free card? Isaac was fine. He was just under the wrong impression."

"Oh?" James sipped what looked like coffee but smelled like a dessert.

"Yes, he was under the impression that I still cared."

James laughed and stood, grabbing his coat. "We're all done here. I'll have the servers clear the dining room and I've got two dishwashers still working. I'll see you tomorrow. Unless you want me to talk to your ex about that job?"

"Seriously? You'd leave me here with Frank?" Mia followed him out of the kitchen and toward the hall where her office was located.

"No, but I'd use the job offer to get him to raise my salary. It's always nice to prove that you're in demand." James paused at the door to her office. "Maybe that's why the ex showed up. He heard you were happy with another guy."

"Maybe, but that's his loss." Mia said goodnight and then went to sit at her desk. Her bag with the high heels was still sitting on her desk. She'd forgotten to change out of her flats. She set the bag aside and started reviewing tomorrow's plan.

A man walked into her office. She looked up at him. It was Todd's brother. The one who had been talking to the other lawyer during the cocktail hour. He looked drunk. "Can I help you?" Mia asked.

He squinted at her and then at the room. "Sorry, I was looking for the head."

"Down the hall to your left. It has a swinging door that says MEN." Mia went back to reading but realized he hadn't moved.

"I know you," he slurred.

"I don't know you." Mia stood. She was beginning to feel uncomfortable.

"I'm Jacob Thompson. You were the one Isaac screwed over, right?" He leered at her. "The two of you were looking pretty chummy tonight. Are you looking for a new sugar daddy? I'm single."

"I can't imagine why." Mia pointed to the door. "If you don't mind, I'm working and this is a private office. Not open to the public."

"Well, then let's make it a little more private. I'll prove that you don't need that wanker, Isaac. He never was good at keeping a woman. I'll show you what a real man is like." He moved to shut the door.

Mia reached for the phone. James was probably gone, but security stayed on all night. She pushed the button, but before anyone could answer, the door stopped moving as a hand blocked its movement.

"The lady asked you to leave." Trent pushed the door open, glaring at Jacob.

"Who the hell are you?" Jacob turned around and squinted. "Oh, a local from your flannel shirt and jeans. Just go back to your woodshed and leave the adults alone, will you?"

Mia realized that security had answered. She had the phone on speaker. "This is Mia Malone. We have a drunk guest in my office who needs to be escorted to his room or kicked out of the hotel. You decide."

The guard responded. "We're on our way."

"You can't kick me out. I'm Jacob Thompson." He glared at Mia and lunged toward her.

All of a sudden, Jacob was jerked out of the office. Mia stood and walked over to where she could see Trent holding him down on the floor with a knee in his back and Jacob's arms pinned behind him. Trent looked up at her. "Your guests from Boise are charming."

"Not my party. This is Mother Adams's doing." She leaned against the doorway and watched as security arrived and took Jacob away. She called after him. "You may want to call Baldwin and see if he has room in his drunk tank."

"That's exactly what I was thinking." The guard she'd talked to earlier nodded at Trent. "Thanks for the assist."

"No problem. He just kind of fell and I didn't want him to hurt himself." Trent grinned at the guard.

"That's not true, I didn't fall," Jacob muttered. He started to say something more, then he must have realized what he'd been stopped from doing. "Just get me out of here."

Trent went over to Mia and stood next to her as they watched Jacob being led down to the security office. "You ready to go home?"

"I just need to text Christina so she's not looking for me." Mia went inside and grabbed her tote and her phone. After she sent the message and got a response, she closed and locked her office. "It's been an interesting night. I'm glad you decided to stay to drive me home."

He chuckled. "Me too."

CHAPTER 11

Saturday morning, Trent had called a meeting with everyone to talk about Todd's death. The group was planning on gathering at the apartment for breakfast since Mia had a catering event later. Mia, Christina, and Trent were cleaning the kitchen and washing dishes when Levi finally arrived. Mia reached for a plate that Trent had just dried and put away. "We still have pancakes and bacon if you're hungry."

"Sure. I guess I better eat before Baldwin comes to put me in jail." He sank into a chair at the table and put his head in his hands.

"I take it you were at the station this morning?" Trent took the plate and filled it with the leftovers they'd kept warming in the oven after the group had finished earlier. "Did he call you in or come visit you?"

"He invited me to come down to the station." Levi poured syrup over the pancakes and started to devour them. In between bites, he told them about the interview. "He wanted to go over my altercation with Todd again. I guess he thought maybe I'd change my story and admit I went back and stabbed him later in the day."

"Or maybe he thought you might have seen someone hanging around when you left." Christina set a glass of orange juice in front of Levi. "Baldwin isn't a bad guy. He has a job to do."

Everyone in the kitchen stopped what they were doing and turned to stare at Christina. Finally, Mia broke the ice. She stepped over and put the back of her hand on Christina's forehead. "No fever. Are you feeling okay?"

"Fine, I know I'm not Baldwin's biggest fan. But he started it. When I first got here, he didn't get my goth look. I think him almost being a dad has changed him a bit. He's softer. He was actually nice to me when I called him and told him I found Todd." She put the orange juice away.

"You're right. Baldwin might have been looking for something else. Or he doesn't know what happened, so he's starting at the beginning again." Mia stepped to the living room where Grans and Trent's mom were sitting and talking. "Hey, Abigail? Do we have some extra cookies downstairs I could take with me to the station?"

"You're going to go talk to Mark Baldwin?" Grans asked. "I haven't heard anything magical about Todd's death. Not since that last session. It might have been an emotional binding not a magical one. Maybe we should just stay out of it."

"I would agree with you, Mary Alice, but my son and Christina are too close to this. I'm sure Mark is looking closely at the kids in this murder. We need to keep them safe since neither of them actually killed that boy." Abigail turned from staring down Grans to Mia. "Yes, we have cookies. And one of Sarah's friends called to hire us to cater a baby shower next week."

"Way to wait for the last minute. Sarah's due any minute." Mia glanced back at the kitchen where Levi was still eating.

"Her mother's coming in this week to stay with them, and Kathy, the friend, wanted to wait until she arrived." Abigail explained. "So, we have an event Wednesday afternoon, if you want to be a part of it."

"I'll have to check my work schedule." Mia hesitated. "Abigail? Have you heard of anyone from the magical community talking about Todd's death?"

Abigail pressed her lips together. "No. Nothing. I'm getting calls to see if Levi's okay but no gossip about Todd and the coven at all. This might just be a fully human murder."

"In Magic Springs? I guess it's possible." Mia thanked Abigail for the cookies and went back to the kitchen. "Okay, so Grans and Abigail think there's no magical component here. We need to find a human killer and motive."

"Which means jealousy is high on the list of motives, and so am I." Levi shoved the last forkful of pancakes in his mouth.

"I heard a couple of interesting things about Todd." Mia sat at the table after refilling her coffee cup. "One, he's been coming up here for a few months now to ski. We need to talk to the owner of that rental and see if he had any company or local referrals. I don't understand why someone would come here to ski rather than Sun Valley."

Levi blinked and sat up straighter. "They wouldn't. I mean, Magic Springs Ski Resort is nice and all, but if you were rich and wanted great skiing, you'd go to Sun Valley."

"I also heard that Todd was running out of money in his trust fund." Mia watched Christina's face for the response.

"You have got to be kidding. Todd said the trust was so big he'd never be able to spend it all. Or even his kids. He got the bulk of his grandfather's estate. I guess the old man didn't like Jacob or Jen much."

"I heard Jacob talking about the trust and how Todd's death took care of their problem." Mia added to the discussion. "Could someone besides Todd have been spending that money?"

Christina shrugged. "I don't think so. When I turned twenty-one, the trustee called me into the office and had me sign a bunch of papers. They said that I was the only one who could withdraw money."

"Isaac said his mom didn't want you to know." Mia felt her cheeks heat. "Look, I just found out last night. Jacob said Todd was trying to get access to your trust to fix their family fortune issues."

Christina laughed. "And Mom thought he had money to take care of me. Boy, she would have been heartbroken to know Todd was just proposing for the money."

"So you know about your trust." Mia rubbed her forehead. She was getting a headache.

"Isaac and Mom don't know that I know. I asked the lawyer to keep Mom in the loop for financial decisions, but anytime she instructs him on something, he calls me for approval. So far, she hasn't tried to take money out so I've let her keep doing the managing. Or at least think she's doing the managing. I know, it's stupid, but she thinks I'm too immature to be in charge of the money." It was Christina's turn to blush.

"You just let her think she's controlling you and your trust." Levi stood and rinsed his plate. "Man, I don't want to play strategy games with you."

"I was planning on telling her. But then she started being nice, and I didn't want to upset the balance we have right now." Christina reached for a cookie from the plate in the center of the table. "Besides, I don't need the money now. Mom's paying for my college. She bought me a car. And my job pays me enough for the rest of my costs."

Mia felt a weight slip off her shoulders. "I'm glad I don't have to tell you about the trust. I didn't want to hold a secret from you. Especially something I think shouldn't be a secret."

"Isaac should have known the lawyer would call me. I know they called him. I guess he thought that me being a girl, I couldn't deal with financial issues on my own." Christina sipped her coffee. "Anyway, if Todd thought he could marry me for my money, he was wrong."

"But what if your mom thought he still had money. Even if she knew about his dad's money issues, she could have still thought Todd had his inheritance. And we all know she was the one who sent him here." Mia finished her coffee. "And it still doesn't explain how he ended up dead. Instead, it points the finger at Christina even more. Maybe she realized what he really wanted from her."

"And I stabbed him a bunch of times because

someone from high school asked me to marry him for my money? It doesn't make any sense. Besides, I don't need validation that badly. One, I knew about my trust. And two," she put her arms around Levi, "I already have a boyfriend. Who liked me even when he thought I was broke."

Levi squeezed her hand. "I think I liked the idea of broke you much better than this heiress status. How much money are we really talking about here?"

Christina kissed him on the head. "None of your business. But maybe we can start talking about a vacation. I think I can afford a week somewhere warm, providing you chip in, that is."

Levi laughed. "I'd go, but Baldwin just asked me not to leave town for a bit."

"Okay, so we're back to the same question we had in the beginning. Who would kill Todd and why?" Trent leaned his head back against the wall. "I feel like we're missing something here."

"I'd like to suggest Jacob Thompson. One, he was talking to one of the lawyers last night about Todd's trust. Or someone's trust. I guess it didn't have to be Todd's." Mia tried to remember the conversation exactly, but it had been a while now. She wrote his name down on her notebook. "And two, he's a jerk as Trent and I found out last night. We need more information about what's going on in Jacob's life."

Christina held up her hand. "I've got to go chat with Mom anyway. She wants me to come have lunch with her at the Lodge. I guess I need to tell her that I know about the trust. Especially if Isaac's trying to pull Mia into their deception."

Mia held up her hands too. "As long as you

don't say I told you. I don't need her hating on me again."

"Don't worry about it. I'll blame it on overhearing Jacob. It might bring her to chat about what's going on with the Thompsons." Christina glanced at the clock. "What else are we doing?"

"Before I go to work, I'm running to see Baldwin. I want to know what he's thinking. And I think I'll point him toward Jacob and the issue of Todd's money." Mia tapped on her notebook. "Does anyone know who owns the house Todd rented?"

Trent raised his hand. "Me. I used to date Andie."

"Andie?" Mia wrote the name down in her book. "What's Andie's last name?"

"That's all you want to know? Not if it was serious or if the girl broke my heart?" Trent placed his hand on his chest. "I'm wounded."

"No, you're not. So, what's the girl's name?" Mia paused her pen, waiting for his answer.

"Green. Andie, Andrea Green. And no, she hasn't married. She's some sort of computer nerd and turned the house her grandmother left her in Magic Springs into a short-term rental. She lives in Boise in a townhouse by the chip manufacturing factory where she works. But I hear she's here getting the house cleaned up after the incident. I'll track her down."

"Sounds like a plan." Mia glanced around the room. "What else? Levi? Is your alibi secure? You were out of town and someone will vouch for you?"

"I *was* out of town. It's not an alibi."

"Actually, it is. I know you were upset to hear

about Todd, but you can't be two places at once."
Christina leaned on him.

"Unless I did the deed for him," Trent added.

Mia slapped his arm. "Stop making this harder."

"You have to know the idea hit Baldwin as soon
as he cleared Levi from being in town." Trent
rolled his shoulders. "The good thing was I was at
the shop all that day. Several people can vouch
that they saw me there. Probably at the same time
Todd was killed."

"Okay, so we'll makes sure we have those names
too." Mia wrote Trent's employees' names down,
just in case Baldwin asked her. "Okay, everyone
has a job."

"Except me," Levi slouched in his chair.

"Oh, dear. son, you have a job. You and I are
clearing out the attic. It's been years since we've
been up there for more than just bringing out the
Christmas decorations. And with your dad out of
town, I need your help." Abigail stood near the
hallway. She glanced at Mia's list. "I'll take care of
keeping Levi busy while you all do your work. Shall
we meet here again tomorrow for brunch? Or we
could meet at my house? The kitchen's a little bigger."

"A little? That's like saying St. John's Cathedral
in Boise is just a little bigger than the chapel on
the Boise State campus on Broadway." Grans
rubbed Cerby's head. Trent had brought the little
Maltese with him when he'd arrived. The dog had
gone straight to Grans and hadn't left her side.
"Trent, can you take Muffy and this pile of fur
out?"

"I'll do it right now." Trent took the pup out of

Grans's hand. "Hey buddy, do you need to go outside?"

Cerby barked his response and they all laughed
at the tiny sound.

"That dog has you wrapped around its tiny paw."
Mia smiled as the puppy curled up on Trent's
shoulder.

"He's very attentive." He kissed Mia and then
hugged his mom. "Let me know where we're meeting tomorrow. I'll bring Muffy back up to the
apartment but then I need to go."

"I'll walk down with you and collect Muffy.
Besides, I thought you were off this weekend?" Mia
walked him to the door where he grabbed his coat.
Then they started downstairs.

"One of my cart boys didn't show up today. He's
sick. So I'm going in to bag groceries for a couple
hours when things are really busy. I'll call Andie
and see if we can meet up for coffee this evening.
Should I stop by the Lodge when I'm done?" They
went outside and the dogs quickly did their business.

They came back inside and Mia pulled a large
sweater on to take off the chill. "If you want to. I
don't expect Jacob to be around so you probably
won't have anyone to rescue me from."

He grinned. "You never know. I'm sure there's
someone in this group who thinks you're hot."

"Besides you?" Mia picked up Muffy so he
wouldn't go wandering while they talked. "Just figure out who Todd knew in town and why he was
here. I'd love to have another suspect to give to
Baldwin so he could stop looking at Christina and
Levi."

Trent nodded. "Point taken. I'll do my best."

After they left, Mia took Muffy into the downstairs kitchen and found a box of a dozen cookies already sitting in the fridge. Thank goodness for Abigail. Mia took the cookies and the dog upstairs to get ready for her day. It was going to be a long one.

CHAPTER 12

Except for the officer on front desk duty, Mark Baldwin seemed to be alone in the Magic Springs police station when Mia arrived. He waved her back without even waiting for his deputy to announce her. He watched her put the cookies on the desk. "You know I can't tell you anything about the ongoing investigation. Including whether or not your friends, Christina and Levi, are on the suspect list. Even for a box of your cookies."

"Levi said that you guys talked again this morning. You can't believe that he'd have anything to do with this, can you?" She left her coat on as she settled into the visitor's chair. "He's an EMT."

"Those guys can kill in an act of rage just like anyone else." He opened the box and took out a cookie. "Do you have time for coffee?"

"I probably better not. I'm working this afternoon and I've already drank two cups more than usual. I'll be flying around the Lodge, getting ready for this dinner tonight." She leaned in and grabbed a cookie. "Besides, Levi's not the killer and you know it."

"Currently I have two suspects. I'm pretty sure you don't want me looking at the second one. Miss Adams and I have come such a long way." He refilled his coffee, then sat back down in his chair. "Look, I hate to ask, but you don't have any inside information about this mess, do you? I got a call from the Boise City Police Chief offering me help in solving the murder. I guess the victim's family is well connected."

"Yeah, I heard that too." She pretended to think a little, then she leaned forward. She hated planting information with Mark, but if he really didn't have any other suspects, she needed to refocus him. "I heard that Todd's inheritance trust fund was running low. That he asked Christina to marry him to get access to her trust."

"Miss Adams is a trust fund baby? No wonder she's so troubled. Nothing ever comes from raising kids with everything they could want or need. My child is going to have a normal life."

Somehow Mia thought that maybe Mark would be surprised at exactly how abnormal the baby's life was going to be. She felt sorry for him a bit since Sarah hadn't bothered to tell her husband about her special powers. Mia could feel the tiny witch as she grew in her mom's stomach and Mia sent the Goddess a quick prayer for the baby's and Sarah's health.

"Christina's a good kid. She and Levi both are." Mia went on and told Mark about the conversation she'd heard between Jacob and the other attorney.

"This Jacob, he's the guy your security captain filed a report on last night. The one who attacked you?" Mark's eyes turned kind and he softened his voice.

"He was very drunk and apparently has a problem with my ex-fiancé. I was just an easy target." Mia stood and adjusted her coat. "Look, Mark, I know it—"

"Wasn't Christina or Levi. I get it. I even agree with you. I don't think either one of those kids could do something like this. But I didn't have another suspect. Now, I do. I asked my Boise counterpart to send me any reports or issues on anyone in the family, but he was less than cooperative. I may need to go down and ask for a look in his files. I think he felt a little too comfortable in attacking you. Like he didn't think there would be consequences. And, since he was stupid enough to do something in my jurisdiction, I have full rights now to ask about his history."

Mia checked her watch. "I need to get to work. How's Sarah doing?"

"She and the baby are fine. I'm not sure how much longer I can be on baby watch. Every time Sarah moves in the middle of the night, I jump and grab the overnight bag. She's getting annoyed at my hyperawareness." He rubbed his eyes. "And, I'm not getting as much sleep as I need."

"You better figure that out now. When the baby comes I hear you won't get any sleep." Mia stood and walked to the office door. "Thanks for chatting with me. I feel a lot better now."

"You know if either of those two did something stupid, I'll find out." He leaned back in his chair. "I just hope it wasn't this level of stupid."

Mia hurried out of the police station. Mark had told her that he didn't think either Christina or

Levi were suspects, yet, he still didn't have a good one to investigate. Hopefully, giving him Jacob Thompson was enough to put him on the right track. Mia didn't like it when magic was involved in a death. It felt to her like it sullied the entire concept of magic. However, with this death having no magical connections, she felt constantly at a dead end.

Gloria giggled and Mia glanced over toward the school. She could see the trees around it from the station parking lot. What was her familiar trying to tell her? She shook it off and got into her old car. It didn't matter today. She was going to be late for work. That's all that mattered right now.

As Mia finished up the setup for the dinner, someone knocked at her office door.

"Come in," she called out. She looked up, expecting to see James with the dessert he'd planned on serving for the dinner. Everything else on the menu he'd already brought by to taste. She thought he really just wanted to talk about last night, but she was too busy to think about Mother Adams and her dinner theater. Every time she was around the woman, she later found out that there was a hidden agenda. What would have her life been like if she'd actually married into that crazy family.

Isaac walked into the office, a small box in his hand. "Hey, Mia."

"Isaac, what are you doing here? I thought we said everything we needed to last night." Mia dropped her pen and leaned back in her chair.

"We did. I'm not here to try to talk you back

into a relationship. I think I've realized that ship has sailed." He set the blue Tiffany box on her desk. "I've had this for a while. I was going to give it to you for Christmas. I don't feel right keeping it."

"You could give it to Jessica," Mia suggested.

He laughed as he tapped the box. "I don't think she'd see the humor in it. No, it's for you. Consider it a going away gift. A thank you for putting up with me for so many years."

"Isaac," she started but he shook his head.

"I'm not expecting anything from this. No strings attached." He pushed the box closer. "Go ahead, open it. If you hate it, give it away. Or throw it away. I just don't feel right keeping it."

She reached out and took the box. Somehow she felt like she was going to regret this. She opened the box and she saw a diamond necklace. It was mounted in a silver charm that appeared to be a cooking pot with a spoon sticking out. The diamond was huge.

"Turn it over." Isaac pointed to the charm.

She did and saw the engraving. She read it aloud. "Kitchen Witch Extraordinaire."

"I thought mixing the two worlds was cute." He nodded to the box. "The chain is long so you can wear it under your tops. I know you hate to wear jewelry in the kitchen."

"Isaac, it's beautiful. But you could reset the stone for Jessica. This is too much." Mia pushed the box back across the desk.

"Like I said, wear it, trash it, give it away. Sell the stone. I had it made for you and I'm not taking it back." He pushed the box back toward her, then stood as his phone buzzed. "My ride's here. I'm heading back to Boise now. Jessica wants to go pick out a china pattern tomorrow. She's a little nervous I'm here."

"I wonder why?" Mia stood as well. "Isaac, it was nice to see you. I'm glad we talked out the ending a little more."

"I'm glad we used our inside voices for the conversation this time." He leaned in and kissed her on the cheek. "Take care of Christina. I know she loves it here. If this Todd thing blows up, please tell her to use the lawyer Mom hired. She needs to protect herself."

"Don't worry about it, I'm not going to let her do anything stupid. She didn't kill Todd and she's not going to be arrested for it. We may be a small town, but our police chief doesn't just put the blame on anyone." She walked him to the doorway.

"Yeah, but Christina's not just anyone. She has a record in Nevada, remember?"

Mia leaned against her doorway. "You and I both know that was bogus. She was lied to and then the people who hired her got mad when she told them she wasn't doing anything illegal."

"Yes, I know that, but it still looks bad. And she did threaten to kill Todd at the fair the year they graduated. I'm sure someone in her old group remembers that mess."

Mia shook her head. "Wait, he was the guy who was following her around that summer? He was really stalking her. She couldn't go anywhere without him showing up. If I remember right, we had to get the police involved to stop him."

"Yeah, but he just got a talking to by the police, and his dad told him to leave her alone. No one took it seriously. But if your Barney Fife finds some record of the incident at the fair, he might misunderstand and blame Christina." He nodded toward her desk. "I hope you keep the necklace. I'm sorry it took me so long to give it to you."

"Hey, Isaac, why did you keep it?" Mia asked as he turned toward the front lobby of the hotel.

He paused, then looked at her over his shoulder. "I didn't think it was really over. I thought you'd come home."

She let that explanation sit as he walked down the hallway and then turned the corner. He'd thought she would have come back. Even after she'd caught him with Jessica. He'd thought she'd forgive him. Maybe she would have if she hadn't picked up and moved to Magic Springs. She remembered the nights when his calls had gone unanswered. She'd been hurt. Mad. And done. He hadn't realized she wasn't playing his game.

Mia went back to the office and returned to the Excel sheet where she'd been setting up the expenses for the event. The necklace twinkled at her and she reached out for the box. She stared at the small pot and smiled. It was cute. She just wished it wasn't from Isaac. She closed the box and put it away in her bottom drawer. She had too much to think about to deal with jewelry nonsense.

A second knock sounded and James came in with a tray and a covered plate. "Ready to taste test the dessert course?"

"Perfect timing." Mia cleared off her desk. "What do we have here?"

When she got home that night, the lights downstairs were on. Trent's truck and Levi's Jeep were in the parking lot. Apparently, the team was here to talk about solving the murder. Or it was just a slow Saturday night and they wanted to play board games.

The group was gathered in the downstairs lobby area and included Grans as well as Muffy and Cerby. The two pups ran to meet her at the doorway, barking their welcome. "Hey guys, what's going on?"

"We've ordered pizza and it should be here any time. James texted us when you left the Lodge. We thought we needed a games night to clear our heads." Trent followed the pups to greet her. "You have about ten minutes before we eat if you want to take a shower and change."

"That would be nice." Mia rolled her shoulders. She waved at the group. "I'll be right down. Do you want to walk me upstairs?"

He frowned but nodded. "What's up?"

As they made their way up to the apartment, Mia told him about Isaac's visit and the necklace she'd brought home with her.

He held open the door for her. "I'm not jealous of your ex. Even if he can give you expensive gifts."

"I know, I just didn't want you to be blindsided if it ever came up. Actually, I wanted to get your take on what else he mentioned." She sat on the couch as the kittens swarmed her. Mr. Darcy ran to the door and opened it just enough for him to run out. Then it slammed behind him. "He's getting tired of the kittens, I think."

"That's obvious." Trent had Cerby in his arms and he put the little dog down on the floor where he promptly attacked the kittens. "What has you worried?"

She told him about Christina's arrest in Nevada as well as the incident at the fair with Todd. "The Nevada thing looks bad, but if I know Mark Baldwin, he found that out when Christina first came to stay. I don't think he believes it either. But if his Boise contact knew about the threat, I think that might be something Mark takes seriously."

"She was a kid and she was never charged with anything. Now, him stalking her, that's a little creepy. Don't these Thompson kids have any boundaries? The older brother attacks you. Todd stalked Christina. What is the little sister? An MMA fighter?"

Mia laughed as the black kitten jumped on Cerby. The two babies went down in a pile of fur, rolling on the floor. "I've never met her. Maybe she's like Christina and is the normal one."

Trent squeezed her to him. "One can only hope. Now go get ready. Pizza's going to be here soon and you'll be left with the Angry Hawaiian."

"Who puts jalapenos on a Hawaiian pizza?" Mia stood and walked toward the shower. She turned and grinned. "Oh, yeah, Levi."

When she finally got downstairs after locking the necklace in her safe, next to Christina's non-engagement ring, the pizza had arrived. She hurried over to the table and grabbed a plate. There was still some of the Angry Hawaiian left, but there was also her favorite, a combination with lots of veggies. She took a couple of pieces and when she went to sit, Trent handed her a beer. "Thanks. How was everyone's day?"

"I talked to the owner of the house, Andie Green." Trent leaned back in the couch. "She says that Todd's been here off and on most of the ski season. He was a referral from someone else she'd rented to. She looked up his file, she keeps them on all her renters so she can give them that personal touch when they arrive. He came just before Thanksgiving, twice in December, and then rented it every weekend except two since the first of the year. She'd already had bookings for those weeks."

"Wait, Todd was here that much? Why did he wait for this last trip to visit me?" Christina put her pizza on the plate.

Levi bumped her arm with his shoulder. "You're sounding jealous. Did you want him to stop in earlier?"

"No, I mean, I didn't want him to stop by at all. But if he was so over the moon in love with me, why did he wait five months to reach out?" She picked the peppers off her pizza. "It doesn't fit with the summer stalker Todd I knew."

"You're right. It doesn't fit." Mia leaned forward. "I think he was after your money when he asked you to marry him."

Christina twisted her lips as if she'd tasted something nasty. "I think you're right. Somehow, probably Mom, he found out I was here and someone told him about my trust. He was looking for a sugar mama."

"Or a refill to his own trust." Trent glanced at Christina.

"What aren't you saying?" Christina pointed at him. "Don't worry, you're not going to break my heart. Todd wasn't ever the one. I don't even think he was a good boyfriend."

"Andie said he had a woman that stayed with him. She found intimates left over in the hot tub area after one visit and a woman called to make the reservation for Todd on another visit. Of course, it could have been his secretary."

"Todd wasn't working. He'd just graduated from college and he was looking for a job while he waited to get accepted to law school." Christina stood and got another slice of pizza, dropping the hot peppers on her plate into the box. "It had to be a girlfriend. Which makes this proposal all so much sadder. I guess I was okay with letting down delusional Todd. But having someone try to trick me into marrying him? That's horrible."

CHAPTER 13

The next morning, Mia was busy getting the gang ready to move the party over to Abigail's. The two couples had stayed up late playing board games and Mia insisted that they all stay over rather than drive on the icy roads. Levi had grabbed blankets and claimed the couch leaving Trent with the spare bedroom. Grans was up making coffee when Mia woke up. She nodded toward the living room where Levi was gently snoring. "You know you all don't have to pretend that you're not doing anything just because I'm in the apartment. I suspect Levi and Christina sleep together when she stays over at his apartment. I don't understand why you make Trent use the other bedroom."

"Grans, it's not because of you being in the house. Trent and I are taking it slow. And I can't speak to and don't even want to know about Christina's relationship. She was just eight when I started dating Isaac. To me, she's still a kid." Mia poured herself a coffee and sat down. "Sarah's doing well according to Mark. But he's not sleeping."

Grans chuckled as she watched Mia sip her coffee. "Nice change of subject, but Mark needs to be sleeping now. If that baby does have a bit of magic in him or her, the fun is only just beginning. I'm sorry to say, Mark is going to have a rude awakening and not just as a human parent."

"Yeah, I feel it too." Mia glanced at her watch. She'd gotten up earlier than necessary. She grabbed a banana and peeled it.

"Oh, we got an invite for the baby shower. The coven is running it." Grans stared at her. "Sarah's secret is about to be revealed."

"I think everyone except for Mark knows. And maybe Mrs. Baldwin, Mark's mother." Mia pulled her calendar over. "Abigail asked if I wanted to help with the shower on Wednesday."

"That's nice dear, but Elvira knows about Sarah's magic. I'm afraid it's just Mark who is going to be surprised. The kid refused to see any magic at all growing up. I'm afraid he might just pop a gasket if he finds out the normal girl he married isn't so normal after all." Grans studied her. "Isaac is gone. I felt some attachment up until yesterday, but now the cords have been broken."

"Good. I was over that relationship years ago. I guess he was causing the cords." Mia broke off a piece of her banana and ate it. "He had a necklace he wanted to give me."

"It wasn't just him holding on to the relationship. There had to be something in you still feeling in order for the cords to stay healthy."

"That's stupid. I don't still love Isaac." Mia stood and refilled her cup. "I'd felt relief yesterday when he finally broke it."

"I didn't say you loved Isaac. Love and hate are both strong emotions. Either one can leave someone tied together even though they *say* they don't want a relationship." Grans reminded her. She stood and took a book out of a bag behind her on the window seat. She pushed it over to Mia, reminding Mia of Isaac's identical movement with the blue box from yesterday. "I took this out of your library yesterday. You need to read it."

Mia picked up the book, focusing on the title. "*Strong Emotions and Their Effect on the Modern Witch.*"

"Well, modern is a bit of a stretch. The book and the research were done in the sixties, but the resulting analysis is sound." She stood and stretched. "I'm going to get dressed and take Muffy out. I'll let Cerby know I'm going outside as well."

"You mean Trent." Mia said, distracted by the book.

Grans laughed and Mia looked up at her. "No dear, I meant Cerby. You really need to finish that book on familiars I gave you last month."

As well as several other books that were stacking up on Mia's bedroom table. For a while, the magic lessons Gran had given her had been more common sense. A few spells here and there, but they'd had to get through the lessons that most witches got in preschool. Now the lessons were focused on books and a curriculum that the educational body of the International Coven Association had sanctioned. At this level, she should be participating in classes with other kids, except she wasn't a kid. Grans was still working on teaching her, but it was like she was being homeschooled with a plan that included group trainings that she couldn't attend. Trent couldn't help her work out some of the problems since he wasn't even supposed to have magic since he turned his magic gift from his family to Levi.

The magical world was just as confusing with its rules and regulations as real life was for normal people. Since not everyone was ready to go to Abigail's, Mia took the book and her cup to the living room and started to read.

Walking into Abigail's house felt like coming home. The air smelled of cinnamon and sugar with a touch of quality coffee. And bacon. Apparently, their hostess had pulled out all the stops for this meeting.

"I'm in the kitchen. I thought we'd eat in here." Abigail called out as they walked into the house.

Trent led the way to the kitchen, but he didn't need to. Mia could have just followed her nose. If she'd ever had any doubt about leaving Mia's Morsels in Abigail's hands, this morning was proving that Mia had been right. Abigail loved food just as much as Mia did.

"Mom, you should keep the door locked. Especially when Dad's not here." Trent walked over and gave his mother a kiss on the cheek. Levi followed him. "You need to think about safety."

"We have the alarm on the front gate. I knew you guys were here, so I went and unlocked the door. If I don't lock it, your dad locks it remotely and I get a call." She squeezed his cheek. "Stop worrying about me. I've been a grownup longer than you've been alive. Good morning, Mia, and Christina. Where's Mary Alice?"

"Grans decided to stay at the apartment. She wanted to work on some spells." Mia glanced at Christina who nodded. "Since we still have the engagement ring, we thought we might be able to reach Todd's spirit if he's still around and see what he can tell us."

Abigail glanced over at her youngest son. Then she brought a basket of muffins to the table. "I hope she's taking precautions this time with the cats. I hate to see Todd's soul get caught up in one of the kittens. I don't think he'd handle it as well as Dorian has so far. Humans all expect to be in a line to get into the pearly gates when their souls pass. Getting stuck in a cat's body might not be Todd's version of heaven."

"Or a dog. Muffy's at the apartment too," Christina reminded Mia.

Mia sat down at the table. "Don't worry about it. Grans told me she's locking herself into the kitchen and doing the spell work there. Mr. Darcy and Dorian are in charge of the kittens and Muffy. Also, she kind of already sent him away with a spell the first night after he died. I'm hoping he's not around still."

Abigail set a plate of bacon and sausages on the table as well as a bowl of scrambled eggs and another filled with Southern hash browns. "We'll just be optimistic then. Come on everyone. Let's eat and feed our brains. We need to figure out this problem."

"Yes, before Baldwin sends me to jail for hating

the guy." Levi sat and patted the chair next to him. "Come sit by me, Christina. Maybe we could get side by side cells. That way, we'd still have each other."

"I don't think it works that way," Mia laughed as she sat next to Trent on the other side of the table. "Abigail, this all looks wonderful. Thanks for cooking. We could have just gotten muffins from Majors."

"We could have," Abigail agreed. "But then what would I have done to relieve some of this stress. I definitely am not a runner. Especially in this snow." Abigail took some hash browns and passed the bowl. Breakfast was on.

As they ate, Mia caught Abigail up on the events since they'd last talked. She felt Trent's gaze on her when she talked about Isaac showing up yesterday with his gift. But before he could say anything, Christina gave her report.

"That makes sense. Mom said she and Isaac were leaving today and going home. The attorney, Bernard, he's here until the killer is caught or Baldwin charges me. I think if that happens, Mom's flying in the big guns. I was told to stop talking to law enforcement and keep out of trouble. Mom doesn't realize I'm not the same troubled teenager I was when I lived at home. I haven't gone to a rave in years."

"You have better taste in music now," Levi added. "And in men."

"How conceited of you to say." Christina swatted at him. "Anyway, I asked her about the rumors on Todd's trust. She said his trust was secure. That she checked with the family lawyer before she told

him where I was living. He still had money when
he died. A lot of it. Mom told me that she wouldn't
have set me up that way."

Mia wrote the question down in a notebook.
"Okay, I'll steer Mark to check on his assets and his
will. If he had money, that's a motive, especially if
the money was going somewhere else."

"Idaho's a community property state. If Todd
had married Christina," Trent grinned at his
brother when Levi's head popped up, "or anyone
else, wouldn't his trust go to his new wife? That
would be a reason to stop him from marrying anyone."

"Unless they weren't a lawyer." Mia shook her
head.

"I don't understand." Trent waved a piece of
bacon at her. "What do you know that I don't?"

"When we first got engaged, Isaac and I sat
down with his lawyer to discuss a prenup. His
mother was concerned I was a gold digger." Mia
rolled her eyes.

"That sounds like Mom." Christina laughed.

"Anyway, the lawyer explained that the community property only covers what we make together.
So, the house we bought, Isaac put a payment
down for the mortgage, but it was in both of our
names. If we had married, the house would have
been half mine too even if he'd paid for all of it
out of his trust. As long as he put the deed in both
our names. When we sold it, I let him take back his
down payment, and then we split the rest of the
profit in half." Mia explained. "Todd and Isaac's
trusts are separate property and not counted as
marital assets. Anyway, we decided against a pre-

nup. Even if he got an inheritance during the marriage, if he didn't put it in our joint account, it would stay his separate property."

"So if Todd's plan was to raid Christina's trust, he wouldn't be able to without her permission." Trent summarized the discussion.

"I can't even get her to pay for half our dinners," Levi complained.

Christina laughed. "That's because it's not money to live on. No matter what Todd or Isaac or anyone says. A trust is for emergencies. Or big purchases, like a house."

"So your trust is big enough to buy a house? Are we talking about Sun Valley big or a condo in Twin Falls?" Levi leaned toward her.

"None of your business big." Christina turned toward Mia. "You're saying if someone killed him to keep me from getting his trust, it was a waste of effort."

"Yeah. And Jacob, his brother, was talking to a trust lawyer at the dinner. I'm thinking that's not the motive."

"Darn, I really wanted that guy to go to jail for something," Trent said.

"I said that couldn't be the motive, not that Jacob didn't kill his brother." Mia focused on eating her breakfast while she thought more. She'd been a little hopeful it was Jacob as well. Jealous brother issues, the story was an old one going back to biblical times. "With as many times as he was stabbed, there was a lot of rage. Maybe the fight was about something besides money?"

"Did you date this Jacob person too?" Levi leaned away so Christina couldn't slug him.

Instead, she just laughed. "No way. Jacob graduated the year I was a freshman. He was a total nerd. He talked for years about going to an Ivy League school, then getting his law degree. He applied to Harvard and Yale. We didn't hear about him for a few years, but later I heard he'd gone to Yale and his dad paid for it; he just didn't come back home on breaks."

"Tough choice." Trent grabbed more bacon. "Mom told me I had Boise State or if I did really well, University of Idaho. Other than that, I was on my own."

"You got a good education. And we didn't have to pay back any parent loans after any of you kids graduated." Abigail stood and refilled the bowl of hash browns from the pan on the stove.

"I didn't say I wasn't grateful," Trent clarified. "Going back to the murder, we're thinking money's not the issue?"

"I don't think he was here to marry Christina for her money. But then, why did he wait so long to reach out? If he was madly in love, he would have pushed the issue earlier." Mia thought about the question.

"If he was madly in love, he wouldn't have waited four years. No matter what 'plan' he thought they had." Levi pushed his empty plate away. "And I'd love to stop talking about Christina like she was chattel."

"Oh, that's so sweet of you," Christina leaned over and kissed him, "but we need to understand what Todd was thinking. If he was thinking. Or who led him down the path to asking me to marry him. I know he didn't just think of it, and Mom said he came to her. So who put the idea in his head and why?"

"I'm going to see if Mark has found out anything about Todd's will and who gets his trust. It has to be a relative." Mia had a small notebook near her plate. She wrote down a note.

"Andie says the house has been released. She's having cleaners come over later today. If we want to get in the rental, we need to do it now, before the cleaners come." Trent set down his phone after reading the text he'd just received from Todd's landlord.

Abigail set her fork down. "You're talking to Andie again? When did that happen?"

"Just talking to her about the murder. She owns the house Todd rented." Trent met his mother's gaze and she was the first one to drop eye contact.

"That's nice of her." Mia didn't want to know what mental conversation was going on between Trent and his mother about Andie Green. She wrote the info down. "I guess that's our first stop after leaving here. Christina? You need to come with us."

"I'm going too." Levi pulled Christina close to him. "Someone needs to protect this girl from random marriage proposals."

Christina dug her elbow into his side. "Whatever. You can come, but stop being so clingy."

"He always was that way, from the day he was born. The other boys, they attached to their dad almost on day one. But not my Levi." Abigail smiled at her youngest. "Mama's special boy."

"Mom, that's embarrassing." Levi blushed as he

stood. "I'm going to call and get my work schedule for the week. Let me know when we're going."

"You chased him away." Mia watched as Levi went out of the kitchen, phone to his ear.

"He'll be back. He always calls in for his schedule on Sunday mornings." Christina took his plate and her own to the sink. "What if it's not about money? I know I shouldn't bring this up, since it makes me look guilty, but what if it was about love?"

"Or lack of love?" Trent nodded. "What if Todd thought he was marrying Christina for the family, but he'd been seeing someone else. Someone who thought he loved them."

Christina nodded. "I can call some of my old high school friends to see if Todd was dating someone. They might know."

"Okay, so we have a plan?" Mia glanced at the list.

Abigail held up her hand. "I'm going to reach out again in the magical community. It's just strange that you all got so many possible familiars dumped on you this week, right before Todd was killed. It's almost like the Goddess knew you'd need some extra support."

"I'm not sure I'd call the kittens support." Mia laughed. "More like comic relief."

"Laughter is one of the Goddess's gifts to us," Abigail said. "Do you need the book on familiars? I think I have a copy from when Levi was trained."

"No, I have the book. I just need to find time to read it." Mia wrote a note on the paper. She really needed to keep up on her studies. Otherwise, she'd be as old as Grans before she finished. If she still had Grans available to teach her. A pit started to grow in her stomach at the thought.

"There's always people here who can train you, Mia." Abigail put a hand on Mia's shoulder as she walked by. "Mary Alice is doing her best, you just need to learn what you can from her and leave the worrying to another time."

CHAPTER 14

An attractive blonde woman was standing outside Todd's rental when they pulled into the
driveway. She went to greet Trent by his door. Mia
climbed out the passenger side, and with Levi and
Christina, walked over to meet the landlord.

"Trent, it's so good to see you. I don't think I've
run into you since that time we went fishing and
the truck got stuck. Thank goodness you had a
sleeping bag in Old Blue or we would have frozen
by the time the tow truck got there." Andie leaned
in and gave Trent a hug.

Mia knew the game. Establish your claim for the
new girl. She just didn't want to play. She waited
for Trent to peel the woman off him, nicely, since
they wanted a favor. Then she leaned in and stuck
out her hand. "Good morning, I'm Mia Malone.
I'm so grateful you are allowing us some time in
the rental. This is my friend, Christina, and you
must already know Levi."

Andie looked at Mia's outstretched hand, then

after a second of hesitation, she shook it. "So nice to meet you. I'm surprised we haven't run into each other before now. But I hear you don't attend coven events, I guess that's why."

"Yeah, I'm not so much into organized get-togethers. And I'm super busy with my new business, and now working at the Lodge. But soon. I've promised too many people that I'll check out the coven." Mia nodded to the house. She was ignoring Andie's games. "Trent said that Todd rented your house several times this year?"

"He's been a regular since the snow got deep enough for skiing. I appreciated his repeat business, even if his friends tended to leave stuff around like they thought he lived here. Of course, maybe he didn't tell them it was a rental." She pulled out her keys. "Come on, I'll let you in, then I need to run and get another client set up. I've got three rentals now and they keep me busy. Especially during ski season."

Andie crossed over to the door and unlocked it. "Just leave it unlocked when you leave, the cleaners are supposed to be here by noon, but with it being a Sunday, I'm expecting them to show up later. As long as I can get a new renter in here by next weekend, I'll be fine."

Mia thanked her and went inside.

Trent said a quick goodbye and hurried after Mia. "Look, about what she said, that was before you moved to town."

"You don't call your new truck Old Blue, right?" Mia smiled at him. "You had a life before me. I have to say I'm shocked."

"I traded him in just before you arrived. I'd had that thing since high school and it was getting undependable." Trent put his arm around her waist. "So we're okay?"

"We're fine." Mia stepped into the living room where Todd was killed. "Except for where we are. This is horrible."

Mia snapped pictures as they walked through the house. In the kitchen, the bags from Majors still sat, empty on the counter. "So, he'd gone shopping or had food delivered."

"I'll check with the store." Trent opened the fridge. "He was planning quite the dinner. Rib eye, mashed potatoes, asparagus, and a bottle of Dom was chilling."

Levi glanced at Christina.

"What? I told you I was bringing the ring back. I wasn't going to say yes to a proposal. I don't marry for money." Christina smiled at him. "No matter what my mom would prefer."

"Nice to know." Levi glanced at the dining room. "I didn't see ski stuff."

"It was outside the house. Maybe Mark had his officers stow it in the garage." Mia went over to the door that led to the garage. She flipped the lights on. A black Escalade sat in the middle of the two-car garage alone with two sets of skis, poles, and suits. One set of ski equipment appeared to be for a woman.

Christina walked over and put the pants next to her. They were way too short. "So who was he ski-ing with? These aren't Andie's. They wouldn't fit her either."

Mia took a picture of the ski apparel. "Good question. I wonder if Mark has an answer."

They walked through the rest of the house but didn't find anything else that seemed out of place.

Christina shrugged as she went through the chest of drawers. "I'm not even sure what I'd look for. Todd and I weren't close. We did things together, yes. And Mom liked setting me up for charity events with him. But the guys at school I was interested in weren't like Todd. They had lives that were outside of the world Mom and Dad lived in. Todd did debate. I was on the cheerleading squad. Even when we were out on these charity balls, the only thing we had in common to talk about were our families. He hated going to the events as much as I did."

"Did he keep a journal?" Mia picked up the book that was on the nightstand. It was a political biography of a recent president.

"He never said he did. But he made fun of me when I mentioned my diary. So, I bet he didn't." Christina pointed to the book. "We didn't even agree on politics. I'm not sure why my Mom thought we were a good fit."

"He was rich." Levi said. Then he stepped out of the room.

Trent met Mia's gaze. "I'll go out with Levi. We'll wait for you. Let me know if you need something before we leave."

Christina sank onto the bed and sighed as Trent left the room. "I don't understand why Levi's acting this way. I wasn't going to marry Todd."

"He sees the differences between his life and what yours could have been. I think Isaac got lost in all that money and status stuff after we were together for a while. He knew I'd never fit into that mold so that's why he went elsewhere. Levi feels that maybe you're going to do the same thing." Mia watched her friend.

"But I'm not." Christina sighed as she looked around. "I shouldn't have to prove myself over and over."

"True, but on the other hand, this situation is a little extreme. It's not just the fact your mom doesn't like him. He has to deal with the fact you came from money. This isn't going to be the last time you two run into this. He needs to know that you're the same girl he fell in love with." Mia went through Todd's closet. "I think this was a waste of time. I don't think we found anything here."

"Except the snow suit. Someone had been skiing with him this trip. And left their expensive skis and ski wear here. Why haven't they been here to get it? If Andie is ready to clean the place, it's going to be either put in Todd's car and sent to his family or thrown away." Christina tapped her finger. "I bet someone at the ski lodge saw them together. And maybe they know who she is."

"That's a great idea. Do you know people there?"

Christina grinned. "Some, but since Levi's on the ski rescue team, he knows more people. I think he and I will head to the slopes."

When they got back to the apartment, Grans was still in the downstairs kitchen, working. A piece of paper was taped to the kitchen door with the words, STAY OUT. Christina and Levi went to the ski lodge to talk to people while Mia and Trent went upstairs. He pulled Cerby out of his pocket.

"Have you had him in there all this time?" Mia smiled at the little guy.

"He likes going with me. Mom said when I left him with her, he sat by the door and whined until I came back. So, he's a pocket puppy for a while. This coat is perfect since he can stick his head out

while I walk around." Trent sat him on the floor
and he ran and attacked the sleeping kittens.
"Typically, hellhounds are black and of the pit bull
or bulldog breed. I've even heard of a mastiff
being chosen. But never a white Maltese puppy.
What was the Goddess thinking?"

"Maybe she's helping you hide your power. If
you showed up with a normal hellhound, people
might suspect you still have magic." Mia suggested.

"Well, it's working." He glanced at his watch.
"I've got some work to do at the store. Do you
need anything before I leave?"

"Just a hug. I'm going to call Mark and see if I
can get an appointment with him for Monday after
my staff meeting. Then I'm going to put my feet
up and watch a sappy movie for a while. I'm tired
of all the angst around here. Christina's worried
about Levi. Levi's making snide remarks because
he thinks he's not enough. You have a local girl
wanting your attention."

"That's not fair. I only called her to find out about
Todd." Trent started explaining, then stopped.
"You're messing with me, aren't you?"

"Totally." She watched as Cerby chewed on the
black kitten's ear. "I still need to find homes for
these guys. Did your mom say anything more about
taking the striped one? I should have asked."

"No, but I'll call her later. I don't like her alone
in that house when Dad's out of town so I tend to
call after dinner most nights."

Mia laughed. "Lately she's been here most
nights."

"Yeah, having something to do has kept her
busy." Trent grabbed Cerby as he started chewing

on the coffee table leg after the kitten had escaped. "Okay, I'll talk to you later."

"Sounds good. I'm going to finish reading the book on familiars today after I touch base with Mark. Then Grans gave me a book on emotions."

He chuckled. "I hated that book. I felt like I was being scolded for having romantic feelings. Christina might think her mom is all in her face about the right marriage match. She has nothing on the coven's rules for a potential mate. As kids, we're taught that emotions shouldn't be an indicator of who you should spend your life with. That the coven leadership might swoop in at any time and set your life plan. They have even arranged marriages between covens, just to strengthen ties."

"Okay so that explains why Amethyst and Tok's marriage into a witch family was so unexpected." Mia had been called in as an emergency wedding planner for their wedding when the original, and human, planner had been fired from the magical wedding. And then she was killed, but that was another issue. "I suspected that much. Which is another reason on my list to NOT join the coven. At least until after I'm married. Then I'm only subjecting my future offspring to their rules."

He laughed and gave her a hug. "That's why I love you. Always looking forward."

After Trent was gone, Mia called Mark and made an appointment for tomorrow at ten thirty at the station. Then she made a cup of tea, turned on a movie she'd seen several times, and started reading. The kittens all cuddled up next to her on the couch and Mr. Darcy took his place on a nearby chair. Muffy sat on the other one.

When Grans came up from the kitchen, Mia put a bookmark in to hold her place and sat up. "How did it go?"

"Badly. Either Todd has already crossed or he doesn't want to talk to me. It feels like he's still around, but confused and angry. I thought I'd come up and cook dinner while I process what I know. Maybe another way will come to me." Grans gave Muffy a rub. "Do you need to go outside?"

"I can take him." Mia started to stand, but her grandmother waved her away.

"I'll do it. Like I said, I need time to process. You keep reading. I'll be back in a few and start dinner. I'd like to talk next week about that book and the emotions one and do some practice spells. What days do you work?"

Mia went through her schedule, including the baby shower. "We don't have catering on Friday so my Thursday's free."

Grans smiled as she went out the apartment door. "Not anymore. We'll start training at eight so make sure to have both of those books read. I'll pull you some more reading material tomorrow."

"I still have four books on my nightstand," Mia called after her.

"Well, you better read faster then," Grans said as she closed the door.

Mia put her feet back up and went back to reading the chapter on Your Familiar and His Special Connection. A lot of this she'd known. But there were some surprises. Like the rarity of getting a hellhound assigned to you. It didn't happen much but as she read more, it appeared to be a sign that a conflict was coming.

She didn't want to think of what that might be.

The smell of potato soup and bread baking made her stomach growl as she finished off the book on familiars. The movie had ended over an hour ago and she'd put the television on a remodeling show. She liked the idea of turning old things new, of course, she tended to do that with the buildings she'd bought in her life already. What would it be like to start with a fresh canvas? Probably not as fun.

She went into the kitchen and Grans had already set the table for two.

Grans looked up from stirring the soup. "Christina called me. Your phone must be on silent. She said Levi's taking her to dinner, but she'd be home about ten."

"They need some time together." Mia sat down and held the book up. "I didn't realize the power of using a familiar."

"You've always had contact with the Goddess, but until you finish your training, you don't want to increase that connection." Grans filled a bowl of soup and set it in front of her. "Did you read the section on familiar gifts?"

"Like how Cerby arrived? I finished the book." Mia took a sip of the soup. Somehow, her grandmother's soup always tasted better than what she made. Like home. She knew it was probably some twist of magic, but she didn't care. The soup made her feel like everything was going to be all right.

"Cerby and the kittens. We need to find out more about who dumped them here. If they truly are from the Goddess, you might have to keep all of them."

Mia looked up from her soup haze. "What? You've got to be kidding. The apartment isn't big enough for four cats."

"Don't worry about it yet." Grans set her soup on the table and brought over a basket of fresh rolls. "I haven't totally ruled out that someone just dumped them."

"Has anyone picked up that mama cat from the pound? Maybe we should bring her over too?" Mia said, then shook her head. "Now I want another one?"

"I'll call Robert tomorrow morning. If she's been picked up, we can go talk to the owners and see why they dumped the kittens. I'm not sure it will be a pleasant chat, but at least we'd know if it was coven related. If you asked the human who dropped off Cerby to Trent, they'd tell you they did no such thing. If these humans remember doing it, the animals aren't familiars." Grans broke open a roll and put some butter on it.

"The black kitten seems like she's got a touch of magic." Mia watched as the kittens chased a small ball down the hallway.

"I've noticed that, but it might just be natural ability." Grans tapped on the book. "Like the book said, familiars are bred through a specific line, especially cats. They have linage back to colonial times here in the states."

"So we might just have three kittens to give away?" Mia shrugged her shoulders. "I was going to put a sign up in the employee break room next week."

"I'd rather you hold off until we check the origins of the group. If the mother cat Robert was telling me about got picked up, we can go over early next week while you're off. Maybe Tuesday?" Grans glanced at the black kitten who was watching them eat. "Then we'll announce their adoption status at the baby shower. Nothing gets people thinking about caring for another life like a baby shower."

"Okay." Mia couldn't help but smile at the small kitten who now was curled up in a corner going to sleep. Mr. Darcy meowed loudly from the window seat. "Fine, I get it. If they weren't sent by the Goddess, we'll find them good homes and get them out of your apartment."

Mr. Darcy made a sound like a grunt, then curled up on the window seat. He kept one eye open, just in case one of the kittens was coming to ambush him.

Mia turned back to her soup and saw her grandmother watching her. "What?"

"I just realized how strong your connection with Mr. Darcy has become. I wonder if Dorian's been training him." Grans glanced at the book again. "That's not supposed to be possible. The only connection Mr. Darcy should have is with you."

"Yet he talks to you and Abigail. I just assumed that was Dorian." Mia took a roll and spread butter on the still-steaming inside.

"I did too, but now I'm beginning to believe it's actually Mr. Darcy, not Dorian talking. I need to go into the library and look to see if it has any advanced books on familiars. I feel like we're missing something." She finished her soup and put her bowl in the sink.

"Do you want me to go with you?" Mia hurried to finish her dinner.

Grans put a hand on her shoulder. "Slow down.

I'll leave the door open and take my phone just in case. The sun hasn't set. You go get some more reading done when you're through with dinner. Don't worry about the dishes, I'll get them when I get back."

"Are you sure?" Mia didn't like the idea of her grandmother going into the library alone. The ghosts that lived there weren't the friendliest, even though they'd left Mia and the other livings alone for the most part.

"I'll be fine dear. But if I'm in there longer than an hour, come and get me. I tend to lose track of time when I'm reading there." Grans grabbed the keys and headed out the apartment door.

Mr. Darcy let out a loud yowl and jumped down off the window seat and ran to the door to sit next to Muffy. He turned back and stared at her.

Mia met his gaze. "I know, I don't like it either, but you know how she gets."

She set an alarm on her phone for an hour. Hopefully Grans would be back long before that.

CHAPTER 15

Grans was back in fifty-five minutes. By the time the door opened, not only Mr. Darcy, but also Muffy and the three kittens were watching for her. Mia must have been projecting her emotions, like she'd just read about. Mia had just put a bookmark to save her place when she heard the door latch.

"Did you find anything?" Mia stood, letting the relief flow through her body and setting the book on the coffee table.

Grans looked around at the animals, then at Mia. "I was fine. I brought back some light reading."

Mia then noticed the four thick books in Grans's arms. She reached over and took the books from her grandmother. "I take it that the library had some information."

"You have to realize that this building wasn't just a teaching facility. The coven used the library for research purposes. And when a witch died without any heirs, her library would be added to the shelves.

The collection is amazing, if a bit dated." She sat down on a chair and pointed to the books that Mia had set on the table. "There's another stack I pulled on the first table. Will you go and get them? And lock the library?"

"Sure, key?" Mia held out her hand.

Her grandmother pulled the key and holder out of her jacket pocket. "Thank you. That will give me some time to warm up. It's always so cold in the library."

Mia had a theory that the ghosts were trying to make it as uncomfortable for the livings as possible. The room had two banks of windows that should catch the morning and afternoon sun, warming the room, but even on sunny days, she needed a jacket to hang out for more than a few minutes. Adding the library to her own living space had been her original plan, but the ghosts had rejected that idea. So, until they went on to their next destination, Mia was stuck with a cold, barely usable, library. She grabbed her jacket off the hook by the door. "I'll be back in a few minutes. And I'll clean up the kitchen. You look like you're drained."

Grans grimaced. "I am a little worn out. The library can do that."

Mia watched as Muffy jumped up on Grans's lap and cuddled in. The dog knew what his owner needed, that was obvious. Mia thought she'd make some tea when she got back.

When she got into the library, the books were where Grans said they would be, in the middle of the room. However, the table wasn't empty. A small girl sat there, reading a book and swinging her legs as the chair was too tall for her. Mia took a breath. "Hello, what are you reading?"

The ghost girl didn't look up. It was the same specter that Mia had seen on her first visit to the library. "I'm reading about familiars. Mama says I can get a cat or a dog. My brother has a dog and he's always barking, so I'm thinking about a cat."

"I have a cat familiar. Mr. Darcy. He's grey and black. Maybe you've seen him. He has a little magic so he's always going off where he shouldn't be." Mia stood near the bookcase on the left, hoping to not scare her away.

"I've seen him in the hallway. Sometimes he lets me pet him when I'm sitting in the sunshine. He doesn't like how cold my fingers are now." The little girl looked up at Mia. "I'm not getting a familiar, am I?"

Mia saw the sadness in her face and decided to be honest. "I don't know."

The little girl nodded. "The guardian tells me I'm supposed to go on but the house is holding me here. He says I can stay with him."

"I'm trying to figure out how to fix the wards. Do you want to leave?" Mia asked. She'd spoken with the guardian before. He didn't want the girl or any of his ghostly companions to leave him.

A crash sounded from the back of the library. The little girl startled, looking behind her. "I've got to go."

"I'm Mia, what's your name?" Mia called after the disappearing spirit, hoping she'd answer.

"Ruth." The girl and the name disappeared in the wind.

Mia gathered the books Grans had collected

and headed to the door. She turned off the lights and locked the door. The school felt empty as she walked the short hallway to her apartment door. She had really taken on too much when she bought this building. Not only the remodel, but the history behind it. If she'd known she'd have ghosts living next door to her apartment and outside on the grounds, she would have thought twice about her choice.

However, as Grans would say, Mia had made this bed, now she had to sleep in it. Which, as she thought about it, was a really dumb saying. People changed their minds all the time. And sometimes, they did things that were the best idea at the time. Like Christina being nice to Todd because her mom asked her to. She never considered marrying him. Yet, he showed up with a ring in his pocket and a fully formed plan for their future in his head.

As she opened the apartment door, Grans sat back down. "Oh, good. I was afraid something had happened. I felt like I was being watched while I was in the library."

"You probably were. I talked to Ruth, she's the little girl. She says Mr. Darcy lets her pet him if they're sitting in the sunshine in the hall." Mia hung up the key on the rack and set the books on the table. "I don't think he goes into the library, even though he could."

"She's so sad. I'm glad she and Mr. Darcy have become friends." Grans ran a finger down the pile. She nodded and picked back up the book she'd been reading. "However, it's odd for a spirit to communicate with a familiar. Yes, the familiar can see the spirit, but it's usually not likely to make friends with it."

"Maybe it's Dorian who's reaching out, not Mr. Darcy." Mia checked the lock on the door. "I'm going to go clean up the kitchen, then I'll take the book into my room to read. I'm worn out."

"I'll be out here if you need to talk through something you read." Grans didn't look up, just focused on her book.

Having Dorian around made reading Mr. Darcy's intentions confusing at best. Dorian watched the wards for the house, let her cat in and out of the apartment, and the building, if Mia was correct. And even gave him treats. There needed to be a new handbook on how to handle your familiar when a witch spirit had invaded his body. Of course, since Mr. Darcy was the only cat to have that happen, maybe there was no need for a handbook. She just needed an expert in familiars.

Mia went to the kitchen to clean up dinner and think about what she'd learned that day.

Monday morning, Christina and Abigail were already downstairs in the kitchen preparing deliveries for the next day when Mia came out of her room. Tuesday was delivery day. Then Wednesday, they'd be prepping for the evening baby shower. Mia was still in her pajamas, going through her email for her Lodge job. She opened one from Jenna who'd been the staff member to leave early on Friday. She'd been right on time Saturday working her full shift. The email was apologizing again for leaving early.

Mia responded with a no problem message. Getting good help took a while. And if she was able to give them a little leeway at the beginning, staff usually came around. They just needed time to learn the routine. At least she hoped that was the issue. Sometimes, they just didn't work out.

Mia made a note in her planner to meet with Jenna next week to talk about schedules and how important it was to keep her shift commitments. Maybe she didn't know how to ask for time off.

Then it was time for staff meeting. She logged into the meeting site and listened as Frank droned on about budgets and staffing. He was trying to prove to upper management that they were a profitable hotel, even with being a smaller property on the company's books.

When he asked if there were any additional items for discussion, Mia jumped in.

"Frank, I'd like to talk about communication around taking new projects without proper notice. Last week, I found out on Wednesday about an event on Friday. That really changed my staffing and budget for the week. When I'm surprised like that, I can't keep overtime down because I can't plan or add new staff that quickly." She paused, seeing the look on Frank's face.

"That situation was unusual, and we were fairly compensated for the short notice. It's not an issue with overtime." Frank glanced at his notes. "Any other issues?"

"Sorry, I assumed this whole budget and staffing discussion was based on last week's numbers. Numbers that included the impromptu dinner event. An event we had issues with getting appropriate supplies to match the customer's needs."

She focused on James who was unusually quiet. "Right, James?"

Before James could answer, Frank broke in. "Well, I'm sorry I gave you that impression. Like I said, we were compensated for the additional costs so that event is an outlier. Now, if there are no other issues?"

The rest of the attendees shook their heads. They didn't want Frank's ire. Not after Mia had stirred the pot. Mia sighed and shook her head as well.

"Okay then, we'll see you all later this week. Mia? You'll be in on Thursday?"

When she replied, he nodded. "Great. Can you stop by my office? I'd like to talk about Friday's events. You got some very positive comments about the event I'd like to share with you."

When the meeting ended, her phone buzzed. It was James. As soon as she answered, he jumped into his question. "Are you crazy? Frank's going to fire you for sure."

"Why would he fire me? He just said the event got positive comments." Mia added check in with Frank to Thursday's to-do list. Along with interview a few more job applicants if there were any applications. And then she realized she'd told her grandmother she'd be free.

"That's got to be code. No one talks to him like that. Not in a full meeting in front of other people. I stuck my neck out for you to get you hired. Now I'm going to have to work with an idiot because you couldn't keep your mouth shut."

"He's not firing me." Mia said, but this time, she wasn't quite as sure. Frank was hard to read in the best of moods. James was right, she'd pushed the limits on the discussion. Next time, if there was a next time, she'd voice her concerns in private.

"Call me as soon as you're out of his office on Thursday. I'll be praying for you until then." A crash sounded behind him. "Great, now I've got scrambled eggs all over the kitchen floor. What a morning."

After the call, Mia pushed the worry away. A tactic she'd been using a lot lately. She needed to go see Mark and find out about Todd's will or lack of one. If Mark would even tell her. His willingness to be open and share information with her went back and forth. If he was frustrated with a case, he'd leak more than he planned when she asked. If his case was going well, he tended to follow procedure more and she'd be told to stay out of his case. Mostly she thought he used her as a sounding board.

Hopefully today was a frustrating day for Magic Springs's police chief. The fact that his wife was just about ready to give birth and he'd been losing sleep was in her favor. Mia went to get changed into jeans and a sweater from her pj's. Then she grabbed her keys and headed out to unthaw her car so she might actually make their appointment time.

When she walked into the police station, Mark was out front, talking with the front desk officer who frowned at her entrance. Officer Gerald definitely didn't appreciate her visits. Even when she brought cookies. She ignored him. "Hi Mark, I hope I didn't keep you waiting."

He glanced at the clock on the wall. "Sorry, I'd

forgotten you were coming in today." He put the paper down and drew a line near the middle. He turned to Officer Gerald. "Call the guys from the top to that line and give them their weekly shifts. I'm still working out the swing shift schedule."

Mia followed him into his office. "Sorry, I come empty handed. It's a busy week for Mia's Morsels and Abigail kicked me out of the kitchen when I tried to snatch something."

"It's this stupid baby shower my wife is having on Wednesday. I think the entire town has been invited as well as any of our friends and relatives. We just had one at the church. I don't know why we have to have another one." He ran a hand over his thinning hair. "This baby isn't even here yet and it's screwing with my life."

"I hear it gets worse until it gets better." Mia smiled at the prospective father.

"When will the better part start?" Mark lay his head on the desk calendar.

"College graduation is what I hear, as long as he or she doesn't rebound and start living with you again." She laughed as he groaned.

"What other good news did you bring? Why are you even here?" He didn't lift his head.

Now was the crucial time. "I was thinking about Todd's murder and wondered who got his inheritance. I overheard his brother and an attorney talking during Friday's dinner about the trust."

"Yeah, I've got an appointment with Todd's legal team later today. They want an update on the investigation. I'm using that time to get answers to the questions they keep ignoring. According to Idaho law, the estate should go back to his parents.

But if the trust had a listed beneficiary, it might go somewhere else." He leaned back in his chair. "Is your Miss Adams expecting a windfall from this?"

Mia shook her head. "Christina says no. But she also didn't know the guy was going to spring that proposal on her. So, if he did change the beneficiary on the trust, she's unaware of any 'windfall' as you call it going her way."

"The rich are funny. Every time I get one of these cases where there's any money involved at all, everyone clams and lawyers up. With all those stab wounds, the death had to be personal. So love or money are my two primary motives so far." He straightened his files. "Have you talked with Levi Majors lately?"

"Yesterday. Why? You can't be thinking Levi did this. He has an alibi." Mia tried not to lean forward to see if there was something on Mark's desk.

"An alibi we haven't been able to confirm. The guy he went to Boise with hasn't shown up for work for the last few days. I'm sure it's nothing." Mark stood, indicating their time together was over.

Mia's vision wavered through the tears she fought off as she made her way back to the car. Crying was the first sign that she was either getting sick, or she was furious. This time the anger was swallowing her. He'd accepted her meeting to chat just to see if she knew something. A voice tried to ease her and a line from the book she was reading popped into her head.

Uncontrolled emotions feed the flames for unexpected magical results. Be calm.

She got into her car and started it, taking several deep breaths. Finally, her anger slipped away.

She looked up at the window into the police station and Mark was standing there, watching her. She faked a smile, then waved, backing her car out of the parking spot. Levi wasn't a killer, no matter what Mark thought. She'd just have to work harder on proving it.

Instead of heading back to the apartment, Mia headed to Majors Grocery Store. She needed milk, but she also wanted to see Trent. She went straight to his office as soon as she got to the store. A young woman sat in his chair, with Cerby on her lap. When she saw Mia, she stood up quickly, putting Cerby back down in his bed.

"Hi, I'm looking for Trent." Mia watched as the woman's face turned pink. What was going on?

"Hi, Mia. I'm Tiff. I work here. I mean, I'm on break right now and I just stopped in to see Cerby. He's so adorable. And Trent doesn't mind if we come visit if we're on break." Tiff's words were coming out fast. If Mia didn't stop her, she'd know all about the woman in the next few minutes. "I have several cats at home."

"I have a cat as well. Anyway, do you know where Trent is at?" Mia quickly inserted a question into a space where the woman finally took a breath. She picked up Cerby and the little pup licked her cheek. "Hi, Cerby, I'm happy to see you as well."

"I think Trent's on the floor, stocking. Our guy didn't come in last night so we've been stocking when it's slow at the checkout counters." Tiff glanced at her watch. "Sorry, I need to go back to work."

Saying no one was stopping her was probably a little testy. Mia decided not to let her bad mood affect her words. "Nice to meet you."

As Tiff walked by Mia, her face turned beet red. Apparently, Tiff must have a little crush on Trent since she knew who Mia was or maybe Tiff was in the coven. That would explain it as well. Mia was certain her name had come up in several coven discussions, mostly since she hadn't joined or even attended one of their recruiting events. Either way, it didn't matter. Mia had more things to worry about than Miss Tiff.

Like how she was going to tell Trent about Levi's less-than-solid alibi.

CHAPTER 16

Mia took Cerby down to the store floor with her. She put him in her tote where he could look out, but not be considered a health hazard. At least she thought he was safe there. Trent was working with another guy in the canned fruit section and had just finished taking cans of crushed pineapple out of the last box from the cart. She called out a greeting, "Hey."

He looked up and smiled. Mia felt her heart flutter and Cerby barked out a greeting. "Hey, what are you doing here?"

"Just wanted to see if you had time for lunch?" Her stomach had just growled so she hoped it wasn't too early for him to step away.

"I do if it's quick. Let's go to the diner across the street. They don't seem to mind if I bring Cerby along. I hate to have him stuck in the office all alone all day while I work." He rubbed Cerby's tiny head. "Ben, let everyone know I'll be back in an hour."

"Oh, I don't think that's a problem." Mia smiled as they walked back to Trent's office to grab his coat.

"I know, he sleeps a lot." Trent grabbed his coat and keys.

Mia followed him out of the store. "I don't want to get anyone in trouble, but your staff seems to spend most of their breaks with Cerby. Is it just because he's cute, or is he singing some kind of siren song to bring them in. Tiff seemed embarrassed that she was even there."

"Tiff loves animals. Her husband keeps giving her crap about bringing home strays all the time. But now that you mention it, Cerby might be drawing people in so he doesn't have to be alone. I'll put up a ward around the office to stop him from persuading anyone else from stopping by. I hate for him to think he can get his way all the time." He took a menu from the waitress and smiled up at her. "What's the special?"

"If it's Monday, it's meatloaf. But I think you knew that." She handed Mia a menu. "What can I get for you to drink? Trent's a regular so I know what he wants."

"Actually, I'd love a hot chocolate. I'm freezing." Mia looked for a nametag. "Thanks, Peggy. Hey, what's your favorite item on the menu?"

"I'm partial to the French Dip sandwich myself. Especially on chilly days like today. But you can't go wrong with anything on the menu. It's all great. And I'm not just saying that because my husband is the chef." Peggy tapped her unpainted nails on the table. "I'll be right back."

Trent watched her leave. "Well, you made a new

friend. Peggy isn't much of a talker, which is weird considering she works as a waitress. I think the diner is more Joey's dream than hers."

"She seems nice. I like the fact that she teases you. You must come here a lot." Mia glanced through the menu and decided to take Peggy's advice and get the French Dip. She set the menu aside. "Anyway, I'm glad you had time to step away, I needed to talk to you."

"Okay, but aren't we talking now?" He set the menu aside and Peggy came over with their drinks. She took their order and left them alone again. Trent leaned back. "Is this about what happened between you and Isaac? Is this going to affect our relationship?"

"What?" Mia frowned as she sipped the hot chocolate. "No, this isn't about me. And nothing happened when I talked to Isaac. Well, something did, but it didn't change us."

"So what happened? You've been off since Friday night." Trent leaned back, watching her.

Mia wiped her mouth. Peggy had added a lot of whipped cream to the top of the steaming hot liquid. She considered her words. "I hadn't realized I had been acting differently. I thought we talked about what he said. But here's the recap again, in case I missed something. He made a mistake and shouldn't have torpedoed our relationship. He wanted to get back together. I told him I appreciated his apology, but I was in a relationship and didn't have any need to go backward. I think I also told him I thought this was just cold feet since he and Jessica had announced their engagement. What I didn't tell him is how crazy it was that he would even think I'd come back after he had done the exact same thing to me that he was currently doing to Jessica. I do regret not saying that."

"You're full of self-restraint," Trent sipped his cola.

Mia laughed at his joke. "I know, it was so unlike me. Anyway, if you were having doubts about my feelings, there they are. Grans said the connection between me and Isaac finally broke this weekend. I guess I was holding onto some anger."

"Sorry, I guess Levi's insecurities are wearing off on me. He's flipping out that Todd proposed to Christina." Trent leaned forward. "I think he has ring envy. He's been looking at rings for a couple of weeks now and they're crazy-expensive."

"Christina doesn't worry about things like that. Her mother does, but not Christina. But if he's thinking about popping the question, he should wait a bit until this whole thing is settled." Now Mia felt like a jerk bringing up what Mark said about Levi. But he needed to know. "Look, I'm just going to say this so don't kill the messenger. Baldwin told me that he can't verify Levi's alibi. The guy he was with isn't around. He's missed a couple of shifts too."

"Derek? That kid is notoriously unreliable." Trent paused as Peggy brought their meals. He picked up his fork and laid it back down. "So Mark Baldwin can't take Levi off the suspect list because no one can verify where he was. And he had motive to be mad and the stabbing was violent."

"Yes, and yes." Mia put her hand on Trent's. "I'm sure this Derek guy will show up, but Levi needs to figure out if there's another way to prove he was in Boise when Todd was killed. Maybe a store caught him on camera or he has a receipt?"

"Those are good ideas. I'll talk to Levi this afternoon." He nodded to her sandwich. "Go on and eat. I've got to get back to the store and finish stocking."

"I'm sorry to be the one to tell you this." Mia picked up her sandwich and dipped it into the au jus.

He shrugged. "You can't fix what you don't know. Levi didn't kill Todd. Now we just have to prove it or find another suspect. You were thinking Todd's brother had some involvement."

"I think Jacob is a cruel individual and I wouldn't put it past him to kill his own brother. But unless Todd's trust money was stolen, which Mother Adams and Isaac told me it wasn't, I don't know what the motive would be." Mia set her sandwich down. "I feel like we're missing something."

"Didn't you say Todd had a sister? Where does she fit into this whole thing." Todd cut into the meatloaf and took a bite.

"Good question. I'll do some research there when I get back to the apartment." She pointed to the food. "Is this our Monday date?"

Trent laughed. "I always take you to the best places. But no, I'll come over about seven and pick you up for dinner. That should give both of us time to do some research."

Mia headed home after lunch and took the yearbooks over to the couch with another cup of cocoa. She'd been planning on doing a big push on the hot cocoa mix for Mia's Morsels this year, but it had slipped through the cracks. Trying to be creative and time-sensitive on things like marketing blitzes was hard when she was working another job. By the time she got home, she was worn out and all her creative juices had been depleted. She needed to start doing her planning for Mia's Morsels before the rest of the day exhausted her.

Mia stood and grabbed her planner from the kitchen bookshelf. She blocked out time from six to eight Monday to Wednesday and then set her alarm for five thirty for those three days. If she didn't plan it in, the good idea would be lost, again.

Satisfied she would at least save some of her time and energy for her own business, Mia put the yearbooks in order and went looking through Todd's high school career. The yearbook had an index, so she went back and looked at the pages where he was listed. Three entries. She opened the second book. Three entries. Huh. She glanced at the page and looked for Jacob's name. Nothing.

She went back to the first yearbook's index. Here, Jacob had twenty-five entries. More than most of the people on the same page. Overachiever, much? She wrote down the page numbers for Todd and scanned the pages where he was listed. His class picture as a freshman, the chess club, and the school writing group. Mia wondered if they'd just missed attributing him in more of the casual pictures. She found a casual shot in the library with a stack of books in front of him. And one where he was at a football game, watching from the stands.

There were four or five more pictures where he'd been included in the crowd. In the crowd, but obviously, alone.

There was one where he was with Christina at the Winter Formal. Christina grinned at the camera but Todd's face was more closed off. He stood behind her, his hands gripping her like he was afraid of her flying away. Christina was listed as one of the Winter Wonderland's princesses. Todd was listed as "her date."

Even when he was in the limelight, he wasn't seen.

Mia slowly worked her way through the four yearbooks. When she got to senior year, Todd's listings increased to five. A huge difference between his popular brother and Todd. This didn't match the press she'd read about Todd in the paper. As Mia scanned the pictures where Christina was highlighted, Todd was usually there, in the background.

"Stalker much?" Mia asked the picture showing Christina cheering on the basketball team. Todd sat behind her, not watching the game. Instead, his focus was on Christina.

Mia closed the book she'd been reading. Grans set a cup in front of her on the coffee table. She picked up one of the books. "I thought you were studying magic?"

"No, I was trying to figure out who Todd was and see if it gave us any clue on who could have killed him."

Grans sat next to her on the couch. "Any luck?"

"No, but I hope Mark doesn't look at these.

Todd was a complete creeper when it came to Christina, at least in high school. If she had killed him, it wouldn't have been surprising."

Grans opened a yearbook. Mia had put stickers on all of the pictures with Todd. She found one where he was watching Christina. She closed the book and shivered. "That energy, it's still active, even with him dead. Teenage angst stays around for a long time. And that attention, it wasn't light and fluffy, like a crush. His feelings were dark and controlling. I think it was a good idea for Christina to turn this guy down. I don't think a marriage with him would have been healthy."

"Yeah, I got that feeling too." Mia picked up the cup and took a long drink. "This is my third hot cocoa today, but I need the energy."

"If you're going out with Trent tonight, you need to get ready. I have a feeling he's on his way." Grans pushed the yearbooks away from her.

Mia looked at her watch and groaned. It was six forty-five. "I'll go get ready now. If he gets here before I'm ready, just buzz him in."

It took Mia less than ten minutes to get ready, but Trent was already sitting in the living room with her grandmother when she came out of the bedroom. She nodded to the yearbooks stacked in front of him. "Sorry, I got caught up with those."

Trent held up the one he had been thumbing through. "I get it. These look like my yearbooks, but the kids have a lot better clothes than my classmates had. We were all jeans and T-shirts or hoodies if it was cold. Did you see Todd's sister? She didn't have a stickie."

Mia sat down next to him. "No, I didn't even

look. I found his brother in the first book. When did his sister come into the school?"

"Christina's senior year. Jennifer Thompson. If you thought Todd was antisocial, she makes him look like prom king. I only found two mentions. Her class picture and one for a library club." He pointed to the page where the freshman class had their pictures. "She's right there. Mousy little thing."

Mia stared at the picture. It looked like someone she knew, but she couldn't put her finger on it. "Where's the other one?"

Trent turned to the next page where he'd put a different color of Post-it. "Here. She's in the back row, almost out of the frame, but she's listed. I wonder why one of the kids was Captain Quarterback and the other two were so unpopular?"

"That's a good question. I'll talk to Christina when she gets done with your mom." Mia glanced at her watch. "Or when we get back from dinner. They're working late."

"Actually, Mom and Christina were both heading out the door when I came inside. She said she was meeting Levi." Trent closed the yearbook. "We better get going. Our reservations are at seven thirty."

"Yeah, okay." Mia stood and pulled on her coat. "Grans, do you want us to bring you back something?"

"No, dear. If I don't feel like cooking, I'll grab one of your frozen dinners. I can feed myself." She turned to Trent. "Cerby will be fine here with me and Muffy."

Trent rubbed Cerby's head. "Now I have to figure out who's babysitting my dog. He got upset from being left in my office alone today after I stopped his siren song. He transformed into his other persona. I have black-singed footprints on my door and the fire alarm went off."

"You're kidding." Mia glanced at the small white ball of fluff sleeping by Grans on the couch. "Are you sure it's safe to leave him here?"

Grans blew out a breath. "Please. If I can't handle a tiny hellhound, you might as well put me out to pasture."

"The alarm scared him and he changed back immediately. I blamed it on someone lighting a cigarette in the back office. I don't think I'll leave him alone at work anymore. Mom says she'll watch him or Dad will during my work hours. Doggy day care. I'm totally domesticated." Trent held the door open for her.

"Being a pet owner comes with a lot of responsibility," Grans reminded Trent. "And when the pet is also a familiar *and* a hellhound, well, you've got your hands full."

Gloria giggled.

Trent rolled his eyes as they left the apartment. On the way down, he grumbled, "I don't mind being lectured by your grandmother about my responsibilities, but having Gloria laugh at me is a little unnecessary."

"Sorry about that. She has a wicked sense of humor." Mia opened the front door and looked out on the cold evening. "Maybe we should stay in tonight?"

"No way. Date night is sacred. And we both need to unwind a bit. I talked to Levi about what Baldwin said and he's worried. He said he's tried to call Derek too with no luck. I guess the guy can be a little flaky and takes off when the powder is better somewhere else."

"Skiers are all a little flaky. That's one of the reasons I wasn't sure Levi and Christina would work. For all of her wild-side persona, she really likes stability in her relationships." Mia hurried over to Trent's truck and climbed inside. When Trent came in the other side, she asked "Are we heading to the Lodge?"

"Yeah, I thought it would be the best." He started the engine. "Unless you want to head to Twin. That steakhouse wasn't bad."

"No, the Lodge is fine. Maybe we'll get lucky and run into one of Levi's friends who knows where Derek has gone." Mia stared out at the darkness around the building. "I need to get more outside lights. It looks a little abandoned at night."

"If you buy them, I'll install the lights. We can check out the solar powered ones so we don't have to get an electrician out here." Trent pointed up to the building's top floor.

Mia watched the house as it disappeared from view on their way to the Lodge. "That's a good idea if we get enough sunlight here to power them."

"Okay, maybe we should call an electrician. I've got a guy who works at the store. He's reasonable. I'll reach out and see if he has some time. We can go to the home improvement store in Twin this weekend if you're not working." Trent turned down the road to the Lodge.

When they came inside the Lodge, a security guard came up to Mia. "I was just about to call you."

Mia exchanged a look with Trent. "What's happening?"

"Levi got in a fight with a guest outside the dining room. We have them both in the security office but the guest is claiming that Levi threw the first punch. We haven't called the police yet. Levi and Christina disagree with the guy's claim. We're pulling up the security video to verify." Carl, the head of security, led the way back to the office. "I don't want Baldwin to arrest the wrong man."

CHAPTER 17

It didn't surprise Mia that the guest, sitting in the security office, was Jacob Thompson. Christina was in the outer office. She came running as soon as Mia and Trent came inside. "Levi didn't start the fight, Jacob did. He said some horrible things, then Levi told him his brother was a creep and deserved to die. Then Jacob swung. He started it."

Mia moved Christina back to a chair. "If that's what happened, the tapes will show it. Just give Carl and his guys a few minutes to review them. I take it you guys came for dinner?"

Christina took a tissue from a box that was sitting on the desk near her. "Yes. Levi wanted to talk, so as soon as Abigail and I got the cooking done for tomorrow, he came and got me. I didn't expect Jacob to still be in town or we would have gone somewhere else."

"I'll call the kitchen and let them know we'll be late for dinner." Mia picked up the phone and called the dining room. A woman picked up and announced her name. "Hi, Holly, this is Mia Malone. Trent Majors and Levi Majors each have a reservation for tonight. We'll both be late, but just go ahead and set us at a table for four." Mia saw Carl come out of the video room. He gave her a thumbs up.

"What time should we expect you?" Holly asked.

"Give us fifteen, twenty minutes tops and we'll be there. We're all in the building, we're just finishing up something." Mia hung up and stepped over to Carl. "So Levi's good?"

"We need to see if he wants to press charges, but if he doesn't, yes, he's good to go. Mr. Thompson is going to be asked to leave the hotel tomorrow morning." Carl glanced at a video monitor that showed Jacob sitting in an office. "This is the third strike for him. I don't care who his father is, that boy is trouble."

"Wait, this is his third incident?" Mia exchanged a look with Trent. "I only know about two, this one and when Trent had to pull the guy off me on Friday night."

Carl stepped over to a desk where a file sat. He opened it up. "It was the weekend before. He got into it with his brother, Todd. When we broke it up, Todd said he didn't want to press charges, although the evidence was clear that Jacob threw the first punch in that fight too."

Mia watched as another officer got Levi from a different room and took off the cuffs the guards had put on him and Jacob. Christina ran to him, enclosing him in a tight hug like he'd been held at a jail or penitentiary for years rather than just a few minutes in the hotel security office.

Mia turned back to Carl. "Can you do me a favor and fax the paperwork on Jacob's incidents over to Mark Baldwin? I don't think he knows about the fight with Todd."

Carl glanced over at Christina and Levi who were waiting by the door. "All of it?"

Mia nodded. She'd have to trust Baldwin to see the pattern as a Jacob thing, not evidence against Levi. Trent held her gaze for a moment, then dropped it. "Come on guys, let's go get some dinner."

Trent didn't bring the issue up until they were done with dinner and back in his truck, waiting for the frost from the windows to clear. "I hope you know what you're doing."

"We both know that Levi didn't kill Todd. Baldwin can't prove that he did. And he's not going to railroad him. If Carl had sent only the one incident and he'd been asked why, it would have looked like we were trying to hide something." Mia rubbed her hands together, then put them against the heater vent. "We need to be totally upfront with Baldwin. That's the only way Christina and Levi aren't going to be looked at harder in this whole investigation."

Trent didn't look at her as he put the truck in gear. "Like I said, I hope you're right."

The next morning, Abigail came early to get ready for delivery day. She knocked on the apartment door right at seven. Mia had been expecting her. Magic Springs was a small town.

"You couldn't have left Levi's name out of that

report?" Abigail stood at the door, her cheeks red. Mia didn't know if it was from anger or the morning chill.

"Come in and let's talk. I made some cinnamon rolls this morning." Mia held the door open wider and stretched out her arm. A wave of energy flowed over her and Mia realized Abigail had just used magic on her. She let the wave finish, then looked up at her friend. "Did you find what you were looking for?"

This time, Abigail blushed. "Sorry, I had to know. Levi's my baby. I needed to know that you had his best interests at heart. I love Christina like a daughter, but your intentions may have been to protect her, not Levi."

"Come in. I might have the same questions. Anyway, my intentions are to protect both Christina and Levi. I know Trent doesn't agree with my decision last night, but I know it was the right thing. Jacob started that fight, not Levi. Mark needs to know everything in order to find the killer. Not what we think will protect those we love." Mia shut the door after her as Abigail came inside the apartment. She picked up her protection amulet and put it back on. "I don't know if this would have stopped your truth spell, but I didn't want Grans to think I was under attack."

"So you were expecting my actions. I must not have been as covert as I thought I was being." Abigail went and poured herself a cup of coffee. "Look, I'm sorry I doubted you."

"Again, not a problem. But maybe next time you could just ask." Mia dished up two rolls. "Are deliveries set for the day? You're on track for Sarah's baby shower tomorrow, right?"

"Keeping busy is the only thing that's keeping me from going crazy." Abigail took a bite of the roll. "Oh, and cooking. I made a quiche for Thomas this morning. He got home last night. I've been up for a few hours."

"I think that's why I went into catering. Cooking soothes me and when it doesn't, at least it distracts me." Mia broke off a piece of the roll and popped it into her mouth, licking the icing from her fingers. "Hey, any surprises from the magic community on Todd's death?"

"No. No one seems to have had him even on their radar. I think this is a mortal thing." Abigail took another bite of the roll. "Love, envy, lust, and anger. All strong emotions surround the death. At least this is what I'm feeling when I open up my senses and focus on him. The odd thing is the emotions aren't dissipating. I know it's not evidence we can take to Baldwin. But if Todd was killed in a fit of rage, his death hasn't calmed the killer. If anything, it made the killer more upset."

"Which leads us to Jacob again. From what Carl and Christina said, Jacob was itching for a fight. And he was plenty angry when he tried to attack me." Mia finished her roll. "I just hope Mark finds a bloody knife with Jacob's fingerprints soon."

When Abigail left to go get the van packed with Christina, Grans was still in the kitchen.

"Abigail spelled you this morning. That was rude." Grans stirred her coffee.

Mia shrugged. "I was expecting it. That's why I took off my amulet."

"I get it, but Mia, that's there to protect you. If you take it off, something besides what you expect could happen. What if that hadn't been Abigail?

What if someone had glamoured into her body and was trying to find out what you knew?"

"I thought our wards were charged to keep glamoured witches out?" Mia pointed out.

Grans sighed. "That's not the point. But yes, our wards wouldn't have allowed it, unless they were tampered with as well. You never know. I thought you watched horror movies when you were a teen. The monster always comes when your guard is down. Or when you think you're safe."

Mia laughed as she rinsed out her coffee cup. She had hit her caffeine level. "I didn't think you watched those movies."

"I wasn't going to let you watch them alone. They might have had inaccurate information regarding your new life." Grans reached down and gave Muffy a head rub. "Besides, some of them were good. Totally fictionalized, but it's always good to hear what the normals think of our secret world."

"Speaking of normals, has anyone sat Mark down to talk to him before the shower tomorrow? Like his mother?"

"You think Elvira Baldwin is going to take a chance her son doesn't adore her anymore? No, I'm afraid he's on his own tomorrow night when he finds out that Sarah's been keeping secrets. She can't tell him now, he'd flip. It has to come as a surprise. Hopefully, he'll be open-minded."

"This is Mark Baldwin we're talking about. You've known him since you babysat him as a kid. He went into law enforcement because he sees the world in black and white. Now you're going to turn on the technicolor and expect him to not blow a gasket?" Mia felt bad because Mark was going to have a *really* hard time with this announcement.

"It's better that he find out before they're at the hospital. Witch babies can be a little tricky to control those first few moments after birth." Grans took the last bite of her cinnamon roll. "I suppose we need to have our sex education class sooner than later."

"You want to tell me about the birds and the bees? Grans, you're a little late." Mia wrapped the last two rolls in plastic and put them into the refrigerator.

"Oh, have you had sex with Trent already?"

Mia almost dropped her plate. "Not talking about this with you."

"Okay then, I see you haven't. It's different when you're talking about two witches. You'll see. I'll grab those books from your library, and we can talk about them this week." Grans picked up a pen and started writing down titles of books. "I find that when I alert the library that I'll be coming by writing down the books I need, something pulls them for me and they'll be waiting on one of the tables." Grans tapped the paper. "It's very helpful."

"It's a little weird, if you ask me. Maybe we could ask the house to start cooking dinner as well." Mia opened her planner. She had things that needed to be done before she went back to work. She ran her finger down the to-do list and frowned. "I need to go talk to the humane society. Has Robert said anything about the mama cat?"

"You know, I forgot to call him yesterday. My phone's in my room, charging. Let me give him a jingle and I'll let you know." Grans stood and left the kitchen.

The kitchen was clean. She needed to refresh the cat box. Change sheets. Do laundry. She decided to start with the cat boxes. Once that was done, she went to her bedroom and changed the sheets. Housework wasn't quite as calming as cooking, but it needed to be done. Mia was putting the dirty laundry into the washer when Grans finally came out of her room. She turned to her grandmother. "Well?"

"The mama cat has been picked up. Apparently, the cat got out while the owners were on vacation." Grans followed her into the kitchen. "Robert didn't say anything about kittens. Maybe this is the wrong mama cat?"

"Maybe. Or the lack of information means the Goddess had something to do with the kittens arriving here." She checked off several items on her planner. "Anyway, I'm heading to the humane society to see if I can get the owner's name and phone number so I can ask them about the kittens. We could have one mystery solved today."

"Or more questions," Grans warned Mia.

"Please don't jinx me." Mia grabbed her keys and tote before heading downstairs to get her coat and boots. "Okay, let's say one of my to-do items *might* be checked off the list."

"I'm not responding since you won't like what I say. Go run your errand and I wish you good luck." Grans sat on the couch and turned on the television. "Either way, it's time for my show."

Mia arrived at the Magic Springs Humane Society right at eleven. She went straight into a cheery lobby with an empty reception desk. She could hear dogs barking in the back. "Hello? Is anyone here?"

A male voice called out from an open doorway. "Hold on a second. I'll be right out."

Mia scanned the bulletin board as she waited. Lost dog signs, lost cats, even a lost ferret had a poster. But no batch of kittens. A younger man came out with a husky on a leash. The dog ran up and put his paws on Mia's legs. She gave his head a rub, then smiled up at the man on the other end of the leash. "Hi, I'm Mia Malone."

"Jeff Conrad. This is Aspen and she seems to like you." He gently pulled on the leash and the dog sat quietly, watching them. "Are you here for an adoption?"

"Actually, no, I'm sorry Aspen." She turned to the man. "Actually, I have three kittens that were dropped on my doorstep about a week ago."

"If you want to bring them in, we can take them off your hands. Kittens are easy to place. Everyone wants a baby they can train." He glanced out to the car. "You didn't leave them in the vehicle, did you? It's kind of cold today."

"No, they're home at my apartment. I'm not actually here to drop them off. I was wondering if you've heard of any missing kittens." Now Mia felt a little foolish. Whomever had dropped them wouldn't put out a flyer saying they were missing. "That sounds silly, right?"

"No, but if they dropped them, I don't think they'll be looking for them." Now Jeff was staring at her. "I'm not sure how I can help you."

"I heard you had a mama cat that you found last

week. One that appeared to have had kittens recently? I've been told that she was picked up by her owners." Mia tried a different path. She wasn't explaining this very well, but she couldn't come out and say she was wondering if her magic Goddess had materialized the kittens to her.

"Oh, Fluffy. Yeah, she was here for a few days. She was so sweet, but you could tell she had an attentive owner. The woman had been out of town." He went around the reception desk. "And there's a note about the kittens. We all assumed it would be a long shot to find them now."

"Does it say what they looked like?" Mia stepped toward the desk but he had the file angled and she couldn't read it.

"No, but there were three of them. If you'd like, I can call Fluffy's owner and see if she wants to talk to you. What do the kittens you have look like?" He closed the folder and started writing on a Post-it.

Mia described the kittens. Then she gave Jeff her name again along with her number. "Can you have her call me? Or call me if these aren't her kittens? I need to know if we can give them away or not."

"Please be careful with the black kitten. People have been known to do, well, just be careful who you give her to if these aren't Fluffy's kittens." Aspen barked at Jeff. He looked down and nodded to the dog. "Sorry, it's time for a walk around the building. I'll try to call her as soon as Aspen's back in her cage. If you know of anyone who needs a good dog, send them our way."

"I will and thank you." Mia headed to the door

but paused and looked back. Aspen was watching her. She nodded, then headed to the car. Now she wanted a dog. Or more specifically, she wanted to bring home Aspen.

When she got into the car, she sent a wish up to the Goddess for Aspen to find a new home soon. She already had Mr. Darcy and the three kittens to worry about. Not to mention Muffy who visited often and now Cerby, who would be around if Trent was at the apartment. A husky wouldn't fit into her life. Even so. Mia started the car and put it in reverse. She didn't need a dog.

The thought of Aspen stayed with her as she drove to the Lodge to check on mail and any changes to the upcoming Friday event. She had Saturday and Sunday off, at least she did now, before she opened her office door. And she had plans with Trent to run to Twin on Saturday.

She went through her mail and email quickly. No surprise catering events had been put on her calendar. She answered a few calls, then she messaged James to see if he had time for a quick lunch. She was waiting for his response when a knock sounded at her door. "Come in."

Jenna opened the door a bit and popped her head in. "Is this a good time?"

"Of course. Come on in. I see James has been keeping you busy this week waitressing. Are you ready for our next catering event on Friday?" Mia pointed to a chair. "Sit and chat with me if you have a few minutes."

"Sure." Jenna moved from the door and sat primly on the chair. Her posture was perfect and reminded Mia of the way Christina sat when she first met the girl. Now she slouched more often than not. Unless her mother was around. "I'm enjoying working here. I'm always busy."

"That's the joy of the hospitality career. You're always in demand and always busy." Mia leaned back in her chair. "Tell me a little bit about yourself. We haven't talked much yet. Do you have family here in Magic Springs? Or, no, you're going to school in Twin with Christina. Sorry, I forgot that for a second. So do you have family in Twin?"

"No, Boise. I went to the same high school as Christina. And then last fall I started in the culinary program here at Twin. Boise State's program is a little more established, but I liked the idea of getting out of town to go to school." Jenna smiled as she talked. "I think living somewhere besides where you grew up shows maturity. And since I hated my siblings when I lived at home, it gives us some distance."

"I don't have siblings. But I feel like Christina is the little sister I never had." Mia decided not to mention how she almost married into the Adams family. Her computer beeped and she saw a message from James about lunch. "I'm being called to a meeting. We'll chat more soon."

Jenna popped out of the chair. "Thanks. I just wanted to apologize again for leaving early on Friday. It won't happen again."

"People get sick. I'm not worried about you missing one shift. I just need to know it's not going to be a pattern. We count on you being here." Mia smiled as she turned off her computer and stood.

"I promise." Jenna stood and followed Mia out of the office. "Thank you."

"It's fine, really." Mia waved at James who was standing in the hallway outside the small ball-room. "I'll see you on Friday."

When Mia reached James, he held the door open for her. "That looked intense. Don't tell me she's quitting. She's actually very good."

"No, she was apologizing again for leaving early on Friday." Mia shook the nagging feeling that she was missing something. "So, what are we eating for lunch?"

CHAPTER 18

When Mia arrived home, Christina was already in the apartment curled up on the sofa with all the kittens surrounding her. She looked up when Mia came inside. "Did you find their owner?"

"Not yet. But the guy at the humane society was going to call and see if these are their kittens. How did delivery day go?" Mia locked the door and sank into a chair. Mr. Darcy ran from the kitchen and jumped in her lap. He hissed at the kittens before making three circles and curling up to sleep.

"It was fine. Abigail has the delivery process set up on a computer route. We just hit the button and the GPS tells us where to go. She's cut two hours off the process so far and we are doing more deliveries." Christina paused the movie. "She'll be here tomorrow at eight to start cooking for the baby shower. Are you helping or do you have to work?"

"I will be in the kitchen with you. I worked at

the Lodge this afternoon and cleared my schedule." Mia rolled her shoulders. "I'd forgotten how much paperwork there is when you work for a corporation with lots of employees. I had to finish off my hiring folders for Jenna and the others so I could get them to HR by the end of the week. Friday, I'll have to check time sheets for payroll. I got used to only having one employee. You were easy. In this role, I'm not only hiring, firing, checking time sheets, but now I also have to set up mandatory HR trainings. I guess I was supposed to do these in January, but no one told me."

"When I worked at the casino in Vegas, I had a week of trainings before they even started to train me in my server job." Christina let a kitten bat at her finger. "I missed a week of dance auditions since the training time was all eight-to-five stuff even though I was working a night shift."

"Well, the first two days of the first week of next month have just been declared training days for my staff. I sent out an email telling them to sign up for a Monday or Tuesday. Then I bet I'll have to do a makeup day for the ones who miss those days." Mia opened her planner and crossed off Monday's planning time for that week. "Mia's Morsels is getting the short stick with me working at the Lodge."

"Abigail's doing fine. And you knew it was going to take some time to adjust. You are always trying to stick with a plan, even when it's a little ambitious. Like when you redid all the bathrooms in the house at the same time. Man, Isaac was mad. He had to go to Mom's and shower for over a week."

"That worm. I was using the shower at the hotel's pool room before my shifts. He said he was going there too." Mia laughed as Mr. Darcy grabbed her hand and bit at her fingers. "And yes, I can have tunnel vision when I want something."

Christina didn't look up. "Levi says Baldwin's still got him on his short list."

"His alibi, Derek, is missing." Mia could hear the worry in her friend's tone.

"He didn't, he couldn't have killed Todd. Levi's not like that." Christina moved the kitten off her lap. "I'm going to call him. He's on shift tonight."

Mia watched as Christina left the living room. All three kittens followed her. Mia hoped Mark would find the killer soon. She grabbed the book on emotions and the modern witch and started reading again. Maybe if she stopped feeling everything for everyone she could find some piece of information that would help the police find Todd's killer.

A girl could hope.

When the women of Mia's Morsels arrived on Wednesday afternoon to set up the food, the community center rec room was dolled up in pink and blue pastels. The coven that was in charge of the shower had taken care of setting up the room, all Mia's team, or actually, Abigail's team, needed to do was bring in the food. Mark had thought it was Sarah's friend who had set up the party, but the information had come from the coven's social chair.

Mia had been cooking all day with Christina and Abigail. She'd felt like an intruder in her own kitchen. Abigail had her own way of giving directions. Where Mia was more direct, Abigail set up a list of chores that they worked off. Mia had almost finished making the wrong appetizer when she found the checklist. Then she had to apologize and mark the item off the middle of the list.

"No worries," Abigail had chirped. "We just don't want to make a double batch."

Mia had asked where to start after she finished the meatballs. Abigail showed her the clipboard and how to mark off what she'd started and, later, what she'd finished. It was all so organized. Mia hated it.

The packing and unloading of the van had been done by checklists as well. While Mia had to admit that the setup did go faster Abigail's way, she thought the checklists were just a little over the top. Abigail had even changed the order of where the tools were packed for the catering job. Now there were different checklists based on the type of event.

Abigail liked to be organized. All the checklists were making Mia itch.

After setup was complete, Mia found herself in a back hallway in the building that held the community room. She was trying to slow her breathing before she broke and started yelling for no good reason. She had her eyes closed and was silently repeating, "it's just for a short time," when she felt a touch on her arm.

She opened her eyes and saw Christina standing next to her. "Oh, hi."

"Are you okay? Abigail means well. She just wants to do a good job and the checklists keep her focused. I even kind of like them," Christina admitted. When Mia reacted, she quickly added, "But I could hate them, if you hate them."

Mia kicked herself for being upset. She gave

herself an imaginary double kick for showing her emotions. Apparently, the book wasn't helping. "Look, it's fine. It's just hard to step back in when so much has changed. Abigail is doing a great job. And if the checklists work for her, that's great. I'll adjust."

"Mia's Morsels is your baby. You've just hired a nanny to raise it for a while. Sometimes nannies don't do things exactly the way you would." Christina glanced back at the door to the room where the party was being held. "Sarah Baldwin wants to talk to you, if you have a minute."

"Since our set up time was shortened using Abigail's checklists, it looks like I have thirty minutes available for Sarah." Mia smiled to let Christina know she was okay. "Let's go find her."

They walked to the door together and Christina pointed toward the stage side of the room. "She's over there, sitting by herself."

Mia headed across the room but as soon as Sarah saw Mia, she stood and waddled over to meet her. It was uncomfortable to watch. The baby was definitely due sooner than later.

Sarah grabbed Mia's arm, leaning on it as they walked. "Let's go over to the green room and chat."

Mia opened the door to a small room with a sofa and a table. A television hung in one corner and a phone sat on the table. "I didn't realize this was even here."

Sarah lowered herself into a chair and pointed to the wall. "There's a switch on the wall. Throw it and we won't be disturbed."

"Does it lock the doors?" Mia threw the switch and the window on the door turned opaque.

"Yes, and it shows others that the room is occupied. Kind of like those individual bathrooms at truck stops when you throw the latch." Sarah waved her over. "Come sit next to me. I need some advice."

"From me? I don't know much about baby nutrition, but I could do some research." Mia crossed to the other side of the room and sat next to Sarah on the couch. "Or I could find a nutritionist for a referral."

"Ouch," Sarah laughed, rubbing her stomach. "That was a strong kick. Anyway, I don't need food advice. I need help with Mark. I don't know how to tell him. You lived normal for several years before you knew about magic, right?"

"Kind of. I always knew Grans was a kitchen witch, but really, I thought she was just fun and a little strange. When I went to school, I knew she was weird. In a good way. No one else in my life talked about spells or creatures. Mom let me be normal for a while. At least until I graduated high school. Then she told me the truth." Mia thought about the weekend when she and her mother had come to visit Magic Springs and she found out the truth.

"How did you feel? Were you mad about them lying to you?" Sarah grabbed Mia's hand and squeezed it. "Whoa, that was a strong kick."

"Do you need me to get someone?" Mia wasn't quite sure what to do with a pregnant woman. Especially a very pregnant one like Sarah.

"No, I'm fine. It's been going on for a few days now. She or he's very active at night." Sarah blew out a breath. "So answer my question. How did you feel?"

"Sarah, there's a big difference between my

mom telling me and you telling Mark about your powers. Did you consider telling him before you were married?" Mia stood and paced the room. "I can't help but think he's going to see it as a lie."

"I was never going to tell him. I wanted to walk away from that life. From the coven. I wanted a man who loved me for my body and my mind, not what I could do with a spell." Sarah gently made circles on her stomach. "Growing up with magic, high school is horrible. Everyone's pairing off based on your skill level. The kid I was supposed to marry according to the coven's decision was a horrible person. He was mean and stupid and humorless. I can't believe one man was so not a match for me. And there wasn't any love. When I met Mark, I realized that love was powerful in its own right."

"You didn't know that the baby might have powers?"

"I didn't think of it. My parents died right after Mark and I married. A car crash. It wasn't until Mark's mother visited last month and she told me I wouldn't be able to keep up appearances anymore. That I had to tell him." She looked at Mia. "He told his mother he didn't want anything to do with magic when he was a teenager. Now I've passed it on to his child."

Mia went over to the small fridge in the room and took out a bottle of water. "Sarah, if Mark's from a magical family, he passed those genes to his kid too. It wasn't just you."

Sarah blinked as she took the bottle of water. Then again. "But his sister took the magic for the family. Mark didn't."

"I don't think it totally works that way." Mia didn't want to out what she knew about siblings and magic transfer like what happened to Trent and Levi so she had to be careful. "Sarah, coven wisdom on inheriting magic isn't totally accurate. Besides, Mark loves you. Whatever happens with this baby, he's going to love the child too."

Sarah closed her eyes for a minute. Then she wedged herself out of the couch to a standing position. "I hope you're right, at least about him loving me. I'm going to tell him tonight after we get home from this. I'm sure he's going to wonder why the coven threw me a shower. I told him it was a friend, but I don't think that excuse is going to work once the gifts start arriving. He's going to think we're living out a version of *Sleeping Beauty*."

"I don't think it's going to be all that bad. My gift is terribly normal and boring." Mia held out her arm to help Sarah move toward the door.

"Bless you for that. I hope everyone is as thoughtful." Sarah turned toward Mia and smiled. "Thanks for talking with me. Mark respects you and your grandmother. For a while, it made me jealous, but I think he sees you as extended family. I hope we will be able to continue to grow our friendship."

"Definitely. I'm going to be bugging you all the time to see the baby, I'm sure." Mia flipped the switch that had closed off the door. Now she held the door open. "Now go enjoy your party. I hear having an infant is a lot of work. You may not sleep for weeks."

Sarah laughed. "Poor Mark is already there. He tells me it's the recent homicide that's keeping him up, but then I see him reading the 'what to expect' book. He's scared to death to be a father."

"Is he coming to the shower?" Mia glanced around but didn't see Magic Spring's police chief.

"He called to say he was going to be late. He had to reinterview someone who he just found out was in town the day of the murder." Sarah pointed to the center table. "You can drop me off there. I think the shower activities are about to start."

Mia thought that maybe this might be a good time to slip into the kitchen so she didn't have to be part of relay race taking care of an egg or a doll. She didn't see the point in having these silly games at a shower. People didn't do them at anniversary events or house warmings, but throw in a baby or a kid, and people go crazy.

"There you are," Abigail walked up to her as she was moving toward the food table. "I wanted to apologize for today. We just kept butting heads. I should have known to ease up a little on your first event back."

"This isn't . . ." Mia started but then realized, it was the first time she'd helped with an event since putting the business in Abigail's hands. "You're right, it is my first time back. And I didn't even realize how much you've changed the process for the better. I'm the one who is sorry for acting like a child."

"There's enough hardheadedness for both of us to take our share. But today did make me realize I need to run some of the changes by you so you're at least aware of them. Especially if we take on new staff." Abigail replaced a serving spoon that had fallen on the floor when a guest had been filling her plate.

"I've decided I need to focus some more time on what I want from Mia's Morsels and have blocked off some planning times. Why don't we meet for breakfast at the diner by Majors on Wednesday morning. That way it's neutral ground. You can tell me what you've been up to and I can tell you what I'm dreaming about." Mia smiled at a woman who was trying to listen in on their conversations as she filled her plate with egg rolls. "Mrs. Kramer, you're going to love those egg rolls. They're amazing. You should try some of the sweet/spicy/salty sauce on those. It's Abigail's secret recipe."

"Oh, yes, I was just going to get some of that." Mrs. Kramer moved to the sauces and out of earshot for Mia and Abigail's conversation.

"Well, we're going to be a conversation topic." Abigail rolled her eyes. "Edith Kramer can't keep a secret if her life depended on it."

"And the story will be about how you hate the woman your son's dating and whose business you're running." Mia held up a hand when Abigail started to argue. "Don't worry about it. I was the one that was out of line today. We just need to talk more."

Abigail gave her a hug, then disappeared into the kitchen to refill one of the serving platters.

Mia watched the party attendees. Christina was in the middle of the pack. She was great at this social stuff. Mia would rather be working in the kitchen, out of sight. Not for the first time that week, her thoughts went back to her life with Isaac. He'd been the schmoozer of the two of them. Mia was the workhorse. She didn't want to go back to that relationship, but it had been nice to know he regretted torpedoing it.

She was just about ready to go sit in the kitchen when she heard the loud noises. An older woman was yelling at someone in the crowd. People moved out of the line of fire and then Mia saw who had drawn this woman's attention. Christina.

Mia moved in to break up the incident as did Mark Baldwin. She could see him moving from Sarah's side to the middle of the floor where the yelling was going on.

"You led him on for years. All he wanted was to love you and you broke him by saying no. But that wasn't enough for you, was it? You had to kill my boy." The woman reached up to slap Christina, but a male hand grabbed her arm.

Mark Baldwin stepped forward. "Mrs. Thompson, this is not the place or the time."

Chapter 19

"That is Marion Harriot Thompson, Todd's mom. And she hates me." Christina told Mia after she'd pulled her into the green room. "I didn't lead Todd on. I told him we could only be friends. I wasn't interested in him."

"Yeah, that was clear from the yearbook pictures. Todd looked like a creeper." Mia handed Christina a box of tissues.

Christina wiped her eyes. "You could tell that in the pictures?"

"Everyone could see that, including Grans and she likes to focus on the best in people." Mia kept watch from the room's window. "It looks like Mark is making her leave. I wonder how she even found you?"

"Small town. Everyone knows we were doing the catering for the event." Christina sank into the couch that Sarah had been sitting on. "Baldwin really needs to solve Todd's murder. First Levi's getting investigated, now I have people accusing me of killing him while I'm trying to do my job. What am I supposed to do with that?"

"Good thing your boss knows you're innocent." Mia pulled a stool over to the window so she could sit while she watched the unfolding events. "Your mom's still in town?"

"She's not supposed to be. She told me she was leaving days ago. Why?"

Mia nodded to the window. "Because she's out there, talking to Mrs. Thompson and trying to get her to calm down. Do you want to talk to her?"

"No. I bet she's the one who told Mrs. Thompson where she could find me. What was Mom thinking? Like the week isn't stressful enough."

Mia watched the women talk. Finally, Todd's mother left with a younger woman holding her arm around the weeping woman. "It appeared that Jacob was the golden boy of the family. Todd seemed a little on the edge, like he was a second thought. But why didn't she like her daughter? Jennifer's freshman year photos list seemed a little sparce."

"I didn't even know she attended Bishop Kelly High School that year." Christina adjusted her skirt. "Rumors around campus was Jennifer wasn't a full-blooded Thompson. That she was an aunt's kid that the Thompsons had adopted after Mr. Thompson's sister left town."

"Wait, the daughter was really a niece? No wonder she looked like a redheaded stepchild in the picture." Mia stood. "Your mother's on the way here. Do you want me to distract her?"

Christina groaned and stood up from the couch. "No, I'll deal with her. She's going to take Lemon Shortcake away from me, I know it."

Mia laughed at the name Christina used for her car. "She can't. The title was sent to the house and it's in the safe. The car is in your name as is the registration. It was a gift. No takes backs."

"You don't know my mother well, do you?" She stared at the door. "Five, four, three, two . . ."

Mother Adams burst into the room. "What in the world are you doing hiding in here? An Adams never hides from a fight."

"I wasn't going to scream at Mrs. Thompson. She's had a bad couple of weeks." Christina stepped forward to greet her mother. "I thought you were leaving on Sunday?"

"I didn't say which Sunday now, did I?" Mother Adams kissed her daughter on the cheek and turned toward Mia. "I should have known you'd be here. You always did have a knack for being where the trouble was happening."

"Good to see you too, Mrs. Adams." Mia glanced at her watch. "Christina, it's almost time for us to pack up the food and get everything back to the school. Do you want me to leave so you and your mom can talk?"

"No," Christina answered.

At the same time, Mother Adams said, "Yes."

"Well, on that note, I'll be packing up the food. Nice to see you again, Mrs. Adams." Mia started out the door, but Mrs. Adams put a hand on her arm, stopping her.

"I wanted to thank you for being nice to Isaac when he asked to reconcile. I know you were upset when he broke off the engagement."

As Mother Adams took a breath, Mia corrected her. "I broke off the engagement when I found him sleeping with Jessica in my bed. He didn't have the decency to break it off with me before finding someone new. Someone I heard you were a fan of until he proposed to her. Doesn't she have all the right family names and pedigree?"

Christina took in a sharp breath as her mother just stood there, anger seething out of her. "Mia . . ."

"Christina, this is not your fight. I should thank the Goddess that I found out Isaac's true colors before we married and I had to divorce him. I wish him and Jessica and you all the luck in the world on the new wedding. You're going to need it." Mia shook off Mother Adams's grip. "Just try not to mess Christina up any more than you already have. I think she has a chance to be normal."

Mia gave Christina what she hoped was a supportive smile, then she tried not to run out of the room. She'd said more than she'd planned. What was up with her today? She'd been mad at Abigail for doing her job. Now, she was lashing out at Mother Adams for the way she'd been treated years ago. She didn't care about Isaac or his proposal or even his mother. She did care about Christina, and she guessed that had been the trigger today. That and Isaac asking her on Friday to come back.

She really needed the Adams family and the Thompson family to leave Magic Springs sooner than later. They were messing with her mojo.

Mia ran into Mark Baldwin as she was making her way to the food table to help Abigail pack up. "Congratulations on the new baby. You and Sarah are going to be amazing parents."

"Thanks. She wants to talk after this. That's never a good thing. Anyway, Miss Adams can come out of hiding. Todd's mother is gone." He glanced over to the entrance of the room where Christina and Mother Adams were talking. "Although, her mom is still here. Parents and children. It makes me wonder what I've gotten into with having this baby."

"Yes, they're talking. I feel bad for Christina. Her mother thought Todd would be the perfect son-in-law. Even though Christina never liked him. What ever happened to falling in love?" Mia met Mark's gaze. "Please tell me she's not on the suspect list anymore."

"I'm close to getting her off it. I'm waiting for copies of her bank accounts and the family is being a little lawyerly on giving them. All I need to see is she didn't hire someone to kill Todd for her and she's done." He shifted from one foot to the other. "Levi on the other hand . . ."

"You still haven't found Derek. Or proof that Levi was in Boise?" Mia felt her shoulders sink with the news. "He didn't do it."

"I don't believe he did. But I have to prove it. I have another interview set up with Jacob Thompson which probably caused his mother going crazy on Christina. According to her, that boy came out of the womb as an angel. But my sources in Boise tell me he was in trouble as a teen." Mark's gaze found Sarah who was holding up a onesie for someone to admire. "I guess it's hard to see your kids' faults, right?"

"I've heard that's true." Mia nodded to Abigail who was watching her. "Look, I need to help Abigail get packed up since Christina's tied up. Tell Sarah it was a lovely baby shower."

"I'll talk with you later. And don't worry, I'm trying to clear Christina and Levi." He turned and hurried over to the table where Sarah was starting to pack all the gifts into bags. "Hold on missy, I'll take those out to the car."

Mia grabbed a tote and started to fill the empty containers and serving tools into it. Abigail nodded to the tote lid. "There's a checklist on the top."

"I know. I set up that system." Mia grinned as they worked to clean up the area. There wasn't any leftover food. The coven members were known for their ability to clear a buffet. "How did everything go? I thought people were having fun, at least until the thing with Christina and Mrs. Thompson. After that, I was stuck in the green room, keeping them separated."

"The baby shower was amazing. No one brought crazy coven gifts so Mark didn't freak out. Most of the coven is respectful about Mark's lack of knowledge." Abigail tied another trash bag closed.

"Sarah asked me what it felt like when I found out about magic. I told her I'd probably always known, but even then, it was a shock. I think she's telling him about the baby tonight." Mia lifted up one end of a tablecloth and waited for Abigail to grab the other side so they could fold it.

"I could feel the baby's power while I was mingling. She feels a lot like you. Warm and inviting. I wonder if she's going to be a chef too." Abigail mused as they folded the last tablecloth.

"With her mother's culinary skills, it wouldn't surprise me." Mia put the lid on the last tote. "You could feel her?"

Abigail nodded. "But kids are kind of my specialty. I think it's because of my own family. I knew the boys before they even arrived. Or maybe it's our ability to connect intellectually with others."

"Read minds, you mean." Mia grabbed a tote.

Abigail laughed as she picked up a second one. "You make it sound so bad."

When they got home, Mia let Abigail and Christina finish unpacking. She went upstairs and drew a bath. She wanted some time to think. Todd had been killed by someone who was emotionally invested in his life. An ex-girlfriend maybe? A brother? Someone he'd tormented or took advantage of in the past? Christina was kind of an ex-girlfriend, but he'd offered her his life. Marriage. That didn't send most women into a murderous rage. Of course, if another woman had loved him and he'd decided to choose Christina, that would be motive. Who was Todd seeing either in school or when he returned to Boise last fall? Maybe that was the person he'd been seen with at the rental?

Mia had gotten so lost in thinking Jacob had killed Todd. And, she mused, she still thought it might be true but Baldwin was looking at that. However, she'd forgotten to look into Todd's ski bunny visitor. Who had been skiing with him on the other weekends he'd come up to Magic Springs?

She needed to talk to Levi and see if any of his ski buddies had known Todd or anyone who had dated him when he'd visited here. And check with the bartenders at the Lodge. If they were drinking anywhere in town besides the rental, it would have to be the Lodge. The next bar was in Sun Valley and too far to drive back to Magic Springs on a snowy night. Besides, they could get off the mountain and head into the Lodge for a drink or food before they went back for another run.

She sank into the cooling water and washed her hair before the water completely turned ice cold. She at least had a few questions she could poke at while Mark talked to Jacob again. And while they waited for Derek to show up.

When she got out of the tub, she climbed into jammies. She'd warm up some soup later. Tonight, she was going to curl up in bed and read some fiction. Grans might not like it, but Mia needed a night off from learning her craft or investigating, or even cooking or planning her escape from the Lodge. Tonight, she was just going to relax.

"You look comfortable. Are those little hearts on your pajamas?" Trent surprised her as he sat at the kitchen table with takeout from the Lodge in bags in front of him.

Mia glanced at her pj's, then sat across from him. "Yes, they're hearts, and this is my favorite pair. I didn't know you were coming over."

"I thought we'd talk through what happened to Todd. With both Christina and Levi on the line here, I think we should think out of the box and see what else we can come up with. So I brought nachos and a box of tacos. Almost like fast food, but it cost me a lot more than the place in Twin." He started pulling out food from the bags and Cerby started barking. "You ate your dinner already. Go lie down with Muffy."

The puppy gave out one last bark, then followed Trent's instructions. The kittens were all in a pile under the window seat where Mr. Darcy was lying with one eye open, watching them. Muffy was on the other side of the kitchen in his dog bed. He moved over to give Cerby some room.

Mia stood and grabbed plates. The gang was all here, at least the animal one. "Where's Grans and Christina?"

"Robert came to get your grandmother a few minutes ago and Christina went to Levi's to play that medieval fantasy game he likes." When Mia met his gaze, Trent laughed. "He promised her pizza."

"So, we're alone and you want to talk about murder?" Mia took one of the tacos and bit into the crunchy shell. Whatever Trent said, James's tacos were a thousand times better than the fast-food version.

"I'm getting worried about Baldwin's investigation. I heard Sarah went to the hospital with labor pains right after the baby shower."

Mia set the taco on her plate and started to reach for her phone. "Really? Is the baby coming?"

Trent waved her back down. "False labor. The excitement from the shower and the fight between Christina and Todd's mother probably threw her into a state. We need to give Baldwin a viable suspect that isn't one of our friends or brothers. He's going to be a mess when the baby comes."

"Funny, I was just thinking about that in my bath." Mia reached for a chip from the nacho pile filled with toppings. She ate it, then grabbed a second one. "I don't think anyone has looked into Todd's love life, at least beyond Christina. I was going to talk to the ski run guys tomorrow at the

Lodge and see if they remember him with anyone. Didn't your friend say anything about the woman's ski stuff left at the house?"

"Andie said it wasn't hers." Trent grabbed a pen and opened a steno pad notebook. "I need to ask her if she has a security camera on that house too. Maybe we can get a picture of his snow bunny."

"That's a great idea." She focused on her tacos. "Apparently the sister was really a cousin. Well, a cousin that was adopted and raised by Todd's parents. Christina said everyone knew it but they went on with the charade."

"The girl from Christina's yearbooks? She looked so sad. I guess maybe the parents didn't want to raise her?" Trent stood and grabbed two beers out of the fridge. He opened one for himself, then held out the second for Mia. When she nodded, he opened it as well and set it in front of her. "I wonder what happened to her? Did she go away to college? Stay in town? Was she here for the event on Friday?"

"I don't think so. My gut is that Mother Adams set up that event so she could be here to help in case Christina had killed the guy. What a complete show of faith, right?" Mia took one more taco and curled her legs under her. She'd been hungrier than she thought.

"But Mrs. Thompson was here and crashed the baby shower. And Jacob has been here since Friday at least. Is he one of the lawyers in the Adams firm? Or did he come because of Todd's death like his mother. And where is his father? Home working through his grief? This family is all over the place." Trent held up the taco box. "Two left. Do you want another one?"

"No, I'll eat this and then work on the nachos." Mia wiped a bit of salsa off her lip. "We can do some social media digging tonight. At least, it might give us some sort of a timeline for everyone's arrival to Magic Springs. And I'll call the Lodge and see who's checked in and how long they've been there."

After finishing dinner, they cleaned the kitchen and took their laptops to the living room with a couple of notebooks. Mia smiled as she settled into the couch with Trent. "We have the most interesting date nights."

"We could be setting up a roleplaying fantasy game," he reminded her.

"Oh, please, kill me now." Mia picked up her phone. "Frank should be gone by now, let me call the front desk and see when the Thompsons showed up."

He nodded and started scrolling through Facebook to see what he could find.

When the front desk picked up, Mia was happy that Felicia was on duty. The girl liked to talk. She asked her to look up any reservations since the week before Todd's death under the name of Thompson.

"Sure, give me a minute, I'll get you that information." Felicia paused. "Oh, I'm glad you called. I heard Jenna McDonald is working with us now. Do I need to change her room charge to the employee rate? And if so, what was her start date? She's going to be thrilled she's saving so much money, but I told her she needs to find a room to rent from one of the locals. Staying at the Lodge is going to eat up her entire paycheck. Anyway, I'll be right back."

"Wait, Jenna McDonald is living at the Lodge?
Mia asked, but Felicia had already put her on
hold.

Trent looked at her. "Problem?"

Mia shrugged and wrote down Jenna's name.
She slid the note toward Trent. "Not sure, but
maybe you should add this one to the social media
stalking list."

CHAPTER 20

By the time Grans came home from her date, Mia and Trent had set up a timeline of when the Thompson family had arrived in Magic Springs and, at least according to their reservations, when they were planning on leaving. She'd also updated Jenna's billing to show that she officially became an employee last Friday. Mia grabbed her planner and made a note to talk to Jenna on Friday about alternative living situations. Felicia was right, a catering server couldn't afford to live at the Lodge.

Jennifer Thompson was another story. All they could find on her were notes about her time at BK. After her freshman year, she'd joined more clubs and had even been part of the concert band, playing flute. She'd gotten several scholarships but when Mia tried to research Boise State to see if Jennifer was a student, she ran out of luck. Mia leaned back, putting her head on the back of the couch. She was beat and finally the adrenaline from working the baby shower was starting to wear off. "The sister didn't go to Boise State."

"With that kind of money? I would expect at least U of I. Anyway, Cerby and I are heading out. I've got a delivery coming tomorrow at five." Trent closed his laptop and ripped out the papers he was using to make notes about each person. "Here's what I have. The Thompsons give away a lot of money. They go to a lot of charity events. And they like to show off their Warm Springs house. It's been on the last three Parade of Homes to raise money for the restoration of historic Boise. They have three children. Jacob, a lawyer with the Adams firm, Todd, our victim who was working for the same nonprofit to save historic homes, and finally, Jennifer, who is attending Brown University in Rhode Island."

"And you let me spend the last ten minutes searching the Boise State rolls." She swatted at him with a piece of paper. "Thanks for nothing."

"I didn't realize that was what you were working on. Communication, it's not just for breakfast." He scooped Cerby up into the crook of his arm. "Come downstairs with me and we can let Muffy out before I go."

"That would be lovely of you, Trent." Grans looked up from the book she'd been reading. Robert had dropped her off about an hour ago after their dinner. "As soon as Christina's not on any suspect list, I'll be heading back to my house. That way I don't have to go down three flights of stairs to let Muffy outside."

As they waited for the dogs to do their business, Mia and Trent stood in the doorway watching them. "I could come by around ten if you wanted me to help you with the ski bums. Then we could run over to where Andie's staying and talk to her about her security system. I should have thought about that before. She uses the same company that you have."

"Are you sure that's wise?" Mia pulled her coat closer.

He leaned in and kissed her. "If she won't talk to me because of you then I don't need her friendship. We're a package deal."

Muffy ran back into the house, followed by Cerby. Trent grabbed the pup and put him in his pocket. "So I'll pick you up at ten?"

"Sounds great." Mia watched as Trent made his way to his truck that he'd started earlier. She closed the door and scanned the area for Muffy. He was sitting in the middle of the stairs, watching her. "I'm coming. I'm ready to crash just like you are."

The next morning, Mia had finished going through her work emails by the time Trent arrived. She met him at the front door with a thermos of coffee for each of them. "Good morning. I got an email from the front desk this morning that Mrs. Thompson is checking out soon. I guess her chat with Baldwin yesterday made her reconsider her stay in Magic Springs."

"Okay, so now all we have to deal with is Christina's mom and Jacob." Trent took the coffee and they walked back to the truck.

"Maybe Jacob has been asked not to leave by

Baldwin. I know Mark said he was going to talk to him again." Mia watched as they drove up to the ski runs that ended behind the Lodge.

"We might be putting too much hope on Jacob as a suspect. Yes, he's a jerk, but he doesn't seem like he's concerned about being charged in his brother's death. If I'd killed Levi, I'd be on a plane to somewhere that didn't have extradition. Especially if I had money like the Thompson family."

"Fair point." Mia pointed to the shed where the ski patrol and the people managing the runs hung out. "Let's go chat with some ski bums."

It took almost an hour and they were down to their last five people on shift before they found someone who recognized Todd.

"Yeah, he's the guy who got stabbed last week. I kept thinking the cops would come talk to me, but so far, it's just been the two of you." Flynn Robins unzipped his coat and moved toward the fire. He'd been out on a run when Mia and Trent first arrived. "Did anyone talk to his chick?"

"He had someone skiing with him?" Mia opened a notebook. "What did she look like?"

"Short, maybe five-four, and long, brown, curly hair. Or what stuck out from her cap. She seemed over-the-top happy. You know that fake kind of happy when your aunt gives you a box of saltwater taffy?" Flynn rubbed his hands and held them up to the fire.

"Did they ski together often?" Trent asked. "Or did he ski with anyone else?"

"Nah, he either came alone or with her. From what I saw of her, she was here, two, maybe three times. But last week, she was here but she wasn't smiling then. He was. I heard him say that he'd been planning this wedding in his head for years and now it was finally going to happen, no matter what."

"He talked about a wedding? Do you remember the day of the week?" Mia asked.

Flynn laughed and pointed around the room at the rest of the group. Some were sleeping, others drinking coffee. "We're understaffed. And they aren't going to hire anyone else since we'll all be out of work as soon as the snow melts. I work every day. I'm not even sure what day it is today. I saw his picture in the paper after that last day, but I'm not sure if it was the next day or the day after that."

A bell rang and a number on the board lit up. "I've got a lesson. I'm sorry I wasn't more helpful."

After they got back in the truck, Trent turned the heat on full blast. "At least we have someone who saw Todd with a girl. One that wasn't happy to hear about the wedding."

"Todd must have been horribly insensitive to talk about marrying one woman when he was out with another." Mia sipped her coffee, letting the heat from the liquid warm her from the inside out.

"Or he didn't see her as a date. Men are like that. She must have been in his friends zone." Trent said, putting the truck in gear. "Let's go see if we can find a video of this woman."

Andie Green's condo was just a few blocks from the rental where Todd had been killed. As they drove past the site, Mia saw the crime scene tape had been removed and there was a car there with a cleaning company's name on the side.

At Andie's condo, they went up to the steps and knocked. No answer. They knocked again. Trent's phone rang. He looked at the name and then answered, putting the phone on speaker. "You forgot you were meeting us."

"No, I got called away to another house. I've got a broken pipe here since the renters turned the heat off. What did you need?" Andie didn't sound happy.

"I was wondering if you had the tapes from Todd's visit to your rental." Trent met Mia's gaze.

"Tapes?"

"From the security cameras?" Trent prompted her.

A sigh came from the phone. "Look, I don't want to advertise that I spy on my guests. And they're just outside cameras. They're activated by motion."

"Perfect. And you have the ones where Todd rented the house?"

"Actually, they dump every thirty days. I have this last stay though. I saved it just in case the police ask to see it."

"Can you send it to me?"

A long pause followed the question. "You want to review my security tapes."

"Just for that weekend. We're trying to clear Mia's friend and Levi." He let that sink in while Andie paused a little longer.

"I'll send it to you. You still at the same email address?"

"Yes, thank you, Andie. I appreciate this." He grinned at Mia.

"I'm not doing it for you. I'm doing it for Levi. I always loved that kid." Andie hung up and the call ended.

"Andie's not happy with you." Mia said as they walked back to the truck.

"She hasn't been happy with me since we broke up a few years ago. We were still dating on and off when you and I met. But before we went on our first date, I ended it. I wasn't in love with her. It wasn't fair to pretend otherwise." Trent glanced over at Mia. "I guess I could have mentioned this before, but Andie and I were just casual. At least in my mind."

"Trent, you don't owe me a list of everyone you dated before we started seeing each other." Mia sipped her coffee as Trent drove her home.

"I know, but Magic Springs is a small town. So we're probably going to run into anyone I dated since high school if they hung around." Trent reached for her hand. "At least your exes have to make a special trip to see you."

"Like Isaac did last weekend. That still surprised me." Mia stared out the window at the snow-covered landscape. "I think he's still working through his commitment issues. Especially since he and Jessica just got engaged. The timing is suspect."

Trent laughed. "Only you would psychoanalyze your ex when they came to tell you they were still in love with you."

"Since I'm not in love with him, it was an easy process. Kind of like stepping back and actually seeing what was going on for so many years. It's cathartic." Mia nodded to the school. "Are you coming in for coffee or I could make lunch if you're hungry?"

"I'd love to but I've got to get back to work. One of my checkers called in sick." He pulled the truck close to the door. "I'm glad we got to spend some time together. Now that you're working at the Lodge, I don't see you as much."

"Not true, we just have to work around two schedules." Mia leaned over and kissed him. "I had way too much free time when I ran Mia's Morsels. You could take advantage of my availability."

"I like spending time with you." He laughed when he saw the grin on Mia's face. "You're messing with me."

"A bit. Anyway, it's okay. I need to do some reading. Grans is talking about doing a lab session tonight and then one every day before she heads home. Where's Cerby?" Mia realized she hadn't seen the little dog since Trent picked her up. "Did you set him up in the back?"

"No, I wouldn't have left him in the truck when we went into the ski shack. I'm not a monster." He put the truck in park but left the motor running. It was too cold to be without heat, even for a short chat. "I left him with Mom. She said she wasn't working Mia's Morsels until next Monday so he'll be there today and tomorrow. And Saturday if we're still going to Twin."

"I really need those lights, so yes, Twin's still on the plan. Unless something comes up and you can't go." Mia grabbed her tote.

"Unless Mom can't watch Cerby, I'm game. We can go to that Thai place you like for lunch." He nodded to the front door. "Can I walk you in?"

"Seriously, is this 1960? I can find my front door. And I haven't been attacked in the school for what, two years now?" Mia opened her door. "Call me later?"

"Of course." Trent watched Mia as she walked the short distance to her door. It was unlocked so Christina or Grans must have seen her coming.

Which was the good part of having a security system.

She waved as she stood in the open door and Trent put the truck in gear and headed out of her parking lot. Mia went inside and locked the door behind her. No lights were on in the lobby so no one was in the prep kitchen. She headed upstairs, but when she got to the third floor, she heard voices in the library. She wished her grandmother wouldn't go in there when she was gone, the spirits were unpredictable.

Mia dropped her bag at the apartment door, then headed to the library. The door was cracked open a few inches. She pushed it completely open. "Grans? What are you doing?"

To her surprise, Grans wasn't the only person sitting at the large library table in the middle of the room. Robert was there as well as two people she didn't know. And the little ghost girl hovered over a book at the end of the table. The entity that Mia had labeled the guardian, floated behind her.

"Mia, if you're going to disturb us, please come in and be quiet. We're trying to reach the library residents." Grans waved her inside. "You can sit there."

Mia turned to the chair that Grans had indicated. The ghost girl who sat there shrugged.

"They can't see us." Ruth focused on Mia. "Why can you see us?"

"That's a good question." Mia turned to her grandmother. "That seat is taken."

Grans looked up from the book she and Robert were studying. "What do you mean?"

Mia met her gaze and nodded when she saw the

understanding hit Grans. "I thought you'd talked to the ghosts before."

"I have." She pushed the book back toward Robert. "You're telling me that there is a ghost sitting in that chair?"

"Hovering, but yes. It's Ruth, the little girl I talked to earlier this week." Mia sat in a chair next to Ruth. "And the guardian is behind her. He doesn't look happy with what you're doing."

Robert turned to Grans. "I knew I could feel them, but why aren't they appearing to us?"

Grans studied Mia's face. "I don't know. But clearly, we're not going to be successful in releasing anyone who doesn't want us to see them."

"It's not that," Ruth protested. "He says they aren't using the right spells."

Mia picked up one of the books on the table. "Communicating with the dead? The guardian says you're not using the right spells."

The two people sitting at the other end of the table whispered to each other, then they stood. "Mary Alice, we need to discuss this with coven leadership. We may need to call in a specialist."

Mia watched as they left the room. "Who are those guys?"

"Robert thought it might be a good time to help the library spirits cross over. The wards shouldn't be keeping them here anymore. He checked the spell earlier today. Since I knew Ruth was still here, we invited people from the coven assigned to clearing houses." Grans stood and started putting books away on the shelves. "I've been working on this cleansing spell for months now, since we found out they were stuck."

"We're not exactly stuck. At least I'm not. I'm

just not sure I want to go forward. The others feel the same way." Ruth looked back at the spirit behind her. "He said we could stay."

Mia nodded, then turned to Grans. "Ruth says they aren't stuck. I don't think they want to leave. Why are we pushing the issue?"

Grans and Robert stared at her. "Mia, you know spirits can't just stay around. They become angry, like those ones in the graveyard."

"Ruth isn't angry. She might be a little upset that she can't have a familiar," Mia smiled at the little girl whose eyes had widened when she mentioned the conversation. "But they're not like the ghosts that used to haunt the grounds. They don't feel maleficent."

"I'm sorry Mia, now that the coven is aware of the entities, we will need to clear them from this plane of existence." Robert stood and adjusted his jacket. "Mary Alice, I'll call you when the coven contacts me."

As he walked out, Ruth started crying. "I don't want to leave. I'm scared." She turned and flew into the guardian who stared at Mia until they both disappeared.

Mia stood. "I'm not sure what you're doing here, but you're upsetting the ghosts. Tell Robert and the coven that if I want my library cleared, I'll call them. Not you."

Grans put the final book on the shelf. "It doesn't work that way. The coven has rules."

"Which is why I didn't want to join it in the first place. Grans, I won't ban you from the library, but I don't want Robert or any coven member in here without my permission. Do you understand?"

Instead of answering, Grans picked up her spell

book and left the library. Mia heard the door to the apartment slam shut soon after that. She looked around the library which had turned dark. "Ruth, I'm going to fix this. I promise."

As she left the room, she closed the door. The key to the room was in the lock. She relocked it and tucked the key into her jeans. Now she had one more problem to deal with. Great.

CHAPTER 21

When Mia went to knock on Grans door to tell her dinner was ready, Grans called back that she wasn't feeling well and would someone let out Muffy. The door opened enough for Muffy to come out and bark at Mia. "Grans, I'm sorry if I upset you, but the ghosts don't want to leave. And I don't think they should be made to if they don't want to go."

"I understand." Grans said through the now-closed door. "Please let Muffy out."

Mia groaned and looked down at her grandmother's dog. "Do you want to go outside?"

Muffy barked and ran to the living room. Mia followed him. She called out to Christina who was sitting at the table. "I'll be right back. Grans says she's not feeling well."

"Okay." Christina started dishing up the lasagna that she'd made for dinner.

Mia felt the gap between her and her grandmother widening as she headed downstairs. She'd

have to figure out a way to apologize again. But
Grans would know if she didn't mean it. She
hadn't meant to embarrass her in front of Robert,
but he and the coven were wrong about the spirits.
Maybe she could get some kind of permit to allow
them to stay. She rolled her eyes. She really needed
to know more about the workings of the coven before she could fight this. Abigail might be able to
help her. Maybe there was a loophole.

She opened the door to let Muffy out and an
old Jeep pulled into the driveway. A woman got
out. Mia wondered if it was a Mia's Morsels customer. Christina was on the schedule to take walk-
ins tomorrow for take-and-bake meals. Maybe this
woman had gotten the days mixed up. Mia pulled
her coat closer and when the woman got out of
her car and started walking toward her, she called
out, "Can I help you?"

The woman grinned at her. "I certainly hope so.
Oh, it's you. I didn't realize who you were when we
spoke the other day."

Mia waited for the woman to get into the light,
then realized it was the woman who had been playing with Cerby in Trent's office. The woman
who'd been on break. Tiffany, no, Tiff. She'd said
her name was Tiff. "Oh, yeah, we met at Majors.
It's Tiff, right?"

"And you're Mia Malone. I should have put two
and two together when I saw you at the store.
Everyone's talking about you and Trent. How
good you are for him, I mean." Tiff's face was red,
but it could have been from the cold.

Muffy came up and stepped inside the doorway,
watching the two women. "Well, he's done with his
business. Why don't you come inside and tell me

what I can help you with? Our take-home meals department isn't open until tomorrow but I might be able to help you if it's an emergency."

"Oh, no. I mean, I'm not here for food. Dinner's on the table. My mother-in-law is staying with us for a few days. She stayed at our house while we went on vacation and she'll be leaving tomorrow." Tiff followed Mia inside and stamped the snow off her boots. "I'm not explaining myself very well, am I? I always talk too much."

"You're fine. So what can I help you with?" Mia put her coat back on the hook and watched Tiff as she rubbed Muffy's head. She was good with animals, that was certain. Which made Mia like her instantly.

"I got your name from Jeff Conrad." Tiff picked up Muffy and cuddled him.

Mia must have frowned, showing her confusion. "Who?"

"He's from Magic Springs Humane Society? He said you have my kittens?" Tiff looked expectantly at Mia, hope seeping from every pore in her body.

"You're the owner of the mama cat?" Mia felt relief knowing the kittens owner had shown up. "Great. Take off your boots and coat and we'll head upstairs. They're in the apartment."

"Bella is fit to be tied. Of course, the kittens are old enough to go to new homes. My mother-in-law said she thought she was dropping the basket off at the humane society. She doesn't like cats around kids. But it wasn't her call. I have two of the kittens given away already and the woman is heartbroken they disappeared." Tiff let Muffy down on the floor. Then she kicked her boots off and set her coat on the bench as she continued talking.

"She thought your building was the humane society. I think she was worried that someone would call me on my cell so she did it at night. Thank goodness you found them before it got too cold. Are they okay?"

"I have three kittens and they're amazing. Troublemakers all of them, especially the little black girl." Mia laughed as she thought about Mr. Darcy's face this morning when he'd found they had eaten all his dry food.

"Three is all I'm looking for. Bella had a small batch this time. I have her an appointment to be fixed before this can happen again. The black kitten, I've been calling her Ebony, and the tabby, are given away to close friends. I'm still looking for the right placement for the yellow-striped boy." Tiff took a breath as she finished the third flight of stairs. "I worked hard to make sure the kittens all had good homes. I didn't expect Bella to get pregnant so young. I'm a responsible pet owner, I promise. You sure get a workout coming up and down those stairs all day, right?"

"I'm used to it now." Mia liked Tiff. She said what she meant and had an open spirit. She opened the apartment door and when the kittens saw Tiff come inside, they all ran to her. Ebony started climbing her jeans. Christina came into the living room as Muffy ran to sit outside Grans door. Mia heard him scratching to be let inside. "Christina, this is Tiff. She works at Majors, and these are her kittens. Well, her cat, Bella's, kittens."

Tiff was gently crying. All three kittens were in her arms. She smiled at Christina. "Nice to meet you, Christina. Thank you both so much for taking care of my babies."

"Oh my Goddess, what is all the emotion floating around out here. I'm trying to read." Grans
stood at the doorway watching them. "Sorry, I didn't
know we had company."

"Grans, this is Tiff. She's the owner of the kittens." Mia saw the look her grandmother was
giving Tiff. "It was all a misunderstanding. Her
mother-in-law thought the school was the humane
society."

"She must be from out of town." Grans said, but
she smiled at the woman who was still focused on
the three kittens.

"Oh, she is." Tiff nodded. "Pocatello. I can't believe how big they all are now. They grow so fast."

"They eat a lot." Christina reached down and
petted Mr. Darcy who Mia saw was watching the reunion with interest from the couch.

He was probably jumping up and down inside at
the thought of the kittens leaving. Then he did
something that surprised Mia. He reached out a
paw to the kittens to say goodbye. Well, he was a
softy after all. Mia rubbed the black kitten on the
head. "Well, we've enjoyed having them. If you are
still looking for a home for the yellow-striped one,
Trent's mom fell in love with him. You should give
her a call."

"Actually I was going to ask Trent if he knew
anyone who wanted a kitten. He's such a good dog
dad to Cerby. Thanks for telling me." She glanced
around the apartment. "And it looks like you're
just sitting down to dinner. If you need some proof
that I'm the kitten's owner . . ."

Mia held up her hand. "No proof needed. As
happy as they were to see you, that's all I needed.

I'll walk you back downstairs. Do you want me to help you carry one?"

The black kitten reached out for her and Mia took her into her arms.

"Looks like she got attached. I hope my friend will be able to bond with her, too." Tiff walked with Mia down to the front door where she put on her coat.

"If not, let me know. I don't want them to wind up at the shelter." Mia gave Ebony a kiss on the nose when they reached the door and handed her back to Tiff after she tucked the other two into her coat.

"You've got it. You're a good person. Thank you for taking care of them for me. I was about to kill Margo for leaving them outside, but she thought she was doing the right thing." Tiff headed out to her Jeep.

Now, Mia could see a man in the driver's seat waiting for her. He waved as they headed out of the parking lot. He must be Tiff's husband. She shut the door and took a breath. She whispered to the Goddess, "Thanks for getting them home."

An odd feeling came over her. One she typically felt after finishing a catering event or passing a test in high school. A feeling of contentment. Of a job well done. Apparently, she'd passed the Goddess's kitten test with flying colors. She was going to miss the energy the three had brought to the apartment but not the constant cleanup.

When she got back to the apartment, Grans and Christina were sitting at the table, eating. A plate filled with lasagna and garlic bread was waiting for her to join them. Mr. Darcy was on the window seat, watching out the window. She walked over and rubbed his head. "The house is yours again, buddy."

He nodded, then meowed and continued to watch the night out the window.

Mia knew that he was going to miss the kittens, even if he couldn't tell her so himself. She went and sat at the table. "Well, that was unexpected."

"I'm going to miss them." Christina said.

Grans patted her arm in comfort.

Mia focused on her grandmother. "Feeling better?"

"Don't gloat. I realized I was pouting. No use starving myself over some perceived slight. You were right, it's your house and your ghosts. Besides, having the kittens returned to their owner is a big deal. We should celebrate by having a lab night for your witch studies. Christina, you don't mind if we go downstairs for a few hours, do you?" Grans broke off a piece of bread that didn't have butter or flavorings on it and gave it to Muffy. "I'm sure you have a movie to watch or homework."

"I do have homework. And Mia needs to be learning too, so, no, I don't mind. I'll do the dishes after dinner."

As she dug into the pasta, Mia realized that life was back to normal in the apartment. At least as normal as Mia's world got. "Hey, Christina? Has Jenna always been insecure about things? She went home sick one shift and she's been apologizing ever since."

Christina shrugged. "Not sure. I just know her from the program. She asked me one day where I worked and if I knew of any job openings in Magic Springs."

"Wait, you guys aren't friends?" Mia tried to remember what Jenna had said about Christina. Maybe she'd assumed they were closer than Jenna had actually said. She'd check her notes tomorrow. Tonight, she needed to focus on her witch studies. Maybe after this week, she'd be smarter than a fifth grader, at least in the witching world.

Friday morning, Mia went into the Lodge early. Christina was up and working on homework downstairs in the lobby. Grans was still in her room when she left. Today would be a long day at work. They had a fifty-plate dinner to serve as well as an open bar and hot and cold appetizers. But at least it wasn't a tray service. She just needed to make sure people were assigned to keeping the apps available on the table during the cocktail hour before dinner. The good thing was they only had the one event so they could use both ballrooms. One for the cocktail hour and the other for the dinner. She could do this level of catering at the school, but Frank didn't want to outsource even the smaller events. Mia thought when they got busy, he might see the error in his decision. At least she hoped so.

It was almost noon when she finally got a minute to sit at her desk with a sandwich James had brought to her with a firm command to eat before she fell down. Mia didn't think that missing one meal, okay so lunch would have been two, would constitute starving, but she appreciated her friend making sure she ate. Isaac never even asked if she'd taken time to eat before a big event. And he was supposed to be in love with her. Isaac was always all about the business part of their relationship.

She scanned through her emails and made some appointments for Monday afternoon to discuss future events. Next weekend was booked with a wedding and a small business conference that started on Thursday. She sent out a group email warning her staff that they would be needed for probably full-time hours from Wednesday to Sunday next week.

At least the kittens were home where they belonged. Mia smiled at the memory of Ebony snuggling up to her. Mr. Darcy rarely snuggled anymore but he had come into her bedroom last night and slept on her feet until she'd woken up this morning. He was missing the little buggers too.

Thinking of the kittens reminded her she was going to look at her notes from Jenna's interview. It didn't matter, except Mia thought she had said she was friends with Christina. Of course, people defined friends in all kinds of casual ways. Mia thought friends should be a different level than yes, they'd recognize me in a crowd. She had just pulled the file and opened it, when her door flew open and James came inside.

"We have a problem. Dean was supposed to bartend tonight, and he's got the flu. Or something. He probably just has a date and doesn't want to work, but I can't prove that. And he did sound sick when he called." James plopped down in a chair. "Tell me you have a list of servers who have also trained at the bar?"

"I have a couple. I assume your staff is booked at the hotel bar?" Mia closed the file and put it aside, pulling up her staff list.

"I gave Julie the weekend off. She had a bachelorette party in Jackpot." James closed his eyes. "It would be better if our staff didn't have lives outside of work. So much easier to schedule then."

"We are supposed to support work-life balance, remember? It's a corporate policy." She scanned the Excel chart she'd made on employee trainings completed.

"Work-life balance in the hospitality industry means you date someone you work with. That way, they're available at two in the morning for breakfast at a truck stop when you get off work." James leaned forward. "Any luck?"

"I have two servers that have taken the bartender training. I think we'll need both of them since they haven't had much experience. Do you have two servers I can use to replace them?" Mia pulled out the coverage plan she'd just completed and grabbed the Wite-Out.

Thirty minutes later, James's bartender emergency had been solved and it was time to get down to the ballrooms and get them set up. She grabbed the clipboard that had the room setup plans as well as the servers spots and roles for the evening. She locked her door and tucked the key into her pocket. Time to make the magic happen.

Her phone buzzed with a text. It was from Trent.

Got the video from Andie. I'll bring it over tomorrow. I hear Tiff collected her wayward kittens.

She texted back **LOL** and **see you then** and added **working** so he knew she couldn't talk. Then she started directing staff to set up the room for tonight's event.

Mia watched from the door as servers milled around the room, setting up the ballroom where they'd serve the dinner. A tap on her shoulder had her turn around to see Jacob Thompson. He must have seen her reaction to his presence, and he held up his hands.

"I come in peace." He laughed but when she didn't, he nodded. "Fair enough. I just wanted to tell you that I'm leaving Magic Springs. Your Deputy Dog told me I could go back to Boise. I guess my alibi for the time my brother was killed is rock-solid. Sorry, I know you were counting on me clearing your friends."

"I want whoever killed Todd to be found. I just know it's not Christina or Levi." She held her clipboard close to her chest. It wasn't much protection, but she had people just steps away if he tried something, again. "What were you and that lawyer talking about when you said the trust had been spent down. I know now it wasn't Todd's trust. Was it yours?"

"Aren't you clever. Yes. I've been a little loose with my money lately. Too many bad investments. But since I should be part of Todd's will, I'm sure that will be rectified soon. Don't worry about me, I'll be more careful with my money from now on." He glanced around the ballroom. "I still can't believe you chose to work for a living rather than marry that loser, Isaac. I hear your new boyfriend runs a grocery store. You sure know how to pick them—not."

"Working for a living is honorable rather than just waiting for people to die and leave you something. I hope Todd decided to change his will." Mia glanced up and saw a server waving at her. "Anyway, have a nice life and I hope not to see you soon."

"You witch," Jacob called after her.

Mia half expected to feel his hand around her arm as she walked away, but apparently the moment was over. "You don't know how right you are," she whispered in response, then she put on a smile and went to meet her servers.

CHAPTER 22

When she got home that night, Grans and Christina were still awake and sitting in the living room. Mia sank into a chair. She was worn out from the event or from the encounter with Jacob. Or maybe both. "Hey, what are you guys still doing up? It's almost midnight."

"We're on baby watch. Abigail's supposed to call us when she gets the call. Then we have a name to call as well. It's a Magic Springs phone tree." Christina explained as she set down a cup with what looked like coffee. "Well, technically it's a coven phone tree and they aren't calling me, but your grandmother. It's still exciting."

"The baby has magic then?" Mia rubbed her face, trying to wake up. She didn't want to be the last one to find out that the newest coven member had arrived.

"Sarah and Mark went to the coven specialist after she told Mark her suspicions about the baby having powers and the doctor confirmed it. Of course, you never know how much power a child will eventually have, but he could monitor the baby's level. And he did a level check on Sarah and Mark. Both of them have more power than they should. The whole coven's talking about it. Most blame it on our location. We live too close together so any residual power from a parent to a non-magical child is amplified. Or something stupid like that." Grans turned down the television. "The coven always needs to label things."

Mia nodded. "I guess we're having a watch party. Anyone want some popcorn or appetizers?"

"We're already way ahead of you. I've got some egg rolls and other finger foods in the oven. And there's a batch of potato soup if you want something substantial." Christina held out her cup. "And some warm spiced apple cider too."

Mia followed Christina into the kitchen and loaded up her plate. She needed food if she was going to stay up and wait for the little one to arrive. She went and changed into sweats and slippers. "Hey, tomorrow morning I'll make a muffin basket and take it and a coffee carafe over to Mark and Sarah. If they aren't still working on getting this baby to arrive."

"I've got a feeling we'll be hearing about the baby soon." Grans glanced around the living room. "It's quiet here without the kittens. I never thought I'd miss the little monsters, but I do."

"Yeah. Me too." Mr. Darcy was on Mia's lap, purring, and looked up at her when she said that. "I know, I have you. But the kittens were fun."

He sniffed, then lay back down.

Mia rubbed his ears. "My book says that familiars like Cerby coming means there's going to be a need for protection sooner or later. Hellhounds are really rare."

Grans looked away. "Trent needs to keep an eye out for that baby. He's vulnerable now when he's young. After he's past a year, he'll be more able to fight off any influence. But for now, he could be turned."

"Turned?" Christina dipped a mozzarella stick into some marinara. "You mean good versus evil?"

"Child, it's not a fairy tale. Evil exists. I would have thought you knew that by now." Grans stood. "I'm getting some soup. Can I get anything for you?"

"No, we're good." Mia decided to tell Christina about Jacob's visit. She could see the fear growing on Christina's face as she explained.

"Wait, doesn't that mean that Levi is the only one left on Mark's list?" Christina set her plate down. "I need to call him."

"Don't. You don't know who Mark's looking at besides Levi. And we still don't know what Todd's will says. Maybe Jacob had him killed and the money trail will show up once the will is read." Mia was too tired to try to find a new suspect for Todd's death. "Oh, and Trent's got the house video. Maybe Todd had some visitors we don't know about."

"Yeah, maybe the library nerd from high school has been working with the Idaho mob and crossed a drug dealer. Fairy tales can come true." Christina said, taking her plate back.

Mia nodded. "Drug dealer, maybe. There's a lot of money in that family. But I don't know that there's an Idaho mob. Is there?"

Christina laughed. "You're tired. No, there's not

an Idaho mob. At least not that I know of. Todd wasn't the type to do drugs, but I haven't seen him in four years. Maybe. He would have said I wasn't the type to work for a living from the person he knew in high school. And look at me."

"Working for a living. That seems to be a bad trait according to the people in your mom's circle. Jacob said something like that to me tonight. That I should have jumped at marrying Isaac rather than doing catering." Mia sipped her apple cider.

"Dad was so mad when Isaac didn't take the bar after law school. He almost disowned him, but Mom talked him down. He said he didn't work long nights to have his children become common laborers. I guess my choice of career didn't set well either, although he did think I'd marry well which meant I didn't need a real job."

"Your folks are snobs." Grans came into the living room with three bowls of soup on a tray. "It's not like either you or Isaac are digging ditches as we used to tell our kids to get them to stay in school. Although landscaping seems to be a valuable skill based on what they charged me to redo my front yard last year. I brought us all a bowl of soup."

As they talked and watched old rom-com movies, waiting for a call, Mia thought about Jacob's comment. Maybe that was why Todd asked Christina to marry him, to keep her from having to work.

The call came just before two. Mark and Sarah Baldwin were the proud parents of a seven-pound baby girl. They hadn't settled on a name yet. Mia and Christina cleaned up the dishes from the living room and put away any leftovers from the kitchen while Grans made the next call. Then they all went to bed. Trent was coming tomorrow to take her to Twin. The world kept turning.

Saturday morning, Mia got up at seven and texted Trent. She needed a couple of hours to get a muffin basket to Mark and Sarah. He replied saying that he'd be there at nine and they could go to the hospital together to see the new arrival.

Mia was filling the coffee carafe as Trent walked into the apartment.

Christina had gone down to let Muffy out and had let Trent inside. "Look who I found. Can I keep him?"

"Of course, but you have to remember to feed and clean up after your pets." Mia smiled at Trent. "Do you want some coffee and a muffin before we go?"

He held up a thermos. "Mom fed me when I dropped off Cerby this morning. She also sent an ice chest with yogurts and fruit for us to take to Mark and Sarah. She said the coven has meals planned for them starting with lunch and going out a week if not longer."

"It's nice to be part of a community." Mia poured her coffee into a personal sized thermos and then glanced around. "I think we're ready then. Christina, will you tell Grans I'll be home about three if she wants to do a lesson?"

"Sure. I'm hanging around the house. Levi's working today so it's laundry and homework for me. Next week, I've got labs Wednesday through Friday. I liked having video classes this week. I didn't have to drive into Twin." She poured a cup of coffee and sat at the table.

"Maybe you should see if your days in Twin matches up with Jenna's class schedule. That way you can carpool on weeks you have to go in." Mia wrapped a hand towel around the muffin basket.

"Jenna lives on campus. She's in the dorms." Christina replied. "I thought you knew that."

"According to the front desk, she checked into the Lodge a few weeks ago and has a room there." Mia met Christina's gaze. "I wonder if we're talking about the same person?"

"Do you have a picture of her?"

Mia nodded. "At the Lodge. I'll snap it Monday and send it to you. Maybe we just have the wrong person. But she did give me your name as a reference."

"I'm not sure I know any other Jennas but maybe it's short for something else. Or someone I knew told her about the job and she used my name." Christina's phone rang. "That's Levi, checking in. We're probably going out tonight for dinner."

Trent picked up the basket and Mia grabbed the coffee carafe. Before they got into his truck, she snapped a picture of the front of the building. Trent watched her. "I want to make sure we get the right lights."

"Okay." He put the truck in gear and they headed to the hospital. Mia wondered who the woman she'd hired was and if she even knew Christina. She'd check other references on Jenna Monday, just in case. Today, she had other issues on her mind.

A CD sat on the seat in between them. Mia picked it up. "Is this from Andie?"

"That's the video from the last few times Todd rented the house. It only records when there's movement so it's not hours long. I didn't have a chance to look at it, but we can load it into your computer when we get back. I was going to bring it in, then the operation food delivery thing got into my head." He smiled at her. "You and my mother are always feeding other people. It's your love language and kind of nice."

"You work with your gifts." Mia turned up the music. When they got to the hospital, she grabbed her phone out of her tote and tucked the bag under the seat. They had enough packages to carry in. After she got the coffee and Trent got the basket and cooler from his mom, she said, "Lock the truck, will you?"

"Planning on it. Or actually, planning on you doing it. Take my keys from my jacket pocket." He turned and she reached in and found his keys along with a glove. She put the glove back, then locked the truck, putting the keys back in his pocket.

Mia headed to the hospital's front doors and then went to the information desk. "We're here to see Sarah Baldwin? She just had a baby?"

"Fifth floor, check in with the nurses' station first, but she's in room 507." The older woman glanced at the packages. "People usually bring flowers, not food."

"I'm a caterer," Mia said as she walked toward the elevator. "Food is what I do."

Trent leaned against the elevator door as they went up. "Love language, I tell you."

"Have you been reading women's magazines at

the store?" She grinned at him. "Or are you buying relationship books to make sure you're doing it right?"

He winked at her. "I'll never tell."

Mark was sitting by the bed and Sarah was holding the baby when they went into the room. "Welcome, guys. Sarah said that we'd be getting some visitors soon. I take it the phone tree worked last night."

"We heard the good news and wanted to bring you guys some breakfast. Or treats for later if you've already eaten." She held up the carafe. "And real coffee. I suspect the stuff you've been getting is decaf."

"Or watered down." Mark stood and took the coffee from her. "Thank you. I should ask for an IV line for this."

"Or there're cups in the basket," Mia offered. "Along with sugar and fresh baked muffins. Abigail sent the cooler so I tucked the cream in there."

Trent set it down and opened it. "Looks like yogurt, fruit cups, and some sparkling waters."

"You guys are the best. Tell Abigail thank you." Sarah nodded to the baby. "Elisa Marie Baldwin. She was named for both of our mothers. What do you think?"

"I love that name. And look at her hair. And her tiny fingers. She looks perfect." Mia smiled at Sarah and Elisa. "Can I take a picture?"

"Of course, but I think she's asleep." Sarah ran her free hand over her hair. "And I must look a mess."

As Mia focused the phone camera so she'd have a picture to show Grans and Christina, the baby,

Elisa, opened her eyes and looked back at Mia. Then she sighed and snuggled closer to her mother.

"We won't stay long. I suspect you're all tired. But welcome to the world, Elisa Marie." Trent handed Sarah a bottle of the water, then closed the cooler. He walked over and stood by the door, waiting for Mia.

"Thank you both so much," Sarah said as she took Mark's hand. "We appreciate your gifts."

Mia and Trent went to the elevator and while they were waiting, Trent took her fingers in his, weaving them together. "Do you want something like that?"

"A baby?" Mia glanced back at the room that held the Baldwins. "Someday. Yeah, that would be nice."

"We hear that a lot from visitors. Keeps us in business." A nurse who stood by them waiting for the elevator laughed as they all got on. "Nothing like seeing a miracle to make you want one of your own."

As they drove to Twin, Mia kept the conversation on anything but Elisa Baldwin. Babies were scary things. And the nurse was right. It was like a pheromone had seeped into their relationship as they stood there, making them want to procreate.

Finally, Trent turned down the music and looked at her. "Mia, I didn't mean right now. I just wanted to know if you saw kids in your future."

She laughed as she rolled her shoulders. "Newborn hospital wards should have warning signs about the effect of seeing a newborn. She was beautiful, but Trent, I'm not ready now. I still want to get back to running Mia's Morsels rather than working at the Lodge."

"I want a big outdoor wedding maybe by the river. So we'd have to wait until at least summer before we could even get married. Then I'd like to travel for a year or two together when we first get married before having kids." He turned onto the highway that would take them to the bridge crossing the river. "So, it sounds like we've got some time."

"It would be nice to have a family, someday." Mia glanced out the window and watched as they moved from mountain to desert landscape.

"Mia, you have a family. You have your grandmother, Christina, me, and my crazy family. And your mother and probably some I haven't met. We just don't have kids running around. We have Mr. Darcy, Muffy, and now, Cerby. Let's see how we do with raising a pup and get him out of doggie day care before we add kids to the mix." Trent pointed up to the sky as they crossed over the freeway. "There's a hawk."

When they got to the box store, Trent took a double take, then stopped a guy walking out of the building as they were going inside. "Derek? What are you doing? Why haven't you answered your phone?"

"Man, I was down at Shoshone Falls. There's a rumor that pirates buried treasure there that you can only reach if you cross the falls on a full moon. Anyway, I slipped and lost my phone in the water. Come to find out, you can't even dig there. It's against the Fish and Game regulations. I got a ticket I have to pay and now I don't have my phone. I'm using my girlfriend's phone." Derek looked at Mia and smiled a lazy grin. "Hey, I'm Derek."

"You missed your shifts last week." Trent pulled

out his phone. "What's your girlfriend's number. I think Baldwin needs to talk to you."

"No, man, I told Tina at the station I was taking vacation. She'll vouch for me. Can Baldwin really arrest me for not showing up for a shift?" He pulled out his phone. "I'll call you. What's your number?"

Trent gave him his number and the phone rang. He picked it up, then texted the number to Baldwin. "Mark's going to call you to verify that you took Levi to Boise to pick up the new ambulance. You're going to have to talk to your boss about missing your shifts."

"Man, if Tina didn't tell him because she was still mad that we broke up, that's going to be a problem." He tucked his phone away. "I'll call him as soon as I get back to Annie's. She's going to be really upset if I don't get my vacation pay on Monday. I told her I'd pay her back for staying with her this week."

As Mia and Trent made their way into the store, he rolled his eyes. "And that's why having a friend like Derek is a problem. That guy's always half doing things. I bet Tina didn't even know he was taking off on vacation. He just thinks he tells people things. In high school, he was always getting Levi in trouble. Well, at least we found him."

For the rest of the trip, they talked about everyday subjects. Not the future or family or even marriage. When they got back to the school, Trent brought the lights Mia had bought inside and put them in a closet by the door. "I'll call and get the electrician out here sometime next week if that will work with your budget. He'll give you a discount since he does all our store work."

"Sounds good." Mia looked around the lobby area. "I had someone check out the wiring before I bought the place, but you know old buildings. It might be more than we think. I have a slush fund I use for remodel projects. And this is important."

"It's not sexy like adding a classroom but it needs to be done. And you probably need to re-cover the parking lot next year. You're getting some potholes." He held up the CD. "Do you still want to look at this?"

"Of course." She nodded to her office. "Let's go in there. I'd like to see it before Christina does, just in case."

"Just in case Levi comes out dripping in blood? That's not going to happen. He saves lives, he doesn't take them. I'd lay money on Christina if it comes down to the two of them." Trent followed her to the office.

"Christina couldn't have done it." Mia shrugged. "I guess we'll just have to see who was visiting Todd."

After the video played, Mia played it again. She wanted to make sure of who she was seeing. Then she turned to Trent. "Can you take me to the Lodge. I've got to grab something. With him having to call Derek and what I'm bringing him, I think I'm going to ruin Mark's first weekend to-gether as a family."

CHAPTER 23

Mark met them at the Lodge in the lobby. He was on his way home from the hospital to change clothes and pick up some things for Sarah. "Tell Levi I've talked to Derek and his alibi is confirmed. And I know the kid doesn't have the money to put out a hit on Todd. He's off my suspect list. Of course, now I regret letting Jacob go to Boise for his family emergency."

"You may not after you see this." Mia handed him the CD and a copy of Jenna's personnel file. She might be crossing company lines, but she needed to know if one of her staff members was a killer. And she'd tucked the original file into her tote. She'd check with Christina and see if she even knew *this* Jenna. Mia filled Mark in on her suspicions.

"And this woman is living at the Lodge?" He glanced around the upscale lobby. "You must pay better than I thought."

"No, we don't. Which makes me wonder how

she's staying here too." Mia squeezed Mark's arm.
"Sorry to take you away from the women in your
life. Elisa's beautiful."

Mark beamed. "She is, isn't she. I'm a very lucky
man."

"Yes, you are." Mia watched as he headed out of
the lobby and to his truck. Carl came over and met
them.

"Everything okay?" He looked from Baldwin's
police vehicle to Mia.

"Fine, but can you do me a favor and put a flag
on Jenna McDonald's hotel file? If she checks out,
will you call me and Baldwin?"

"I can put the note in for you, but I'd need something from the police department to add Baldwin.
Do you want me to call him and see if he'll do the
paperwork?" Carl glanced around the lobby. It was
a habit Mia had noticed the first time she'd talked
to him. The guy was always watching for something off.

"No, just call me. I'm sure if Baldwin wants to
talk to her, he'll be here sooner than later." Mia
took Trent's arm in hers as they started to walk
away. "Can you take me home? I can make you dinner if you want."

"I'm beat and I still have to pick up Cerby from
Mom's. I'd hate for the little guy to bond to her
rather than me. Besides, Mom needs to know we
found Derek. She's been worried about Levi since
this whole thing started." Trent pulled on a beanie,
and they walked out into the freezing weather.
Rubbing his hands together, he said, "I'm looking
forward to spring."

"You're a skier. Aren't you supposed to be praying to the snow gods for more powder?" Mia teased

as they walked to the truck, the stars in the clear sky winking at them.

A voice called from behind them. Mia turned and saw Jenna following them outside without a coat. "Mia, can I talk to you?"

Mia and Trent stopped and he put a hand on Mia's back as he leaned down to whisper, "Is it safe?"

Mia nodded. "I hope so," and then stepped back toward Jenna. "You're going to freeze out here without a coat."

"I won't keep you long," Jenna smiled up at Trent. "You're probably on a date. You guys make a cute couple. Anyway, I just wanted to tell you I'm available for extra shifts next week if you need me. I didn't have many hours this week."

"We didn't have any caterings this weekend. Check your email. We've got a wedding and a small conference next week. You'll have more than enough hours next week." Mia wondered if Jenna would even be working next week. "Anyway, you need to get inside. I'll talk to you on Monday."

"That's great to hear. I'm sorry I bothered you. I should have thought to check my email." Jenna started rubbing her arms. "I'm so stupid sometimes."

"You're not stupid, Jenna. But you are going to freeze if you don't get inside." Mia smiled at the woman. No matter what she'd possibly done, Mia liked Jenna. She was a little needy and clingy, but nice.

"I'll see you Monday and I'm so sorry." She turned and ran to the Lodge's front door where she turned and waved before going into the lobby.

Trent put an arm around her as they walked toward the truck. "That's the woman we think stabbed Todd?"

"That's Jenna. I have to agree you wouldn't see her as a killer if we hadn't seen her going into Todd's house. She said she was doing personal chef gigs. Maybe she was just there to cook dinner for him and Christina and something went wrong. If she's not the killer, maybe she knows something." Mia decided to leave the why to Mark. It was his job, not hers. But she was going to have to start hiring again if he arrested Jenna.

"Well, I guess we'll see. I'm just glad Levi's off the suspect list. As far as skiing, I have to admit that I'd love a late storm, then sixty-degree weather to have one last run where I could wear jeans and a jacket rather than heavy ski clothes. Levi loves to do his last run wearing nothing but shorts, but he's a little younger than me. I'm starting to feel the cold." Trent opened the door and she climbed into the still-warm truck.

"I have to say, I'm ready for spring to arrive too. It's my second favorite season. Especially when things start to grow." Mia glanced over to the Lodge lobby doors. Jenna was still standing there, watching them. Mia shivered.

Trent turned up the heat. "I'll have you home in just a few minutes."

Mia wasn't sure the chill she felt was due to the dropping temperatures.

Sunday morning, Mia was baking pumpkin bread when a car she didn't recognize pulled into the driveway. She watched as a woman got out of the car and headed to the front door. Christina who had been sitting at the table glanced up to watch the monitor. "Who's that?"

"That's Jenna McDonald. The one who said you were her reference. Do you know her?"

Christina squinted at the monitor. "She looks familiar, but I can't place her. What's she doing here this morning?"

"That's a good question." Mia tucked her phone into her pocket. "Call me in ten minutes if I'm not back here. And if I don't answer, call Mark Baldwin."

"Like he's going to be happy to hear from me on a Sunday morning. Besides, isn't Sarah still in the hospital?" Christina sipped her coffee. When Mia didn't respond, she sighed and went to get her phone. "Fine, if you're not back upstairs in ten minutes, I'll call you and then Baldwin. But I'm telling him that you asked me to call."

"Christina, this is important." Mia didn't want to scare her friend, but on the other hand, she was going downstairs to talk to a person who could have killed Todd. She didn't want to be stupid. On the other hand, if Jenna was innocent, she didn't want to just ignore her. Was she being the too stupid to live character in all the horror movies. She reached up and touched the amulet Grans had given her to protect herself. Hopefully it was good for more than just magic spells.

She left the apartment and headed downstairs to answer the door. She was being silly. But she still was glad she took the precaution. Mia opened the door and smiled at Jenna. "We have to stop meeting like this, people will talk."

Jenna's eyes widened, then she saw Mia was smiling and handed Mia a folded piece of paper. "I was going through some old family recipes. Well, things we had when we were kids, and found this one for a shortbread cookie. I thought you might like it. It's like the one Mia's Morsels had in the delivery box for last week."

"I didn't know you were on our delivery route. I turned that over to my assistant when I took the catering director job at the Lodge." Mia took the paper. "I'll show her this on Monday."

"Christina's not living with you?" Jenna frowned as she tried to look around Mia.

"Abigail, she's the one running my business, not Christina." Mia didn't open the paper. "You know Christina's still in school. There aren't enough hours in the day for her to run the delivery business too."

"Oh, yes, I should have realized. Is Christina here? I'd love to talk to her." Jenna stepped forward but Mia blocked her by moving the door.

"Sorry, she's out with Levi, her boyfriend. I'll tell her you stopped by though." There was no way Mia was letting Jenna into the house. The woman was acting weird.

Jenna pointed to Christina's Land Rover. "Isn't that her car?"

"Levi came to get her this morning for breakfast at the Lodge. I'm surprised you two didn't run into each other there." Mia glanced at her watch. "Sorry, I've got to run. Trent's upstairs working on the area I hope to make my library. Can you imagine how many cookbooks I can put into a real library area?"

Jenna stepped back and nodded. "That would

be fun. You need to try out that recipe and let me know what you think. My brother and I loved the cookies when we were kids."

"I'll do that. See you Monday for the staff meeting, right? Ten thirty, don't be late." Mia waved and shut the door before Jenna could respond. She heard her phone ringing, but she took the time to throw all the locks on the door. From the monitor above the door, she could see Jenna hadn't moved but instead, seemed to be talking to herself.

As she walked away from the door, Mia answered the call. "I'm fine."

"Good, because I was just about to hang up and bother Baldwin. What did she want?"

Mia watched as Jenna kicked at the sidewalk, then at her car before she got in. She appeared to slam her hands against the steering wheel as she continued her monologue. Whatever she'd expected to happen when she arrived at the school, hadn't happened. Mia watched as Jenna drove out of the camera's viewpoint.

"Mia? Are you there?" Christina asked through the speaker on the phone.

Mia moved toward the stairs and answered her. "Sorry, I was just watching Jenna leave. Something is wrong with that woman."

When she got upstairs, Mia sat at the table and unfolded the paper. Like Jenna had said. It was a recipe.

Christina took it. "Funny, this is the same recipe the cook at my house used for these cookies. We were always having these after school because they were Isaac's favorite."

"Jenna said it was a family recipe. Did your cook have children?"

Christina shook her head. "No, Mrs. Hendrickson must have been over sixty. She said that she'd never had kids so that's why she loved making us cookies. She's the one who let me bake with her when my mom wasn't home. Mom would have had a fit."

"So Jenna lied." Mia pushed the paper away. "What the heck is going on with this woman? She's beginning to scare me."

"She just wanted to drop off the recipe?" Christina asked as she refilled Mia's coffee cup.

Mia thanked her, then leaned back in her chair. "No, she wanted to talk to you. I told her you and Levi were at the Lodge having breakfast. I don't know if you were watching, but she didn't take it well. Are you sure you don't know her?"

Christina shook her head. "I don't, but it seems like she knows me."

"Well, if Mark doesn't arrest her for killing Todd, I'm going to have to fire her for being creepy." Mia took the pumpkin bread out of the oven. "Monday I'm calling your school and seeing if she actually attends. If not, that will be enough to fire her for lying on her application. Frank takes that very seriously."

Christina picked up the recipe again. "Todd and his sister used to come over to the house after school when we were kids. Rich kids playdate, I guess. Anyway, we had cookies and cocoa. Do you think Jenna is Todd's sister?"

Mia went to the living room and picked up the yearbook that had the third Thompson sibling listed. "She was three years younger?"

Christina took the yearbook and opened it. She found Jennifer Thompson's picture and stared at it. "It could be her. I really don't remember her. When I was in middle school, I had too many activities to need a playdate so we stopped doing them."

"But maybe Jenna attached to you somehow. Maybe she wasn't happy her brother was trying to marry you?" Mia shook her head. "That doesn't make any sense. If she bonded to you somehow, wouldn't she want you to marry Todd?"

Christina was paging through the blank pages in the back of the yearbook where everyone wrote their favorite memories of high school. Christina's pages were full. Finally, she found what she was looking for. She turned the book and pointed to a page-long scribble. "Unless she didn't think Todd was good enough for me."

Mia read the note from the teenage Jennifer. When she got to the bottom of the page, she stopped and read it a second time. "Wow."

Thanks for being my friend and don't let Todd fool you. He's evil.

"Now that I look at the picture again, I think the woman who showed up this morning was Jennifer, but she's dyed her hair blond. I don't even remember talking to her in high school." Christina leaned back in her chair. "Isn't that sad?"

"Especially if she feels so strongly about your friendship." Mia picked up her phone. "I need to call Baldwin and give him Jenna's motive. Protecting you."

CHAPTER 24

The next week, Mia sat in her kitchen at the table, thinking about the busy week they'd just had. Baldwin had arrested Jenna McDonald, aka Jennifer Thompson. She'd lived with Neil McDonald for a year out of high school and had taken his name. Along with his credit cards. Frank had been called in by human resources when Jenna's hotel bill charges had been reversed. And then, Frank had called Mia into his office regarding her lack of detail in hiring.

The good thing was Mia had done everything right, including asking for a background check, but in order to trim expenses, Frank had changed policy and decided not to send the paperwork to human resources for two weeks after hiring. Jenna's background check came across right after Mark had arrested her, pointing out the inconsistencies in her resume.

Baldwin's office got a copy from an anonymous source that day.

Jenna had issues. And an unhealthy attachment to Christina. According to her confession, she had told her brother that Christina was too good for him. Todd had told her that Jacob had spent Jenna's trust fund. When Baldwin's officers searched her room, they found plans to take Jacob out next.

So much for family bonding.

Elisa had arrived safely home from the hospital and mother, daughter, and new father, were doing fine. Mark seemed more focused. More open to suggestions and ideas lately. Mia didn't know why he'd changed, but she liked this new 2.0 version of Mark Baldwin better.

Mia bit into one of the cookies Christina had baked that morning before she headed to Twin for class. It was the family shortbread recipe Jenna had brought that morning. The cookies were good, Mia had to admit that. Mrs. Hendrickson's baking affected more than just the Adams household. It had given comfort to a young girl who didn't know who she was. No matter what Jenna or Jennifer had done, at least she'd had one good memory from childhood.

Abigail was working downstairs, getting things put away from yesterday's delivery day. Grans came out of her bedroom, dragging her packed suitcase. Muffy was by her side.

"Are you going back home?" Mia stood and reached for her grandmother's suitcase.

Grans nodded. "It's time. Trent has bonded with Cerby. The kittens are gone. And this swirl of activity around Christina and her unexpected marriage proposal has died down. Sometimes you just have too much going on around here. Especially for an old lady like me."

"Except, when it gets quiet like now, you leave and go home." Mia reminded her. "Thanks for catching me up on my witch lessons. When are we meeting again?"

"Tomorrow night. Come to my house. We have a new member to your class."

Mia paused by the bottom of the stairs they'd just come down. "Trent? Is he training again? I thought he went through the stuff I'm learning now."

"It's not Trent dear, it's Mark. He wants to know what his child is going to face. His mother is over the moon that he's taking an interest in his heritage. I think it's more that he wants to be prepared for what might come. Like you can ever really prepare for that." Grans kissed her on the cheek and went outside. The spring temperatures had arrived and the snow was melting. All over. The potholes that Trent had predicted in her parking lot were showing up.

Mia followed her to her car and put the suitcase in the trunk by the box of magical supplies Grans never left home without. Bottles of potions, bags of herbs, and a few books were always close by, based on what she thought she might need. "Whatever excuse you need to come over and stay a while, I'm always happy to see you."

Grans patted her cheek and got into the car. "That's sweet of you, dear. Please remind Trent to keep an eye out for Cerby. Hellhounds have to have a very specific diet. No cheap dog food allowed and it has to be chicken based. At least while he's a puppy. Lamb is also acceptable but no other proteins until he's under control."

"Trent's coming over tonight for dinner. I'll remind him." Mia watched as Muffy curled up in the passenger seat. The drive wasn't more than ten minutes, but the little dog was going to have his nap, no matter what.

When Mia got back to the front door, Mr. Darcy was sitting in the open doorway watching Grans leave. He looked up at her and meowed.

"Dorian, I know you love her, but Grans has to have a life. She and Robert are good together. I promise, as soon as I have the knowledge and the power, I'll release you from Mr. Darcy so you can pass on."

The cat waved a paw at her, then took off outside, moving faster than she could catch him. Message received but not appreciated. She closed her eyes and took a breath. She'd have to trust that Dorian wasn't going to get Mr. Darcy into more trouble than they could get out of. On the other hand, she had a bad feeling about his wanderings.

Mia's phone rang, it was the Magic Springs Humane Society according to the caller ID. "Hello?"

"Hi, is this Mia Malone? This is Jeff Conrad, we talked a few weeks ago?"

"This is Mia. I remember you, Jeff. How can I help you?" Mia wondered if the little black kitten was coming back. An announcement that Mr. Darcy would not be happy with when he came back from his wanderings.

"I just wanted to make sure Tiff got ahold of you

about the kittens. It's been a zoo here. Apparently, this guy died and his will named all the no-kill shelters in the area as his heirs. We had to apply and send all our certifications by a certain date or we'd miss out on our share of the money. I heard it's enough to redo the outdoor dog shelter and add an indoor walking path." Jeff's excitement about the gift bubbled over into his conversation.

"Yes, the kittens are back with their original family." Mia bit her lip, she didn't want to ask, but she couldn't help it. "How's Aspen?"

"She was adopted the same day you came into the shelter. A young guy who wanted a running companion. They stopped by yesterday on their run and Aspen's so happy. You can tell when a dog's happy by looking in their eyes. They smile."

Mia gave thanks to the Goddess for Aspen's new home as well as what appeared to be Todd's money finding a good place to land. That wasn't Jacob's bank account.

"Well, I just wanted to follow up. Thanks for getting the kittens back to their mama." Jeff greeted someone who had just come in the building. "Got to go. Lots to do here."

As Mia hung up, Abigail came out of the kitchen and into the lobby. "Oh, I thought I heard voices. Did Mary Alice leave?"

"She wanted to get home." Mia put her phone in her pocket. "Mr. Darcy's outside so please watch out when you leave."

"They can take care of themselves." Abigail waved her toward the kitchen. "I wanted you to taste test this chicken chili. I think it will be amazing as a delivery option next week."

Mia followed her into the kitchen and gave thanks to the Goddess for things being back to normal. Or at least as normal as things got around Magic Springs, especially for a kitchen witch and her family and friends.

RECIPES

Chicken Gyros with Tzatziki Sauce

Now, I'm not sure this recipe would make a good delivery option, unless Mia's Morsels made up a packet of the chicken, fresh vegetables, pita bread, and sauce in a kit for families to make at home. But it would be a great picnic basket recipe. Especially if you could keep the chicken warm in a wide mouth thermos.

The Cowboy (my husband) and I make this on a weekday night. And have leftovers for lunch the next day.

Enjoy,
Lynn

Cook two chicken breasts on the grill, then shred the meat into a large bowl after they cool. (You could cook extra breasts the night before to save time for this recipe.) Add to the bowl the following ingredients:

3 tbsp sunflower oil
3 tsp minced garlic
1 tsp dried oregano
1 tsp paprika
1 tsp salt
1 tsp black pepper
1 tbsp lemon juice
1 tbsp red wine vinegar
1 tbsp honey

Toss until the chicken is thoroughly coated. Spread on a baking tray and broil for 5 minutes. Mix in ¼ cup of chicken stock and put back in oven for another 5 minutes.

Then put on a warmed pita or flatbread with chopped cucumber, cherry tomatoes, and red onion slices. Top with tzatziki sauce.

Tzatziki – Mix together and chill until serving time.

1 cup Greek yogurt
½ cup grated cucumber
1 tbsp lemon juice
½ tbsp olive oil
1½ tsp minced garlic
1 tsp salt
1 tbsp chopped fresh dill
1 tbsp chopped mint

Are you over the moon about Lynn Cahoon and her Kitchen Witch Mysteries? Don't miss her popular Tourist Trap series. Keep reading to enjoy an excerpt from the next Tourist Trap Mystery . . .

OLIVE YOU TO DEATH

Coming soon from Kensington Publishing Corp.

CHAPTER 1

The business-to-business meeting for May was stuffed with agenda items. The Memorial Day parade and fireworks beach display still needed volunteers to make sure the festival ran smoothly. Darla Taylor, our promotion queen and owner/operator of the South Cove Winery, was wrangling for committee placements as smoothly as a tenured politician. It was too bad Mayor Baylor or his wife, Tina, weren't here to see the way community activism should be handled.

Since Darla was running the meeting, I'd been working on outlining my last paper for my business ethics class on community development, using South Cove's business-to-business group as my example of what happens when people work together. Not having the town politicians here helped make my case that towns could be managed by a council of civic-minded business owners, rather than elected officials. What? It was my fantasy and no one but my professor would see the paper anyway.

If Mayor Baylor read my paper, he'd think I was staging a revolution during my two-hour monthly meeting and probably attend every meeting after he'd made the decision. That wouldn't be in my best interest, especially since I couldn't stand the guy.

Anyway, I had one more paper and I'd have those three little letters after my name, Jill Gardner, MBA. Not as impressive as a PhD or the JD I already had after I finished my law degree, but I was already running my dream business. I owned South Cove's only bookstore, Coffee, Books, and More. And better, I almost owned the brick building the store was housed in.

The building where our monthly meeting was still droning on. The coffee carafes were empty and all the treats I'd put out had been devoured. The mayor had decreased my treat budget last year in his budget, so I limited the amount I set out. I could buy the cookies at the grocery store in Bakerstown cheaper, but I wanted to continue to support Pies on the Fly, my friend Sadie's bakery. As it was, I didn't put any markup on the treats or the coffee from my bookstore, a decision my aunt didn't agree with. I told her it was my donation to the cause.

When Darla finally got the volunteers she needed, she moved to end the meeting.

Josh Thomas, owner of Antiques by Thomas, the upscale antique store that sat next to my coffee shop, stood and raised his hand. "I have one last announcement."

There was a collective groan from the table. Josh's agenda items were never quick. Nor were they usually important. But he was a council member.

"Then you have the floor," Darla looked at me, her question, *What now*, clear on her face. I shrugged. Josh hadn't campaigned for any agenda item before the meeting. At least not to me. Everyone else looked as confused as I was or maybe just tired and ready to get out of the meeting.

Josh shuffled from foot to foot as he stood there. He wore a bright-blue polo shirt and tan khakis, the typical uniform for a business owner in the central coastal section of California. However, it was a far cry from the black suit he'd worn on his oversize frame when I'd first moved here. Josh's dress code and even his appearance had done a complete one-eighty since he'd started dating Mandy Jenson. She ran the farmers market on the highway between my house and the beach. Well, on the other side of the road. And she was a cousin or something to the people who ran the olive farm in the hills above South Cove.

I'd never thought the relationship would continue. Mandy was light, Josh, dark. Mandy was an extrovert, Josh, an introvert. Mandy liked being outside in the sun, Josh loved spending his free time digging through old building and garages for stock for his business. They were complete opposites.

Josh cleared his throat. "I wanted to tell you that Mandy and me, I mean, Miss Jenson, Mandy Jenson and I are engaged. The wedding will be a

small, private ceremony next month and we'll be
hosting a reception at the community hall on June
fifteenth. That's all." He sat back down, his cheeks
red.

No one said anything for a few moments. Finally, Darla stood at the podium and smiled. "Well,
isn't that amazing news. Congratulations to Josh
Thomas and Mandy Jenson on their upcoming
nuptials. I suspect details will be forthcoming on
the reception?"

Josh stood again. He had his hands crossed in
front of him. "Yes. As I mentioned before, we will
have a reception. Everyone's invited to that and it
will be from two to six at the community hall on
the fifteenth."

He sat back down. Then back up. "Gifts are op-
tional."

"Well, with that happy news, I'll end the meeting unless Jill has anything?" Darla looked at me to
confirm but I shook my head. "Okay, then see you
all in June."

Josh stood and nearly ran out of the shop. I saw
him go past the window and toward his shop.
People called out best wishes and congrats as he
passed by them, but I didn't think he heard anyone. He was too focused on getting back to the
shop and away from people and questions.

After people had left, Darla and Amy Newman
Cole, city planner and my best friend, stayed behind to help me get the café back in order.

"Wow, Josh is getting married. Did you know?"
Amy moved a table, then set chairs under it.

I shook my head. "Not a clue. I guess I'm glad

Greg's mom asked us to delay the wedding until fall now. Although I was a little put out by her request."

"A little put out? Girl, I'd be furious. The woman never visits anyway, but then she asks you to change your wedding date because the date interfered with an elective surgery. That's cold." Amy washed another table. "Thank goodness I like Justin's parents. They are super nice. His mom's coming out next month to visit now that we have the new house ready."

"You are still coming to Santa Barbara next weekend for our girls' weekend, right?" Amy had a habit of forgetting appointments and dates. I bought her a planner for Christmas after Greg had gotten me attached to mine.

"Not a problem. I've got it on my work calendar. Greg has already hired a temp to answer phones that weekend so both Esmeralda and I can get away." Amy and I turned to Darla, who had been unusually quiet.

"Hey, I'm in. Don't look at me that way. I've already got Matt and my day manager looped in. I told Matt he can't take any gigs since he has to run the winery that weekend so I'm free. No emergencies. Besides, I'm excited to have the fitting for the bridesmaid dress. I've lost weight since we ordered them. It might be too big." Darla glanced around the room and grabbed her tote bag. "I'm out of here. We've got a beer delivery coming and last time they shorted us two cases. I'm doing the counting this time, not Matt."

"Esmeralda has a reading at lunchtime, so I've

got to be back to answer phones. I never thought that most of my work time would be playing phone dispatcher rather than actual city planning. If I didn't have to also work for the mayor, my job would be perfect." Amy followed Darla out of the door. Esmeralda was Greg's part-time police dispatcher, secretary, and she ran a fortune telling shop out of her house across the street from my house.

I glanced around the empty dining room. The rain had kept people from walking in which was good since I was alone at the shop. Judith had asked for the day off. She needed to run to the city for her annual checkup. I would have asked Aunt Jackie to step in, but then she would have gone off on how irresponsible it was to schedule an appointment on a workday. My aunt didn't like Judith. Since Toby Killian was due in at eleven, I finished my morning shift change tasks and then grabbed a book and poured myself a cup of coffee. The book I was reading was a romance and the fictional couple's back and forth chatter made me wonder about Josh and Mandy.

Maybe I should invite them to have dinner with Greg and me this week so we could commiserate on the pain of wedding planning. Besides, I liked Mandy. Josh, he was an acquired taste, but he'd gotten nicer since he started dating Mandy. *There was always at least one key for every lock.* That was one of my aunt's favorite sayings. Especially around relationships.

I grabbed my phone and called Greg. When he answered, I jumped right into my question. "Hey, you're home Thursday for dinner, right?"

"Don't you have class?" Greg reminded me.

"The professor has a thing so the class got moved to earlier that day. So I'll be home in time. I was wondering if it would be okay for me to ask Josh and Mandy to dinner."

There was no answer on the phone. I held it out to check to make sure we hadn't been disconnected. "Greg?"

"I'm here, I'm just trying to process your question. You want to invite Josh Thomas to our house for dinner, intentionally?"

"I know, but Josh just dropped the bombshell that he and Mandy are getting married next month. I thought it would be nice to have dinner and talk to them about the wedding. Like Amy and Justin did for us."

"We were already friends with Justin and Amy." He paused, letting out a sigh. "But if you want to, I don't care. You'll owe me. I'm not quite sure what horrible thing Josh will say or do, but I know the man. He isn't all sunshine and roses."

"No, but he's a good guy, deep down. I'll keep dinner simple, maybe grilled pork chops, a pasta salad and a cheesecake?"

"Now I'm hungry." Greg smacked his lips like that frog on the commercial.

I laughed and then heard the bell over the door go off. "Got to go, I'll see you tonight."

"Call me when you get back from your run, or text if you're busy. I'd like to know you're home."

"Okay, why?" But then I realized Greg had already hung up. He hadn't wanted to answer my question, so he had ended the call. Was something going on? Or did Greg just want me to check in?

Toby Killian dropped a picture of a little girl on the counter in front of me. "I went into town and saw Sasha last week. I thought you'd like to see Olivia."

"She's getting so big." I picked up the photo to see her smiling face. She had her hair in cornrows with beads at the end. "What grade is she in now?"

"She'll be starting first grade in the fall. I went to the city for her kindergarten graduation last week. I took that at the park." Toby washed his hands and put on an apron. "It was a nice trip."

"So, you and Sasha again?" I handed him the photo but he waved it away.

"Keep it. Or put it on the community board. I bet a lot of people would love to see how much Olivia has grown." He moved the cups to where he liked them by the coffee maker.

"You're avoiding my question." I leaned on the counter, watching him. He and Sasha had been a thing for a while years ago. To the point he had started saving for a house. Then she'd moved to go to school. And then she'd started dating someone else.

He stopped moving and then leaned against the counter. "Maybe. We don't know. She broke up with that guy she'd been seeing. He wasn't putting her or Olivia first. All he wanted was a ready-made family for his career. But she has a good job in the city. And I don't want to leave South Cove, so right now, we're just hanging out again. She might be coming into town to visit this weekend."

"Well, I'd love to see her and Olivia." I knew Toby still had a soft spot in his heart for Sasha. Once he committed to someone, they stayed with

him, even after the breakup. My newest employee
was proof of that. Tessa and Toby had dated in
high school, but then they'd broken up. Toby still
had feelings for her. He was a hopeless romantic
for a police officer and part-time barista. And he
gave me hope for all men, everywhere.

Walking home after my shift ended, I realized I
hadn't stopped at the antique store to invite Josh
and Mandy to dinner on Thursday. When I got to
the house, Emma, my golden retriever, stared at
her leash after I let her back inside.

"Give me a minute. I need to call Josh." I dialed
the shop number and got his machine. I left a message, then went to get ready to run. I'd call again
later if I didn't hear back.

When we were walking to the beach, I noticed
Mandy's small truck at the farmers market. We
crossed the road and I found her in the back, setting up trays for display. "Mandy, Josh told everyone the big news. Congratulations."

"Thanks. It's about time. I asked him to tell
everyone last month, but he forgot." Mandy nodded to a metal folding chair. "Want to sit?"

"Actually, I've been sitting all day. So are you excited? Where is the ceremony going to be?" Emma
sat near my foot, watching us talk.

"Under the oldest olive tree at the farm. I know,
it hasn't been the happiest of places with all the
history, but I want to change that. It's a lovely
place. And a wedding is so filled with happiness
and joy, it should change the tree's karma, right?"

I didn't want to upset Mandy's plans, but the
tree did have a really infamous history. "I don't
know, maybe."

"You sound like Josh. He wants to support me, but he really hates the idea of getting married at the tree. He's a little bit superstitious."

"It's a beautiful spot, that's for sure." I didn't want to get into the middle of this argument. "Anyway, do you and Josh want to come over for dinner on Thursday? We can compare notes about the pain of planning a wedding."

"You've had a lot more time to plan." Mandy laughed. "Yeah, I'll have to check with Josh, but we'd be glad to come. Can I bring anything?"

"Just yourselves. This will be fun." I turned to go toward the highway where we'd cross over to the beach parking lot. A line of eucalyptus trees went from the stand to the corner away from our road. "I didn't realize these were here. Do you get monarchs in the winter?"

"Tons. They swarm the trees. I love watching them as they take off." Mandy stood next to me and pointed toward the ocean. "And sometimes, I get to see whales out there. It's such a blessing living here."

"We're surrounded by nature's beauty, that's for sure." I tightened my hold on Emma's leash. I always worried about her as we crossed the road to the beach. "See you Thursday."

"Okay, maybe we'll have a surprise to tell you when we come over." Mandy waved as we crossed the road and headed over the empty parking lot toward the stairs to the beach.

I was already running before her words hit me. What surprise did she have that she wanted to share, but couldn't so she half shared that something was coming? It was telling but not telling. Was Mandy pregnant? Was that why the quick wedding? I thought about the way she looked and to me, she looked as skinny as ever. But first moms didn't always show, at least not at first.

Josh Thomas with a baby. My next thought was that the world might be coming to an end.

ACKNOWLEDGMENTS

Writing a paranormal cozy lets me play with magic and the good things that could be true. As a teenager, I fell in love with *The Lord of the Rings* trilogy. Being a band kid, an introvert, and lost in my head a lot of the time, I loved the fact that people could be different and still find their family and home on this earth. Or one like it. Kitchen witches spell for good to happen on this planet. And our world could use a little (or a lot) of goodwill today.

Big thanks to the usual suspects on this book. My editor, Michaela Hamilton. All the magical staff at Kensington. And my agent, Jill Marsal.

Visit our website at
KensingtonBooks.com
to sign up for our newsletters, read
more from your favorite authors, see
books by series, view reading group
guides, and more!

**BOOK CLUB
BETWEEN THE CHAPTERS**

Become a Part of Our
Between the Chapters Book Club
Community and Join the Conversation

Betweenthechapters.net